STANDING BY
THE WALL

STANDING BY
THE WALL

THE COLLECTED
SLOUGH HOUSE NOVELLAS

MICK HERRON

SOHO
CRIME

Published by Soho Press, Inc.
227 W 17th Street
New York, NY 10011

Library of Congress Cataloging-in-Publication Data
is available upon request

ISBN 978-1-64129-503-1
eISBN 978-1-64129-504-8

Interior design by Janine Agro, Soho Press, Inc.

Printed in the United States of America

10 9 8 7 6 5 4 3 2 1

To Katie-May & Flossie

STANDING BY
THE WALL

TABLE OF CONTENTS

THE LIST

. . .

Those who knew him said it was how he'd have wanted to go. Dieter Hess died in his armchair, surrounded by his books; a half-full glass of 2008 Burgundy at his elbow, a half-smoked Montecristo in the ashtray on the floor. In his lap, Yeats's *Collected*—the yellow-jacketed Macmillan edition—and in the CD tray Pärt's *Für Alina*, long hushed by the time Bachelor found the body, but its lingering silences implicit in the air, settling like dust on faded surfaces. Those who knew him said it was how he'd have wanted to go, but John Bachelor suspected Dieter would sooner have drunk more wine, read a little longer, and finished his cigar. Dieter had been sick, but he hadn't been tired of life. Out of respect, or possibly mild superstition, Bachelor waited a while in that quiet room, thinking about their relationship—professional but friendly—before nodding to himself, as if satisfied Dieter had cleared the finishing line, and calling Regent's Park. Dieter was long retired from the world of spooks, but there were protocols to be observed. When a spy passes, his cupboards need clearing out.

• • •

There was a wake, though nobody called it that. Most of the attendees had never known Dieter Hess, or the world he'd moved in as an Active; they rode desks at Regent's Park, and his death was simply an excuse for a drink and a little stress relief. If they had to come over pious at the name of a dead German who'd fed them titbits in the Old Days—which were either Good or Bad, depending on the speaker—that was fine. So as the evening wore on the gathering split into two, the larger group issuing regular gales of laughter and ordering ever more idiosyncratic rounds of drinks, and the smaller huddling in a nook off the main bar and talking about Dieter, and other Actives now defunct, and quietly pickling itself in its past.

The pub was off Great Portland Street; nicely traditional-looking from the road, and not too buggered about inside. John Bachelor had never been here before—for reasons that probably don't need spelling out, Regent's Park had never settled on a local—but had developed affection for it over the previous two and a quarter hours. Dieter too had faded into a warm memory. In life, like many of Bachelor's charges, the old man could be prickly and demanding, but now that his complaints of not enough money and too little regard had been silenced by a heart no longer merely dicky but well and truly dicked, Bachelor had no trouble dwelling on his good points. This was a man, after all, who had risked his life for his ideals. German by birth, then East German by dint of geopolitics, Dieter Hess had supplied the Park with classified information during two dark decades, and if his product—largely to do with troop movements: Hess had worked in the Transport Ministry—had never swayed policy or scooped up hidden treasure, the man responsible deserved respect . . . Bachelor had reached that maudlin state where he was measuring his worth against those who'd gone before him, and his own career had been neither stellar nor dangerous. That his current berth was known as the milk round summed it up. John Bachelor's charges were retired assets, which is to say those who'd come in from other nations' colds; who'd served their time in that peculiar shadowland where clerical work and danger meet. Veterans of the microdot. Agents of the filing cabinet. Whatever: it had all carried the same penalty.

It had been a different world, of course, and had largely vanished when the Wall came down, which was not to say there weren't still pockets of it here and there, because friends need spying on as much as enemies. But for John Bachelor's people the Active life was over, and his role was to make sure they suffered no unwelcome intrusions, no mysterious clicks on the landline; above all, that they weren't developing a tendency to broadcast the details of their lives to anyone who cared to listen. It sometimes amused Bachelor, sometimes depressed him, that he worked for the secret service in an era where half the population aired its private life on the web. He wasn't sure the Cold War had been preferable, but it had been more dignified.

And now his rounds were shorter by one client. That was hardly surprising—nobody on his books was younger than seventy—but what happened afterwards? When all his charges expired, what happened to John Bachelor? It was a selfish question, but it needed answering. What happened when the milk round was done? Then the door opened, and a cold blast nipped round the room. Thanks for that, he thought. He was drunk enough to read significance in the ordinary. Thanks for that.

The newcomer was Diana Taverner.

He watched her pause at the larger, noisier group and say something which roused a cheer, so probably involved money behind the bar. Then she glanced his way, or his group's way.

"Oh god," groaned the soak next to him. "Here comes the ice queen."

"She can read lips," said Bachelor, trying not to move his own. They buzzed with the effort.

Taverner nodded at him, or perhaps at all of them, but it felt like at him. He'd been Dieter's handler. It seemed he was in for some line-managed compassion.

It was news to him that compassion was in her repertoire.

Diana Taverner—Lady Di—was one of the Park's Second Desks, and wielded much of the power around that edifice, and not a little of the glamour. In her early fifties, she wore her age more lightly than Bachelor; wore smarter outfits too. This wasn't difficult. He shifted on the bench seat; caught the end of his tie between finger and thumb, and rubbed. It felt insubstantial, somehow. When he looked up his neighbouring soak had vacated the area, and Lady Di was settling next to him.

"John."

". . . Diana."

Ma'am, usually. But this was not the office.

His group had fragmented, its constituent parts repairing to the bar or the gents, or just generally finding an excuse to be elsewhere. But this was a while seeping through Bachelor's consciousness, swaddled by alcohol as it was. He did not want to talk to Taverner, but she had at least arrived bearing more drink. He took the proffered glass gratefully, raised it to his lips, remembering at the last minute to say "Cheers." She didn't reply. He swallowed, set the glass down again. Tried to gauge how presentable he looked: a fool's mission. But he found himself running a hand through his hair anyway, as if that might add lustre, or bring its former colour back.

"Dieter Hess died of natural causes." Diana Taverner's voice was always precise, but there seemed extra edge in it now. More than was called for, fuddled intuition told Bachelor, at a social occasion. "Just thought you'd like to know."

It hadn't occurred to him there'd be any other explanation.

"He'd been sick for a while," he said. "Was on medication. Heart pills."

"Do you remember what?"

Of course he didn't remember what. Wouldn't remember sober, couldn't remember drunk. "Xenocyclitron?" he freewheeled. "Or something like."

She stared.

I did say "*or something like*," he thought.

"When was the last time you saw him?"

"Alive?"

"Of course alive."

"Well then." He gathered thoughts. "That would be last Tuesday. I spent the afternoon with him, chatting. Or listening, mostly. He complained a lot. Well, they all do." He added this to avoid accusations of speaking ill of the dead. Speak ill of the whole bunch of them, and the dead don't feel singled out.

"Money?"

"Always money. They never have enough. Prices rising, and their income's fixed . . . I mean, is it just me, or do you ever think, it's not like they have mortgages to pay? I know they've done their bit and all, but . . ."

Even drunk, Bachelor wasn't sure he was putting his argument cogently. Also, he felt he might be coming across mean-spirited.

"Well," he amended. "Of course they've done their bit. That's why we're looking after them, right?"

He reached for his glass.

When he looked at Taverner again, her face was cold.

"He complained about money," she said.

"Yes. But they all do. Did. I mean, they still do, but he—"

"So he didn't mention an alternative source of income?"

Sobriety had never been so swift nor so unwelcome.

He said, "Ah. No. I mean—" He stopped. His tongue had swollen to twice its size, and sucked up his mouth's moisture.

"Strange that he'd keep that quiet, don't you think?"

"What happened?"

"You were his handler, John," she reminded him. "That doesn't just mean making sure he's fed and watered, and listening to his grouses. It means checking his hide for fleas. You—"

"What happened?"

He'd just interrupted Diana Taverner in full flow. Better men had been sandblasted for less.

"Dieter had a bank account you didn't know about."

"Oh Christ."

"And there was money going into it. Not sure where from yet, because someone's gone to a lot of trouble to hide the source. But that in itself is somewhat suggestive, wouldn't you say?"

He was going to be sick. He could feel the heave gathering force. He was going to be sick. He was going to be sick.

He'd finished his drink.

Diana Taverner regarded him the way a crow regards carrion. Eventually, she picked up her glass. Bachelor craved that glass. He'd kill for its contents. He had to settle for watching her swallow from it.

She said, "It's hardly *Tinker, Tailor*, John. You wipe their noses, feed their cats, make sure they're not blowing their pensions on internet poker, and—and I really didn't think this needed emphasising—and above all, make sure they don't have bank accounts they're not telling us about. You want to take a guess as to why that's so important?"

He mumbled something about being compromised.

"That's right, John. Because if they've got secret bank accounts someone else is filling with money, it might mean they've been compromised. You know, I'm going to go out on a limb here. It very definitely certainly fucking does mean they've been compromised, which means we can't trust anything they've ever told us, and do you have any idea, John, do you have the remotest idea of the headache that'll cause? When we have to go trawling through everything we ever thought we knew about everything they ever told us? To find out where the lies start, and what actions we took based on them?"

"Ancient history," he found himself saying.

"That's right, John. Ancient history. Like discovering your house's foundations aren't made of stone but pizza dough, but what's the harm, right? Now go get me another one of these."

He did what he was told, each action muffled by a sense of impending doom. The floor buckled beneath his feet. Laughter boomed from the youngsters' table, and he knew it was aimed at him. He paid for three doubles, downed the first, and carried the survivors back to land.

Look for a loophole, he screamed inwardly. Just because this is happening doesn't mean it can't be unhappened. He was fifty-six years old. He didn't have much of a career, but he didn't have anything else going for him.

Setting her drink in front of Lady Di, he asked, "How long?"

"More than two years."

"How much?"

"Eighteen grand. Give or take."

He said, "Well, that's not—"

She raised a hand. He shut his mouth.

For a few minutes, they sat in silence. It was almost peaceful. If this could go on forever—if there never had to be a moment when the consequences of Dieter Hess receiving money from unknown sources had to be faced—then he could live with it. Stay on this seat in this pub, with this full glass in front of him, and the future forever unreached. Except that the future was already nibbling away, because look, see, his glass, it was emptying.

At last, and possibly because she was reading his mind, Taverner said, "How old are you, John?"

It wasn't a question you asked because you wanted to know the answer. It was a question you asked because you wanted to crush your underling underfoot.

He said, "Just tell me the worst, would you? What is it, Slough House? I'll be sent to join the other screw-ups?"

"Not everyone who screws up gets to join the slow horses. Only those it'd be impolitic to sack. That clear enough for you?"

That was clear enough for him.

"Dieter was an asset," she went on. "And assets, even retired assets, even *dead* assets, fall on my desk. Which means I do not want the Dogs sniffing round this, because it makes me look bad."

The Dogs were the Service's police.

"And what makes me look bad makes you look redundant."

Her eyes had never left his during this speech. He was starting to get an inkling of how mice felt, and other little jungle residents. The kind preyed on by snakes.

"So. How do you think we resolve this situation?"

He shook his head.

"Excellent. And there's the can-do attitude that's made your career such a shining example to us all." She leaned forward. "If this gets to be an inquiry, John, you won't just be out on your ear, you'll be implicated in whatever crap Dieter Hess was up to. I'll make sure of that. And we're not just talking loss of job, John, we're talking loss of pension. Loss of any kind of benefit whatsoever. The best your future holds is a job in a supermarket, assuming you're still of working age when they let you out of prison. Just stop me when you come up with a plan. Not stopping me yet? It isn't looking good, John, is it? Not looking good at all."

He found his voice. "I can fix this."

"Really? How very very marvelous."

"I'll find out what he was doing. Put it right."

"Then I suggest you start immediately. Because that's how soon I'll expect to be hearing from you."

She put her glass down.

"Are you still here?"

He made it to the street somehow, where he went stumbling

for the nearest lamp post, grabbed it like a sailor grabs a mast, and puked into the gutter, all the evening's drink pouring out of him in one ugly flood.

Across the road, a well-dressed couple averted their gaze.

It might have been the hangover, but the leakage from the headphones of the man opposite sounded like a demon's whisper. John Bachelor was on an early train to St. Albans, his limbs heavy from lack of sleep, his stomach lumpy as a punchbag. Something pulsed behind his left eye and he was sure it glowed like a beacon in the gloomy carriage. The demon's whisper slithered in and out of meaning. Every time he thought he'd grasped its message, his mind greyed it out.

He had not had a good night. Good nights, anyway, were rare—at forty, Bachelor had discovered, you began dreaming of gravestones. After fifty, it was what you dreamed of when you were awake that frightened you most. Could Diana Taverner really engineer him behind bars? He wouldn't bet against it. If Dieter Hess had been in the pay of a foreign power, Bachelor would be guilty by default. Implicating him would be child's play to an old hand like Taverner.

The train flashed past a fox curled up in weeds by the side of the track, and two minutes later pulled into the station.

Bachelor stepped out into light rain, and trudged the familiar distance to Hess's flat.

For the past ten years he'd called here at least once a week. Two days earlier, letting himself in, he had known—was almost positive he'd known—that he'd be finding Dieter's body. Dieter had been sick for a while. Dieter had been an old man. And Dieter hadn't been answering Bachelor's calls—the fact was, Bachelor should have been there sooner. So the sight of Dieter at peace in his armchair, his passing eased by wine, tobacco and music, was, if anything, a relief. If he'd found Dieter face-down on the carpet, frantic scrabble marks showing his attempts to reach the phone, Bachelor would have had to work the scene a little, cover up any appearance of neglect. He'd been Dieter's handler, as Taverner had kept reminding him. Letting his charges die alone in pain didn't look good.

Any more than having them turn out doubles did.

But it was too soon to say whether Dieter had been a double. There were other explanations, other possibilities, for Dieter having had an illicit source of income. All Bachelor had to do was find one.

The flat had been searched, as protocol demanded, but not torn apart—the significance of the paperwork removed from Dieter's desk had only come to light back at the Park. What John Bachelor embarked on now was more thorough. He began in the kitchen, and after spreading newspaper on the floor he went through cupboards, opening jars and dumping their contents onto the paper; reading the entrails of Dieter's groceries, and finding nothing that shed light on his own future or on Dieter's past. All that came to light were coffee grounds and teabags, and surely more jars of herbs and spices than a single man could have need of? No secrets buried under packets of sausagemeat in the freezer drawers. Nothing under the sink but bottles of bleach and the usual plumbing. As he searched, Bachelor found himself working faster, intent on finishing the task in hand, and forced himself to slow down. He was breathing heavily, and on the spread-out newspaper sat a mountain of mess. He should have thought harder before launching into this. He couldn't even make himself a cup of coffee now, which would have been welcome, given the state of his head.

Bachelor closed his eyes and counted to ten. When he opened them again, nothing had improved, but he thought his heart had slowed a little. Was beating at more like its usual pace.

Think, he commanded himself. Arriving here, full of his night-time furies, he'd gone off like a Viking, which would only have made sense if Dieter had been a Viking too. But Dieter had been an old man who'd lived a careful life. A careless one would have proved much shorter. His habits of secrecy were unlikely to be laid bare by a whirlwind uprooting of the contents of his kitchen ... *Think*.

Leaving the mess in the kitchen, he walked through the rest of the flat.

Hess's sitting room—the room in which Bachelor had found him—was the largest, occupying as much space as the others put together. Bookshelves covered three of the four walls; against the fourth, below the window and facing inwards, was Dieter's armchair. His books were the view he appreciated most, and Bachelor had spent many afternoons listening to the old man rabbit on about their contents; sessions that had reminded him of interminable childhood Sundays in the company of his grandfather, whose mind, like his shelves, was not as well stocked as Dieter's, but whose appetite for rambling on about the past was just as insatiable. At least in Dieter's case the view backwards was panoramic. He had studied history. On his shelves was collected as much of the past as he'd been able to squeeze onto them; mostly early twentieth century, and post-war too, of course. He'd once confided to Bachelor—being a handler meant hearing all sorts of secrets: romantic, political, emotional, religious; meant hearing them and passing them on—that he nursed a fantasy of finding, in all that convoluted argy-bargy of politics and revolution, pogrom and upheaval, the key error; the single moment that could be retrospectively undone, and all the messiness of modern Europe set to rights. In Dieter's perfect world, he'd have stayed the German he was born. East and west would have been directions on a map.

Borderline obsessive, had been the verdict from the Park. But then, if your retired assets weren't borderline obsessive, they'd never have been assets in the first place.

There was poetry too, and fiction in a segregated corner, but Hess's taste in that area had been stern. He'd admired Flaubert above all writers, but had a compulsion to arrange, and rearrange, the great Russians in order of merit, as if the bulky tomes were jostling for a place in the starting line-up. Just looking at these novels' width aggravated Bachelor's headache. Their colours were as dull as their contents threatened, but a cheekier red-and-white spine nestled among its beefy brothers and sisters proved to be a paperback of Robert Harris's *Fatherland*. He wondered if that, too, had offered a glimpse of a happier twentieth century for Dieter Hess. One in which the war had fallen to the other side.

He moved on. The flat was near the railway line, and from the bathroom window could be seen trains heading for London and deeper into the commuter belt. It was a sash window and the wood had rotted round the edges of the frame, and its white paint flaked at the touch. It was about a year past the point Dieter should have had something done about it, just as the carpet—fraying around the rods holding it in place at the bathroom and kitchen doorways—was beyond shabby and edging into hazard country. It wasn't a big flat. If you tripped in a doorway, your head was going to hit something—the bath, the cooker—on its way down. Bachelor supposed he should have pointed this out back when it was likely to do some good, but the way things turned out, it hadn't mattered. He opened the bathroom cabinet, then closed it again. He wasn't looking for anything hidden in plain view.

The bedroom was small, with a single bed, and a wardrobe full of old-man shirts on wire hangers, their collars frayed. A faint smell he couldn't put a finger on brought hospitals to mind. The window overlooked the front street, and was near enough to a lamp post for the light to have been a bother. More books were stacked in piles along one wall. On a chest of drawers sat a hairbrush still clogged with old-man hair. Bachelor shuddered, as if something with a heavy tread had stomped across his future. Except even this, even this much, was going to look pretty desirable if he wound up paying the price for Dieter's secret life.

It was all neat enough. Everything where it was supposed to be. What if the only things hidden were hidden inside Dieter's head? What if there were no clues, no evidence, and the bank account was nothing more than his own savings, channeled through various offshore havens in order to, whatever, hide it from the taxman? But would Dieter have known how to do that? He'd been a bureaucrat. He'd known how to open a filing cabinet and use a dead-letter drop, and even that much had been decades ago. Money laundering would have been a whole new venture, and why would he be laundering his own money anyway? Bachelor was grasping at twigs, and knew it. He needed to stop the panicky theorising and get to work.

He was there for hours. He started over in the bathroom, prising the cabinet off the wall and shining a torch into the corners of the airing cupboard. In the bedroom he upturned the furniture and ran a hand round the skirting board, checking for hidden compartments. He worked the bookshelves, because he had no alternative, opening book after book, holding them by the spines and shaking, half-expecting after the first few hundred that words would start floating loose; that he'd drown in alphabet soup. Halfway done he gave up and returned to the kitchen, stepped around the mess he'd made and put the kettle on, then had to rescue an untorn teabag from the pile. He drank the unsatisfactory cuppa upright, leaning against the kitchen wall, glaring at the fraying ends of the carpet where it met the rod at the doorway. And then, because he couldn't face returning to the unending bookshelves, he knelt and prised the rod up. It came away easily, as if used to such treatment, and one of its screws dropped onto the lino and rolled under the fridge. Setting the rod aside he raised the carpet. Below it was an even thinner, disintegrating underlay, part of which came away in Bachelor's hand as he tugged.

In the exposed gap, so obviously waiting for him it might as well have been addressed, lay a plain white envelope.

In a pub on a nearby corner, Bachelor took stock. It was early doors, and he was first there, so he spread the contents of the envelope on his table as he supped a pint of bitter and felt his hangover recede slightly, to be replaced by something larger, and worse. If he'd hoped for an innocent explanation for Dieter's secret bank account, these papers put the kibosh on that. Dieter hadn't been innocent. Dieter had been hiding something. Had hidden it not only in an envelope beneath his carpet, but in code.

3/81.

4/19.

5/26.

And so on . . .

There were two pages of this, the numbers grouped in random sequences: four on one line, seven on the following, and so on. Twenty lines in all. Typed, they'd have taken up less than half a sheet, but Dieter Hess had been old school, and Dieter Hess didn't own a typewriter let alone a computer. And what this was was old-school code, a book cipher. They still taught book ciphers to newbies, in the same way they still taught Morse, the idea being that when it all went to pot, the old values would see you through. A book cipher was unbreakable without the book in front of you. Alan Turing would have been reduced to guesswork. Because there were no repetitions, no reliable frequencies hinting that *this* meant E and *that* was a T or an S. All you had were reference points. Without the book they were drawn from you were not only paddleless, you didn't have a canoe. And one thing Dieter had had in abundance was books—with all that raw material on his shelves, he could have constructed a whole new language, let alone a boy-scout code. An impossible task, thought Bachelor. Impossible. No sensible place to begin.

Then he took the old man's copy of *Fatherland* from his pocket, and deciphered the list.

Two pints later, he was on the train heading back into London. It was mostly empty, but he could still hear that demonic whisper—maybe it was Dieter. Maybe he was haunted by Dieter Hess.

The list had been precisely that: a list. A list of names, none of which meant anything to Bachelor. Four women, six men: Mary Ableman to Hannah Weiss; Eric Goulding to Paul Tennant. Dum de dum de dum de dum. Just thinking them, they took on the rhythm of the railway. Why had Dieter copied them out, hidden them under his carpet? Because it was a crib sheet, Bachelor answered himself. Whoever these people were, Dieter had referred to them often in whatever coded messages he had sent, ciphered letters painstakingly printed in his large looping hand. To save reciphering them every time, he'd copied out this list. It wasn't Moscow Rules—was shocking tradecraft—but to be fair to Dieter, he'd grown old and died before anybody stumbled on his lapse.

Dum de dum de dum de dum. It was the sound of Bachelor's own execution growing nearer. He'd gone to find proof of Dieter's innocence. What he had in his pocket proved the bastard's guilt: he'd been writing, often enough that he needed a crib sheet, to someone with a paperback of *Fatherland* to hand—*3/81* = third page, eighty-first character = M; *4/19* = A; *5/26* = R; *6/18* = Y, and so on, and so very bloody forth … Lady Di would have him flayed alive. Just knowing there were names being bandied round in code: she'd have him peeled and eaten by fish. And god only knew what she'd come up with if it turned out these coded characters were up to *mischief*.

He could abscond, the three pints of bitter suggested. He could flit home, grab his getaway kit—passport and a few appearance-adjusting tools, including fake glasses and a shoe-insert, to give him a limp: heaven help him—but even if the bitter had been convincing, the plan fell apart at the first hurdle, which was made of money. Divorce had cleaned him out, and it had been years since his escape kit had included the couple of grand that was the bare minimum for a disappearing trick. And it was one thing imagining himself a stylish expat in Lisbon, admiring the sunshine from a café on the quay; quite another to picture the probable reality: hanging round bus stations, begging for loose change.

Besides, even if he'd had the money, did he any longer have the nerve? The view through the windows was dreary, a grey parade of unidentifiable crops in boring fields, soon to be replaced by the equally unappetising back-ends of houses, with flags of St. George's hanging limply from upstairs windows, and mildewed trampolines leaning against fences—but it was where he belonged. Everyone needs somewhere to imagine escaping from, which didn't mean they wanted to leave it for good. Those young-man dreams of living each day as if it were your last, they wore off; showed up, in the cold light of after-fifty, for the magpie treasures they were. Live every day as if it were your last. So come nightfall, you'd have no job, no savings, and be bloody miles away. He wanted to stay where he was. He wanted his job to continue, his pension to remain secure. His life to continue unruffled.

Which meant he had to do something about this list before Lady Di got her hands on it.

He could destroy it, but if he did that before unravelling its meaning, he might be storing up grief to come. That was the trouble with the spying game: there were too many imponderables. But a list of names that meant nothing . . . He wouldn't know where to start.

The train ploughed on, and fields gave way to houses. Even after it came to a halt, Bachelor remained in his seat, watching without seeing the half-busy platforms. At length, he stood. He had a plan. It wasn't much of a plan, and involved a lot of luck and twice as much bullshit, but it was the best he could do at short notice.

And let's face it, he told himself as he headed for the underground. You've been coasting for years. If there's any spook left in you, let's see if he can pull this off.

Bachelor was headed across the river. This wasn't as bad as it sounded. In a profession whose every activity came encrypted in jargon, this one was happily literal, and didn't betoken an over-the-Styx moment, or not yet it didn't.

Some who worked there might have taken issue with this. The office complex from which various Service Departments operated—Background, Psych Eval and Identities, among others—was far removed from the dignity of Regent's Park, and a sense of second-class citizenry permeated its walls. Had it been *just* across the river—had it enjoyed a waterside view, for instance—things might have been different, but in this case over the river meant quite some distance over; far enough to leave its more ambitious inhabitants feeling they'd bought a loser's ticket in the postcode lottery. Nevertheless, the phrase was geographical, not metaphorical, which meant that those working across the river were in better shape, linguistically and otherwise, than the denizens of Slough House, which wasn't in Slough, wasn't a house, and was where screw-up spooks were sent to make them wish they'd died.

But not everyone who screws up gets to join the slow horses. Only those it'd be impolitic to sack . . .

He'd made calls, discovered who the newbies were. In an organisation this size there was always someone who'd just walked through the door, and while the training they'd been put through was more intense than most office jobs demanded, they'd still be the easiest pickings. With three names in his head, he checked their current whereabouts with security: showing his pass, barking his requests, to forestall any inquisition into his motives. Two of the newbies were out of the building. The third, JK Coe, was hot-desking on the fourth floor, not having been assigned a permanent workstation yet.

"Thanks," Bachelor said. His card had been logged on entry, and for all he knew this exchange had been recorded, but he'd come up with something plausible, or at least not outrageous, to use if he were quizzed. *Coe. Thought I'd known his father. Turned out to be a different branch.*

Coe, when Bachelor tracked him down, looked to be early thirties or thereabouts, which was old for a recruit, but not as unusual as it had once been. "Hinterland" was a buzzword now; it was good to have recruits with hinterland, because, well, it just was—Bachelor had forgotten the argument, if he'd even been listening when he'd heard it. Somehow, the Service had evolved into the kind of organisation which most of its recruits had joined it to avoid, but that was a rant for another day. Coe, anyway: early thirties. His particular hinterland lay in the City; he'd been in

banking until the profession had turned toxic, but his degree had
been in psychology.

"You're Coe?"

The young man's eyes were guarded. Bachelor didn't blame
him. The first few weeks in any job, you had to be on your
mettle. In the Service, that went times a hundred. Most unsched-
uled events were official mind games—googlies bowled at
newbies, to see how they'd stand up under pressure—and some
were co-workers' mind-fucks, to see whether the virgin had a
sense of humour. Depending on the department, this meant
laughing off anything from a debagging to life-threatening harm,
to show you weren't a spoilsport.

All or most of which probably went through JK Coe's head
before he replied.

"Yes."

"Bachelor. John." He showed Coe his ID, which was about
twenty-five generations older than Coe's own. "You're through
with induction, right?"

"Yesterday."

"Good. I've a job for you."

"And you're . . ."

"From the Park. I work with Diana Taverner."

And there was the word *with* stretched far as it would go; way
beyond where it might snap back in his face and lay him open to
the bone.

From his pocket, he produced a sealed envelope containing the
deciphered list of names. Before handing it over, he scribbled
Coe's own name on the front.

"I want background on each of them, including current

whereabouts. 'All significant activities,' is that still the phrase you're taught?"

"Yes, but—"

"Good, because that's what I want to hear about. All significant activities, meaning jobs, contacts, travels abroad. But I don't need to tell you your job, do I?"

"You kind of do," said Coe.

"You work here, right?"

"Psych Eval. I'm putting together a questionnaire for new recruits? Even newer ones, I mean."

A sheepish smile went with this.

"Maybe you'd like to call Lady Di, then. Explain why you're knocking her back." Bachelor produced his mobile. "I can give you her direct line."

"All I meant, no, nothing. Sure. Here." Coe took the envelope. "Am I looking for anything . . . in particular?"

"Information, Coe. Data. Background." Bachelor leaned forward, conspiratorially. The cubicle he'd found Coe in was surrounded by vacant workstations, but it was always worth making the effort. "In fact, let's say that what you've got here's a network. Deep cover. And you're looking to prove it. Ten ordinary people, and what you're after is the connection, the thread that links them. Which could be—well, you don't need me to tell you. It could be anything."

Coe's eyes had taken on a vague cast, which on a civilian might mean he was tuning out. Bachelor assumed it here meant the opposite; that Coe was drawing up a mental schedule: where he'd start, what channels he'd take. Analysts, in Bachelor's experience, were always drawing mental maps.

He wondered whether he should stress how confidential this was, but decided not to rouse the newby's suspicions. Besides, how stupid would Coe have to be to go blabbing to all and sundry?

He said, "The good news is, you've got a whole twenty-four hours."

"Is this live?" Coe asked. "I mean, is this an actual op?"

Bachelor touched a finger to his lips.

"Jesus," Coe said. He glanced around, but there was nobody in sight. "That long?"

"Banks shut at four-thirty, don't they? News flash. You don't work in a bank any more."

"It wasn't that kind of banking," Coe said. He glanced at the list in his hand, then back at Bachelor. "Where do I bring the product?"

"My number's on the sheet. Call me. Do this right, and you've a friend in Regent's Park."

"Who works with Diana Taverner," said Coe.

"Closely. Who works *closely* with Diana Taverner."

"Yes. I've heard she picks favourites."

Bachelor wondered if he'd made the right choice, a psych grad, but it was too late now.

Coe said, "I spent a night in a ditch last month, in freezing fog. Out on the Stiperstones?"

Bachelor knew the Stiperstones.

"I was told it was part of a reconnaissance exercise. Counted towards my pass rate. Turned out it was a wind-up. Left me so shagged out I nearly failed the next day's module."

Bachelor said, "We've all been there. What's your point?"

Coe looked like he had a point, and it was no doubt something to do with the kind of emotions he'd feel, or the sort of vengeance he'd hope to wreak, if it turned out that Bachelor had just handed him the desk-bound equivalent of a night in a freezing ditch.

"...Nothing."

"Good man. We'll speak tomorrow."

Bachelor left the building still with the ghost of a hangover scratching his skull. Maybe Coe would come up with something he could shield himself with when Lady Di made her next move. More likely this was a waste of time, but time was currently the only thing he had on his calendar.

It might help.

It probably wouldn't hurt.

It depended on how good JK Coe was.

How good JK Coe was was something JK Coe had been wondering himself. The complex knot of his reasons for joining the Service had tightened in his mind to the extent that rather than attempt untangling them, it was simpler to slice right through. On one side fell disillusionment with the banking profession; on the other, an interview he'd read in a Canary Wharf giveaway magazine with an Intelligence Services' recruitment officer. Like any boy, he'd once harboured fantasies of being a spy. The fact that here in grown-up life, the opportunity actually existed—that there was a number you could ring!—offered a glimmer of light in what had become, far sooner than he'd been expecting, a wearisome way of making a living.

It turned out that a psychology degree and a background in investment banking fitted Five's profile of desirable candidates.

That's what Coe had been told, anyway. It was possible they said that sort of thing a lot.

But here he was now, less than a week into fledgling status, and he'd been handed what had looked like a desk job but was rapidly becoming more intriguing. It might be, of course, that this was another set-up, and that Bachelor—if that was really his name—was even now celebrating Coe's gullibility in a nearby pub, but still: if this was a time-wasting riddle, it appeared to be one with an answer, even if that remained for the moment ungraspable as smoke.

Because the names he'd been given belonged to real people. Using the Background database, for which Coe had only ground-level clearance, but which nevertheless gave access to a lot of major record sets—utilities, census, vehicle and media licensing, health and benefits data, and all the other inescapable ways foot-prints are left in the social clay—he'd established possible identities for each name on Bachelor's list, and caught a glimmer, too, of a connecting thread. He thought of this in terms of a spider's web in a hedge: one moment it's there, in all its compli-cated functionality; the next, when you shift your perspective an inch, it's gone.

There were real people with these names, but if they made up a network, it can't have been a terribly effective one. Because almost all of them were lock-aways of one sort or another. Care homes, hospitals, prison . . . Each time he tilted his head, the perspective shifted.

The afternoon had swum away, leaching all light from the sky. Coe hadn't eaten since mid-morning, a bacon sandwich he'd been planning to trade off against lunch, but he hadn't reckoned on skipping supper too. He should call a halt now, but if he did, there was no telling he'd get any further with his task in the morning; odds-on he'd be called to account for that questionnaire he'd barely started. And this was more interesting than devising trip-up questions, and now he had his teeth in, he didn't want to let go ...

But he needed help. Oddly, he had an idea where it might be found.

A lecture he'd attended the previous month had been given by a Regent's Park records officer. She ran a whole floor, it was whispered; ran it like a dragon runs its lair, and it was easy to see how the dragon rumour started, because she was a fearsome lady. Wheelchair-bound, with a general demeanour that just dared you to give a shit about it, she'd held her audience if not spellbound then certainly gobsmacked, through the simple expedient of giving the first student she caught drifting such a bollocking he probably still trembled when reminded of it now. In one fell swoop, the dragon-lady had resurrected several dozen bad school memories. She'd quickly been dubbed Voldemort.

Funny thing was, JK Coe had rather liked Molly Doran, who was every bit as round as she was legless, and powdered her face so thickly she might have been a circus turn. Her lecture—on information collation in a pre-digital era: *not*, she emphasised, an historical curiosity, but an in-the-field survival technique—had been brisk and intelligent, and when she'd finished by announcing that she would not be taking questions because she'd already answered any they might be capable of coming up with, it had been with the air of delivering a tiresome truth rather than playing for laughs. She had added, though, that she expected to see the more intelligent among them again, because sooner or later the more gifted would need her help.

Only JK Coe had offered the traditional round of applause once she was done, and he quit after two claps when it was clear he was on his own. He'd been relieved Doran had had her back to the class, shuffling her papers into a bag, and hadn't seen him.

Two thumbs down from his classmates then, but that was okay. Coe, the oldest in his recruitment wave, felt licensed to divert from the popular opinion. Molly Doran was—no getting round this—a "character," and having escaped a profession which prided itself on its characters, this being how it labelled those who read *The Art of War* on the tube, Coe was gratified to have come across the real thing. Already he'd heard two conflicting stories behind the loss of Doran's legs, and this too was a source of pleasure. The Service thrived on legends.

He could track down people with the bare minimum to go on, he'd proved that much today. It wasn't a stretch coming up with Molly Doran's extension number; nor was it a surprise that she was still within reach of it, down in the bowels of the Park, on the right side of the river.

Legends don't keep office hours.

Coe explained who he was.

She said, "You're the one who clapped, aren't you?"

He could see his reflection in his monitor as he heard the words, and afterwards had the strange sensation that his reflection had been observing his reaction, rather than the other way round. Certainly, it seemed to retain an unusual state of calm for one who'd just been presented with evidence of witchcraft.

She said, "All right, close your mouth. If you hadn't been the one who'd clapped, you wouldn't dare call me now."

"I'd worked that out for myself," he lied.

She asked what he wanted, and he explained about the list; not saying where he'd got it from, just that it was a puzzle he'd been presented with. Besides, he reasoned, Bachelor hadn't sworn him to secrecy.

"And what do you expect from me?"

"Something you said in your lecture," Coe said. "You said don't muck about with secondary sources—"

"I said *what*?"

"—You said don't fuck about with secondary sources if there's a primary available. And that there's always a primary available if you know where to look."

"And I'm your primary?"

"Or you can tell me who is."

"So you're expecting me to point you to someone cleverer?"

"I doubt even you could manage that."

She laughed what sounded like a smoker's laugh. Last time he'd heard anything quite like it, he been sanding off the edge of a door.

"That's right, JK. You did say JK? Not Jake?"

Some jerks get lumbered with Jason. Some saps are saddled with Kevin. But how many poor sods end up with—

"JK," he confirmed.

"That's right, JK, you ladle on the syrup. The ladies always fall for that."

He said, "In that case, I have to tell you, you've got a great set of wheels."

A silence followed, during which Coe's thoughts turned to the essential elements involved in forging a new identity: fake passport, fake social security number, fake spectacles. He'd need to shave his head, too . . .

And then she was laughing again, more like a rusty bicycle chain this time.

"You little bastard," she said.

"Sorry."

"Don't spoil it now. You little bastard."

He counted blessings until her laughter passed.

"So this list," she said at last. "This famous list. You've found a link and you want to talk to someone who might know what it means."

"If it is a link, and not just a coincidence—"

"Don't be boring. If you thought it was a coincidence, you'd not have called me."

Coe said, "They all have German connections. Some close, some not so close. But they all have connections."

"Oh Jesus," Molly Doran said. "I'm sorry, JK."

She sounded it, too.

"You can't help?"

"Just the opposite. I know exactly who you want to speak to."

"Then why so sorry?"

"Ever heard of Jackson Lamb?" she asked.

In his final years as a banker, JK Coe had grown understandably secretive about his profession. In that sense, joining the Service hadn't involved big changes—broadcasting your daily activities was frowned upon—but he still found it hard to avoid feeling himself separate from the general sway. It was ridiculous, stupid, counter-productive—being an agent, even a back-room, across-the-river agent, meant melding in—and he knew, too, that everyone felt this way, that everyone was at the centre of their own narrative. Still, he couldn't help it. Take this trip across town right now, to talk to Jackson Lamb. Standing on the tube, Coe was studying his fellow passengers, gauging their identities. There was a checklist he'd memorised, a cribsheet on how to spot a terrorist; and there was another checklist, allowing for the possibility that terrorists might have got hold of the first check-list and adapted their behaviour accordingly, and Coe had memorised this too. And he was mentally running through them, scoring his fellow travellers, when it struck him there was con-ceivably a checklist for spotting members of the security services, and he was doubtless ticking all the right boxes himself . . . The thought made him want to giggle, which itself was on one of the checklists. But he couldn't help feeling skittish. He was still in his first week, newest of newbies, and he'd shared a clubby phonecall with Molly Doran, and was now on his way to meet Jackson Lamb.

Who definitely figured among the legends he'd been contem-plating earlier.

Lamb was a former joe, an active undercover, who'd spent time on the other side of the Wall, back when there'd been a Wall. So he was definitely the man to talk to if you were looking for dodgy German connections stretching into the past—most of the folk on Bachelor's list were certified crumblies—but he was also someone who came trailing clouds of story, some of which had to be true. He'd been Charles Partner's golden boy once—Partner,

last of the Cold War First Desks—but after Partner shot himself,
Lamb had been hived off to the curious little annex called Slough
House, which was right side of the river, but wrong side of the
tracks. And there he'd remained ever since, presiding over his own
little principality of screw-ups. Some of the stories said he'd been
a genius spy; others that he'd blown a whole network, and was
the only one who'd come back alive. Nobody Coe knew had ever
laid eyes on him. Well, nobody except Molly Doran, and he
couldn't really claim to know her.

He'd phoned Slough House and spoken to a woman called
Standish. When he'd said he wanted to speak to Lamb, she seemed
to be waiting for the punchline. So he'd explained about the list,
and she'd told him Lamb didn't talk to strangers on the phone, and
wasn't terribly likely to speak to him in person. But if he was prepared to head over Barbican way, she'd see what she could do.

What she could do involved opening the door for him. This
was round the back, as she'd said on the phone: Slough House
had a front door, but it hadn't been used in so long, she couldn't
guarantee it actually worked. "Round back" was via a mil-
dew-coated yard. There was no light, and Coe barked his shin on
something unidentifiable, so was leaning against the door gri-
macing when it opened, and he came this close to measuring his
length in a dank hallway.

"Now there's an entrance," the woman said.

"Sorry. That yard's a deathtrap."

"We don't get many visitors. Come on. He's on the top floor."

Trooping up the stairs felt like ascending to Sweeney Todd's
lair. Coe didn't know what that made Catherine Standish, who'd
have been a dead ringer for a woman in white—a lady with a

lamp—had she worn white, or carried a lamp. But her long-sleeved dress had ruffled sleeves, and Coe believed he caught a glimpse of petticoat in the two-inch gap between its hem and the strap of her shoe. But Slough House, Jesus . . . Regent's Park was impressive—a cross between old world class and hi-tech flash—and his own across-the-river complex, if drab, was functional, and had been gutted and refitted often enough that you sensed an attempt to keep up with the times. But Slough House was time-warped, a little patch of seventies' squalor, with peeling walls and creaking stairs. The bare lightbulbs highlit patches of damp that resembled large-scale maps, as if the staircase had been designed by a wheezing cartographer. And in the corners of the stairs lurked dustballs so big they might have been nests. He wasn't sure whose nests. Didn't want to be.

On each landing a pair of office doors stood open. They were vacant and unlit, and drifting from their gloomy shadows came a mixture of odours Coe couldn't help adumbrating: coffee and stale bread, and takeaway food, and cardboard, and grief.

He thought something moved.

"Did I just see a cat?"

"No."

And up they went, up to the top floor, and a small hallway with office doors facing each other from either side. One stood open, and was lit by a couple of standard lamps; the effect wasn't exactly cosy—it remained a drably furnished office—but at least it looked like a space in which things got done. This was Standish's own, Coe assumed. Which meant that the other—

"You'd better knock."

He did.

"Who the hell's that?"

"Good luck," said Catherine Standish, and disappeared into her room, closing the door behind her.

Okay, so Coe was about to meet a Service legend. *Beard him in his den* was the phrase that came unbidden, and he raised his hand to knock again, this time while announcing his name in a pleasing, manly fashion, when the door opened without warning.

So here was Jackson Lamb.

He didn't look like a legend. He looked like a Punch cartoon of a drunk artist, in a jacket that might have been corduroy once, and another colour—it was currently brown—over a collarless white shirt. What a kinder observer might call a cravat hung round his neck, and his hair was yellowy-grey, with clumps sticking out at odd angles. More hair, much darker, could be seen poking through his shirt at stomach level. As for his face, this was rounded and jowly and blotchy; there was a slight gap between his two front teeth, visible below a snarling lip. Yes, like a caricature of an artist, and one in the grip of some creative urge or other. His eyes were heavy with suspicion.

"Who are you?"

"Ah, JK Coe—"

"Oh Christ. I've told her about letting strays in. What are you selling?"

"I'm not selling anything."

Lamb grunted. "Everybody's selling something."

He withdrew into his room, and since he did so without actually telling Coe to get lost, Coe followed.

The room's sole illumination was a lamp set upon a pile of books, which on second glance turned out to be telephone directories. In the feeble yellow light it cast, Coe could make out a desk whose most prominent ornaments were a bottle of whisky and a pair of shoes. In the shadows round the walls lurked what Coe took for filing cabinets and shelves. Blinds were drawn over the sole window, but a cracked blade hung loose, and through the gap some of the evening's dark leaked into the room, offset by tiny reflections of the traffic on Aldersgate Street, blinking in the beads of moisture hanging on the glass.

Lamb didn't so much settle into his chair as collapse into it. The noise it greeted him with was one of resigned discomfort.

"You're from over the river," Lamb said, reaching for the bottle.

"Ms. Standish told you?"

"Do I look like I've time to gossip? She didn't even tell me you were coming. But you're hardly from the Park, are you? Not unless they've widened their entry criteria." Looking up, he added, "It's a class thing. Don't worry about it."

"Lamb is easily bored," Molly Doran had said. "Play him right, and he'll bend your ear for hours. But if he's in one of his moods, forget it."

"But this is work," Coe had said. "It's Service business."

"That's sweet. I remember my first week." Doran paused. "Oh, and one other thing. Don't tell him I sent you. Got it?"

"Got it."

So here, in place of the truth, was Coe's reason for approaching Lamb:

"Everyone says you're the one to talk to."

"Everyone says that, do they?"

"You lived the life. Ran your own network, survived for years. They say—"

Lamb interrupted with a fart, then said in a plummy tone, "I do apologise. That's never happened before."

Coe said, "They say you were the best."

"I was, was I?"

"And my problem's about a network . . ."

He paused. He seemed to be always pausing. This time, he was partly waiting for permission to continue; partly wondering if Lamb was ever going to invite him to sit. But there was nowhere obvious to sit that didn't involve retreating into the shadows, and while he didn't actually believe anything untoward lurked by the walls, he was a little concerned about the floorboards. The air of rot was more pronounced than it had been on the stairs. He figured he was okay if he remained in the middle of the room.

Lamb had closed his eyes, and linked his fingers across his paunch. His feet were visible on Coe's side of the desk, and he was indeed shoeless, which perhaps accounted for some small part of the atmosphere. Lamb's recent emission hadn't helped. He grunted now, and when this didn't spur Coe on, opened an eye. "You don't need to tell me about your problem, son. I already know what your problem is."

So Doran had called him after all, Coe thought. He realised he was caught in the middle of some complicated game between this man and Molly Doran, as intricate as any courtship ritual, but that didn't matter now, because the important thing was, Lamb was going to explain the oddities in this supposed network . . .

"Your problem is, you're lying. Nobody talks about me on the other side of the river, or when they do, it's not to say how brilliant

I am. It's to say I'm a fat old bastard who should have been put out to grass long ago."

"I—"

"And it's not only the lying. You'll never get anywhere in this business without lying. No, your problem's twofold. First off, as you've probably worked out for yourself already, you're no good at it."

"I was told not to tell you—"

"And second, it's me you're lying to."

All of this with just one eye open, trained on Coe. It was extraordinary, thought Coe, how much a badly dressed shoeless fat man could look like a crocodile.

"And you've no idea how cross I get when that happens."

But he was about to find out.

It was after nine when Catherine Standish entered Lamb's room again. Lamb was in his chair, eyes closed, shoeless feet propped on his wastepaper bin. A bottle of Talisker sat on his desk, a pair of thumb-greased glasses next to it. One was a quarter full, or possibly three quarters empty. The other, while not exactly clean, was at least unused.

She knew the routine, a recent parlour game of Lamb's. No point talking until she poured herself a glass. This was what passed, in his mind, for good-natured teasing.

Slough House had been empty of staff for hours, the pair of them apart. For Catherine there was always work to do, a never-ending cascade of it. For Lamb, she sometimes thought, there was nowhere else to be. He had a home; might even—now here was a thought—have a family somewhere. She thought that less likely than finding intelligent life on Twitter, but still: there had to be a reason he spent so many of his waking hours here, even if a goodly fraction of those waking hours were spent asleep.

Without touching the glass she poured a slug of whisky into it, then added a pile of newspapers from the visitor's chair to the bigger pile on the floor next to it, and sat.

She said, "That wasn't very helpful."

He didn't open his eyes. "This is me you're talking to?"

"We're all part of the Service. So someone thought it would be funny to send a Daniel into your den. That doesn't mean he didn't need real information."

"I didn't object to the little bastard turning up. I objected to the little bastard trying to play me."

"Well, I think we can safely say he won't try that again."

JK Coe's departure had been precipitous, making up in speed what it lacked in dignity.

"Did you know him?"

"He's still in his first week. Refugee from banking, but he scored high on the entrance exams and—"

"Entrance exams," said Lamb. "God help us."

"I know," Catherine said. "Just give them a Double-Oh-Seven watch and drop them behind enemy lines. Never did you any harm."

"Well, we can't all be me," Lamb said reasonably. "What's his day job?"

"Psych Eval."

"For a washed-up alky, you're still plugged into the network, aren't you?"

Washed-up was right. Catherine's career, like a castaway's

message, had been sealed inside a bottle and tossed overboard. Slough House was where it had beached, and in the years since she hadn't touched a drop.

The amount of booze Lamb had put away in that time would float a hippo.

"It's funny," she said. "I'm sitting here dry as a bone while you souse yourself nightly. How come I'm a drunk and you're not?"

"Drunks have blackouts," he explained kindly. "And wake up in strangers' beds. I never do that."

"When you start waking in strangers' beds, it's the strangers who ought to be worried."

"You say tomato," Lamb said obscurely. He reached for his glass, balanced it on his chest, and closed his eyes again. "Tell me about the kid's problem."

So she told him about the kid's problem. John Bachelor, one of the Park's old lags, had presented him with a list of names; find out who they are, Bachelor had said. Find out if there's a connection.

Find out if it's a network.

"Bachelor," Lamb said without opening his eyes. "Milkman, right?"

"He's on the milk round, yes."

"One of his mentals just died."

"Mentals?"

"Trust me, they're all mentals." Lamb craned his head forward, caught the rim of his glass in his teeth, and easing his head back again, allowed the contents of the glass to pour into his mouth. He swallowed, then set the glass back on his chest. "When Daniel Craig can do that," he said, "tell him to give me a ring."

"I've made a note."

"Dieter Hess," Lamb continued. "That was the bugger's name."

"Did you know him?"

"God no. I've better things to do with my time than pal around with clapped-out spooks."

It was true, Catherine thought, that you didn't get that adept at handless drinking without hours of practice.

"I know who he was, but not a joe, an asset. Worked in the Department of Transport on the other side."

When Lamb said "the other side," he always meant the Wall. For him, the Cold War had been geography as much as politics.

"He had access to classified info. Troop movements, that sort of thing. Fair play to him, it was useful stuff. How far did Coe get?"

Coe had done the basic searches and come up with a list of possibles connected by a thread: they all had links with Germany. They were offspring of immigrants, or had other family bonds; they had work connections; they'd studied the language and literature to degree level. In some cases, frequent holidays indicated an attachment to the country. It wasn't much, Coe had thought, but it wasn't something he was spinning out of fresh air. It was definitely there.

Lamb grunted. "And means the list definitely came from Hess. So what's the problem?"

"The problem is, most of those on the list are shutaways. In care homes, a lot of them. Elderly. There's one who's younger, thirty-two, and he's never been anywhere else. He's severely disabled. One's been in prison for the last decade, and isn't leaving soon. Of the whole crew, there's only one at liberty, a twenty-one-year-old girl." Lamb wasn't reacting to any of this. Hadn't even opened his eyes. "So what Coe wants to know is, what kind of network is that?"

She leaned back in her chair and waited.

After some minutes Lamb raised his empty glass, using his hand this time. He held it in her direction. Suppressing a sigh she reached for the bottle, and filled it for him. Her own still sat where she'd left it, untouched. She was trying to pretend it wasn't there. If she looked at it by accident—if it looked back—she would turn to stone.

Lamb said, "Any rumours on the late Hess?"

"There was money."

"But not huge great bucketloads, right?"

"Not from what I've heard."

And Catherine heard a lot. She had fallen far—there were those who'd argue she'd fallen further than Lamb—but the only enemy she'd made on the way was her own younger self. In her private life, she double-locked her doors. But at work she kept all channels open, and even Lamb was impressed by the range of her contacts, and their willingness to share with her.

But if she dealt in raw data, Lamb liked to build castles with it.

She said, "You have that look."

"What look?"

"That look where you're about to be clever, and I'm supposed to be amazed."

Lamb belched.

"Though I could be wrong," Catherine said.

"Coe's still slimy with afterbirth, so you can't blame him for being ignorant. But Bachelor's third-rate at best. Know him?"

"Of him."

"Best way. All being a milkman involves is wiping noses and he can't even do that. If he asked Coe to track down these people, it's because he doesn't want to do it via channels, which means he hasn't told anyone at the Park. I expect he found the list after Hess died, and has been crapping himself in case Lady Di gets wind of it. Coe doesn't know enough to work out what it means, and he's too stupid to do it himself."

"But you're not."

"You probably weren't either, before you pickled what used to be your brain. You never get those cells back, do you?"

When he asked a particularly nasty question, Lamb generally required an answer.

Catherine said, "They're usually full of information you don't want to recall anyway. If I ever struggle with your name, there's your reason." She thought for a bit. "The fact that it wasn't much money is a clue, isn't it?"

Lamb lit a cigarette.

She thought some more. Out on the street, a car honked and another honked back. Impossible to tell whether two friends had driven past each other, or one stranger had cut another up. There were times when it was similarly hard to tell what was happening in this room.

Hess had been receiving money to pay the people on this list. But the people weren't any kind of network; they were shut-ins and innocents.

She waved away smoke and said, "It's a ghost network."

"There you go. All you've ever done for the Service is type memos and boil the kettle, and even you can work it out. I despair for this generation, I really do. Bunch of Gideons."

She didn't ask.

Not being asked never bothered Jackson Lamb. "Talentless chancers riding on their family pull and the old school tie. Call me a hopeless idealist, but talent used to count for something."

Catherine stood. "Maybe we'll put that on your gravestone."

She was halfway out the door before he said, "You'll tell him all this, won't you?"

"Coe? Yes, I will."

"Another lame duck. Collect as many as you like, it won't help you fly again."

"I'm under no illusions about my future, thanks."

"Just as well. It's not clear you have one. Unless you count this place."

Catherine turned. "Thanks. And by the way, what *is* that round your neck?"

"Somebody's scarf. Found it in the kitchen." Lamb scratched the back of his neck. "There's a draught."

"Yes, keep it on. Don't want you catching cold."

She went back to her own office to ring Coe, thinking: So that's where the tea towel went.

Lamb finished his drink, then reached for Catherine's untouched glass. A ghost network. He didn't especially approve—in Lamb's lexicon, a joe was not to be trifled with; even an imaginary joe—but the old lag had doubtless done it for beer money, which left Lamb half-inclined to applaud. A ghost network didn't require joes. All it took was a little identity theft; enough to convince your paymasters you were nurturing the real thing: verifiable names, plausibly sympathetic to whatever cause you'd hired out to. In Hess's case, he'd scraped together a crew as near their last legs as he'd been himself, but that didn't matter, because there was no way the paymasters were ever going to get an actual sniff of them. *Too soon*, he'd have said. *Too raw. Bring them on gently*. Phrases Lamb had used himself, in the long-ago, but always for real. And what were they supposed to be passing on, Hess's phantoms? Nothing major. Gossip from the corridors of power, industrial tittle tattle, maybe hints of policy shifts; or possibly Hess had gone for something riskier, and pretended one of them was actually in the pay of the Service. Thinking about it, Lamb suspected the old boy could have made that fly. Milked John Bachelor for office gossip and passed it off as product, explaining the lack of substance everywhere else as being early yield; a thin harvest from a too-green vine, but let it grow, let it grow . . .

And it was only small sums of money.

He supped from Standish's glass. A low murmur from across the hall told him she was on the phone, giving the lowdown to Coe, who'd doubtless be puppyishly grateful, and just like that Standish had another resource to call on. Networks everywhere . . . And who could be surprised, really, that a worn-out spook had found a way to supplement his pension? Hess had been an asset, and here was a thing about assets: you could never be sure they weren't going to turn 180 degrees. Lamb accepted that now as he had done then. He hated a traitor, but defined the breed narrowly. Assets switching pavements was part of the game. Because they were the ones doing the risky business, while their paymasters risked only papercuts.

"So no harm done," he muttered. Least of all to John Bachelor, who'd be able to pass the whole thing off as an old man's petty

larceny; if, indeed, he bothered to pass anything on at all. Ghost
networks were only a problem if you believed in ghosts. Bachelor
probably scraped by without that superstition.

So no, no harm done.

Unless somebody does something stupid, Lamb thought, but
really; what were the chances?

Information is a tart—information is anybody's. It reveals as much
about those who impart it as it teaches those who hear. Because
information, ever the slut, swings both ways. False information—
if you know it's false—tells you half as much again as the real
thing, because it tells you what the other feller thinks you don't
know, while real information, the copper-bottomed truth, is
worth its weight in fairy-dust. When you have a source of real
information, you ought to forsake all others and snuggle down
with it for good. Even though it'll never work out, because information, first, last and always, is a tart.

This much, John Bachelor knew.

So the best thing to have, he also knew, was an asset; someone deep in the enemy's bunker—and for information purposes,
everyone was an enemy—passing back knowledge that the
enemy thought was his alone. But even better than that was
knowing the enemy had an asset inside your own bunker, and
feeding him, feeding her, information that looked like the real
thing, that nobody dared to poke at, but which was false as a
banker's promise.

And best of all, better than anything else, was having it both
ways; was having someone the enemy only thought was their asset
inside your own bunker, so while your enemy thought he was

feeding you mouldy crumbs and harvesting cake, the reality was the other way round.

All of this, Bachelor wanted to explain to Di Taverner before he got on to anything else, but that wasn't going to happen. For a start, she knew it all already. And for the rest, she had other things on her mind.

"They should have taken the carpets up," she said.

"He was an old man."

"Your point being?"

"Nobody was expecting this. Dieter's been—had been—defunct for years. As far as anyone knew he was sitting at home reading Yeats, and drinking himself into oblivion. Cleaning up after him was a matter of respect, that's all."

"If they'd respected him more, they'd have taken the carpets up," she said.

They were in her office in Regent's Park, and it was mid-morning, and the artificial lighting was pretending it was spring. On her desk lay the list; Dieter Hess's coded original. The copy of *Fatherland* with which Bachelor had unwrapped its secrets sat next to it.

"And these people," Taverner said—the people on the list—"they're all real?"

"They exist, but they're not a network." He'd told her this already, but it was important to emphasise the point: that Dieter Hess had not—had *not*—been running a coy little op behind Bachelor's back, but had simply been filching pennies to ease his days; to pay for his wine and his books; to ensure, god help us all, that he could turn the heating up. So Bachelor laid it out again, this information that had seeped down from Jackson Lamb to

Catherine Standish; from Standish to JK Coe; from Coe to John Bachelor, and was even now being soaked up by Diana Taverner: that the people whose encoded names had been laboriously printed on that sheet of paper in most cases probably didn't know what day of the week it was, let alone that they were spies. Dieter Hess had picked their pockets, though all he had taken was their names.

"Why them in particular?"

"For their German links. He needed people the BND would believe in."

The Bundesnachrichtendienst was the German intelligence service.

"Do me the smallest of favours and don't treat me like an idiot. I meant why people in homes, in hospitals? Out of circulation?"

"Safer. He didn't want anyone who was going to make waves. You know, win the lottery or something. Get in the papers. Draw attention."

"Then what about the younger one? Why doesn't she fit the pattern?"

"He wanted a live one. Obviously."

Her eyes flashed danger. "What's obvious about it?"

"I didn't mean obvious, I just meant I've been thinking about it." Jesus. "He wanted someone he could demonstrate was live and kicking, if he needed to."

"Like when? How did this scam work? If it was a scam. The jury's still out."

"It worked on old-school principles," Bachelor said. "The kind that mean, if you've got an agent in place, you don't put them on parade. Hess was known to the BND, of course he was. He

defected, after all. Ancient history, but still. So if he claimed, I
don't know, regret, or willingness to make amends now the
Fatherland's reunited, he'd have found a willing ear. He was a
persuasive man. That's how he survived doing what he did. So
anyway, he made his contact, and yes, *mea culpa*, *mea culpa*—I
should have known he did that."

If he'd been hoping Diana Taverner would wave his guilt away,
he was disappointed.

"Anyway." Moving briskly on. "Having made contact, he convinces whoever, let's call him Hans, he convinces Hans he's built
up a network of people prepared to pass on whatever titbits their
professional lives offer. The same kind of thing we'd be interested
in ourselves. Now, I know you're going to say, 'But they're on our
side—'"

Because it was his firmly held principle that when trying to
seduce, you bowled the odd full toss.

"For god's sake, John. Who do you think you're talking to?"

For information purposes, everyone was an enemy.

"Sorry. So anyway, Hans takes the bait, and in return for a small
amount of money, peanuts, he's acquired a string. But strictly sight
unseen, of course, because he can't go round kicking tyres, can
he? Not with a stable of spooks. All he can do is give thanks, open
a bank account so Dieter can feed the fledglings, and sit back and
wait for product."

"Which is what?"

"That's the beauty of it. Hess would've claimed to have
long-term agents in place, the kind that take years of cultiva-
tion. So there's not going to be major product. Not right away.
Which keeps Hans quiet and doesn't worry Dieter one jot,

because by the time his debts fall due, and his agents are expected to be coughing up the proverbial fairy dust, well, he'll be dead. He knows how ill he is. He's not expecting a miracle recovery."

Diana Taverner's eyebrows were drawn to a point. Partly she was assessing Bachelor's story; partly his demeanour. He seemed to believe his tale, but then, he was invested in it—either Hess's list was the harmless petty larceny Bachelor was selling, or the old fool had really had been up to something, in which case it had been happening on Bachelor's watch. And while her warnings to him about prison time had been for effect, her other threats had been real. Taverner had a strict policy about mistakes. She was prepared to accept her subordinates made them so long as they were prepared to take the blame. She didn't like finding other people's messes on her desk. From a distance, they might look like her own.

On the other hand, surrendering the list was a point in his favour. He could have pretended he'd never found it, and worked up a legend to explain Hess's secret funds. Along with her policy on mistakes, Taverner had one on cover-ups: provided they came with full deniability, she could live with them.

He'd stopped talking.

She said, "And all this for a few extra quid."

"Don't discount it. We don't exactly bed them down in clover—"

"Don't talk to me, John. Talk to the Minister. And she can talk to the Treasury."

"Well, quite. But anyway, a few extra quid, a couple of grand a year, makes the difference to Dieter between a nice bottle of wine

and a supermarket offer." Bachelor paused, having been struck by
a vision of his own future. Where was he? Yes: "And besides . . .
He was a game old bird. He probably enjoyed it."

"Maybe so," she said.

The moment's silence they shared was more of a wake for
Dieter Hess than the evening in the pub had been.

She said, "Okay. You screwed up, which I'm not forgetting,
but for the moment, no harm done. Hans'll no doubt come looking for his strays once he's sure Dieter's safely forgotten, so Hess's
phantoms are on your watch list. I don't want to read about various shut-ins being smothered in their sleep when a vengeful
BND spook finds he's been conned."

Bachelor didn't reply. He was staring at a fixed point in space
that was either high above London or somewhere in the back of
his own mind. Lady Di scowled. If anyone was going to fall prey
to reverie in her office, it was her.

"Still with me?"

"There's another possibility."

"Enlighten me."

"You're right. Hans, whoever he is, will wait for the ashes to
settle before he comes looking for Dieter's lost sheep. Which gives
us a window of opportunity."

Lady Di leaned back. "Go on."

"This younger girl, the one Hess must have meant for show
. . . What if we turn her?"

"You want to recruit her?"

"Why not? If she's suitable . . . We run the usual background
checks, make sure she's not an idiot or a nutjob, but if she fits the
asset profile, why not? Hans already thinks she's on his side, and

she doesn't even know he exists. We'd have a ready-made double. How much of a coup is that?"

"Running an op against a friendly?"

"It wouldn't be an op as such. If Hans is planning a recruitment drive on our soil, it serves him right if he gets his fingers burnt. Don't pretend you don't like the idea."

As far as Diana Taverner was concerned, she'd pretend whatever she liked. But she allowed the idea to percolate while she told Bachelor to leave, and he departed to float round Regent's Park, wondering whether he'd done enough to save his career.

Recruit one of Hess's phantoms . . . It had a nice circularity to it. Was the kind of scheme which could become a case study, a model for future strategists to ponder; how to seize an opportunity, turn it into a triumph. Backdoor views into other states' intelligence services were always welcome. Like having the chance to rummage through your best friend's cupboards. An opportunity you'd publicly deplore, but so long as they didn't find out about it, you were never going to pass up.

And as so often with Second-Desk decisions, it was the money tilted the balance. When the money side of it occurred to her, a slow smile spread across Diana Taverner's face; a smile that had been known to draw men her way, until they got close enough to notice that it never reached her eyes. Hans had been paying Hess to maintain his network; he'd be disappointed when he discovered nine tenths of this network was fake, but if he thought the girl was genuine, he'd continue paying her upkeep. Which meant the Park wouldn't have to. A detail that would bring her a standing ovation once she ran it past the Limitations Committee.

She had Bachelor paged, and gave him the go-ahead.

• • •

The waves were mostly froth: great fat spumes hurling themselves at the Cobb's sides, then spitting as high as they could reach before collapsing back into the roiling puddle of the sea. Again and again the waves did this, as if reminding the Cobb that, while it might have graced this harbour for hundreds of years, the sea had been around significantly longer, and would prevail in the long run.

That particular scenario wasn't troubling Hannah Weiss, however. Mostly, she was enjoying the figure she must cast to anyone watching from the quay. With a red windcheater and jeans in place of a black cloak, and her dark-blonde hair pulled into the briefest of knots at the back of her head, she was a far cry from Meryl Streep, but still: there was no denying the inherent romance in the scene. The waves splashed against the stone, and the grey sky was tinged with purple on the horizon, threatening rain later, and here she was; lingering on the stone arm Lyme extends into the sea, curled protectively round its bobbing fleet of boats.

And she was here with romantic purpose, of course. The man who had dropped into her life a mere fortnight earlier had brought her here, or perhaps summoned her was a better way of putting it; or perhaps—to be blunt—had sent her the rail ticket: first class return (big spender!), a cottage for the weekend, and he'd join her, within an hour of her arrival, on the Cobb. Sorry they couldn't travel together, but he'd explain all soonest. Clive Tremain, he was called. He wore a tie all week and polos all weekend, enjoyed country walks and well-earned pub meals after, and was going to do his damnedest to borrow a dog for this particular mini-break, so they could throw balls on a beach, and watch it jump across waves to collect them.

He'd turned up at a party two weeks earlier, an old friend of an old friend of the party-giver, and had cornered Hannah in the kitchen for an hour, hung avidly on her every word, then wooed her number out of her before mysteriously disappearing. She'd been on tenterhooks for forty-eight hours, which was her upper limit for tenterhooks, before he'd used it. Since then they'd been on three dates and he'd improved on each occasion, though had yet to make any significant moves in a bedward direction. And then came the weekend-in-Lyme-Regis idea, which struck Hannah as perfect, definitely one up on any invitation any of her girlfriends had yet received. Clive Tremain. A bit sticky-looking at first sight—sticky-looking as in, might just have a stick stuck up him—but that didn't detract from his looks. He had the air of one who'd taken orders in the past, and might not be above dishing them out in the future.

And now here he came, for this surely must be him—a man approaching the Cobb from the road. Wearing a black overcoat at which la Streep herself might not have turned her nose up, and bareheaded, and on the Cobb itself now, near enough for a pang of disappointment to reach her, because it wasn't Clive; was a much older man . . . She turned, glad she hadn't embarrassed herself with a wave, and keen to resume her solitary vigil over the sea, striking just the right attitude for the real Clive to admire, once he arrived, which he surely would do any minute.

"Ms. Weiss?"

She turned.

"Hannah, yes?"

And that was all it took for her to know that Clive Tremain wasn't coming to collect her; that Clive Tremain wasn't showing up in her life ever again. That Clive Tremain, in fact, had never existed at all.

Hannah Weiss. Born '91, parents Joe and Esme—such a lovely name John Bachelor had to say it again, for the sheer pleasure of the sound: *Esme—née* Klein, the rest of whose family were scattered across Germany like so many seedlings: Munich mostly, but enough of a contingent in Berlin for there always to be a cousinly bunk for Hannah to bed down in when, as so often during the noughties, she had spent summer vacations there; enjoying the feeling of being truly European, with a language under her belt, and friendly faces to speak it to. Then a degree at Exeter, a proper one: history. And then the Civil Service exam, and now a first-rung job at BIS, which John Bachelor made a bit of a production out of not being sure what it stood for: something to do with business, I'm guessing, Hannah, yes? Something clever to do with business? He was a different man today, John Bachelor, having donned handler's garb, which for Hannah he had decided meant Favourite Uncle.

"Business, Innovation and Skills."

"The department for," he said. "Well done. Very well done."

They were in a pub off Lyme's main street, the one that curled uphill in picturesque fashion, and Bachelor had already laid a world of apology at Hannah's feet for what was obviously unforgivable—what couldn't possibly be countenanced for any reason other than the one he was about to produce—and had commenced wooing her with the best the pub had to offer, which was a not-bad prawn risotto and a decent Chablis. The rocky part, he hoped—if only the first of many rocky parts—was over, because she had after all listened to him when he'd explained that Clive wasn't going to be able to make it actually, but that he himself would very much like a quiet word.

Laying that snare for her—the word was honeytrap—was risky, but Bachelor had deemed it necessary; partly to remove her from her usual sphere, because recruitment was best done in a neutral zone, one in which the object of desire had nobody, nothing, to rely on but her own judgement. But it was partly, too—though this could never be spoken—to establish a certain willingness in advance: the object of affection was here to be wooed, true, but the end result was already flagged up. The atmosphere had prepped a "yes." The food was warm; the wine was chilled. Outside, rain danced brightly on the road and pavements and the roofs of parked cars, for the weather Hannah had watched approaching from the Cobb had arrived to complete the scene.

He would like to buy her lunch, he had explained, to make up for Clive's absence. And afterwards, she could head back to London—first class—or, if she preferred, make use of the cottage Clive had booked. Bachelor himself, he hastily added, would not be included.

"There's something going on, isn't there?"

He could scarcely deny this.

"You're not planning on drugging me for sex or anything, are you? You don't look the type, I must say."

He was grateful for this, until she added: "Too wrecked looking, really." She'd looked back towards the sea then, and the purple-fringed cloud in the decreasing distance. "I take self-defence classes, by the way."

"Very wise," said Bachelor, who knew she didn't.

"Okay." This had been abrupt. "If that sod's not coming, you'll have to do. Buy me lunch."

Over which he asked her about herself and her family, and checked her answers against what he already knew, which was almost everything.

"And why did you stop going to Germany, actually, Hannah? Fall out with the cousins?"

"Well, I haven't stopped going," she said. "I just haven't been in a while, that's all. I was in the States one year—"

Coast to coast, Bachelor mentally supplied; a six-week roadtrip with three friends from Uni. Hannah had split with her half of the male couple within days of arriving home.

"—and just been *really busy* since, but I'll certainly be going back next time I get a sniff of a chance at a decent break. They work you awfully hard, you know."

"Oh, I'm sure it'll get easier after a while."

Later, when the rain had passed over, and the sun was making a valiant attempt to regain control, they took a footpath leading out of town, and Bachelor explained a little more of the circumstances that had brought him to her.

"So you mean . . . What, this man stole my identity?"

"In a manner of speaking."

"But he wasn't racking up huge debts or anything?"

"No, nothing like that. He was using your name and your background, that's all, to convince some people that he had recruited you as what we like to call an asset."

"A spy."

"Not really. Well, sort of," Bachelor amended, when he noticed a certain shine in her eyes.

"So that's what you are too. You're a spy."

"Yes."

"And Clive too."

"Clive's not really his name."

"Will I see him again?"

"I see no reason why not," John Bachelor lied.

But there was something in her attitude that hinted that Clive, anyway, had already been written out of her future.

"So what do I do about it?" she asked. "Do I have to give evidence in court? Something like that?"

"Good heavens, no. Besides, he's dead now."

She nodded wisely.

"Lord, don't think that. He had a bad heart. He was unwell for a long time. It was only afterwards that we—I—found out what he'd been up to."

"So nobody knew."

"That's right."

"And nobody would still know—I mean, I wouldn't—if you hadn't just told me."

"That's right."

In the very best of cases, the object of affection wooed herself.

"So that means you want me to do something for you, doesn't

it? I mean, you're hardly telling me all this just to keep me informed. Spies keep secrets. They don't go round blabbing them to all and sundry."

"They're certainly not supposed to," he said, thinking of JK Coe.

They were under trees, and a sudden gust of wind shook loose some hoarded rain, sprinkling their heads. This made Hannah laugh, and Bachelor had a sudden pang—when she did this, she seemed about thirteen, which was far too young to be wooed or honeytrapped; far too young to be recruited. But when her laughter stopped, the look she directed at him was old enough that he shook those thoughts away.

"You want me to make it real, don't you? To become what he pretended I was. Except you want me to do this while really being on your side."

"It's not something anyone's going to ask you to do," he said. "It's simply an idea that's been . . . floated."

As if the idea had risen out of nowhere, and was bobbing even now between them like a balloon, red as the coat she wore. She could burst it with a word. If she did, he would do nothing to attempt to change her mind. Nothing at all. He swore this to himself on everything he kept holy, if anything still bore that description. And even if his failure to recruit her swept him straight back into Lady Di's black books, he'd deal with that— even unto being cast out of Regent's Park, into the pit of unemployability that awaited a man his age, with what was effectively a blank CV—sooner than strong-arm this young woman into leading a shadow life.

Because that's what he'd been leading, these decades gone. A shadow life. Scurrying round the fringes of other people's history, ensuring that none of it ever raised its head in polite company.

She was looking up into the trees, awaiting the next shower.

John Bachelor knew enough not to say anything.

He watched her though, and marvelled again at what it must be like to be young, and know that you hadn't yet messed everything up. In Hannah's case, he thought, she'd continue looking young well into age. Bone structure counted. He might be trying to steal her soul, just as dead Dieter Hess had stolen her identity, but ultimately Hannah Weiss would hang onto everything that made her who she really was. That, too, he marvelled at, a trick he'd not managed himself.

She said, "Will it be dangerous?"

"Not like in the films."

"You don't know what kind of films I watch. I don't mean car chases and jumping out of helicopters. I mean going to prison. Being caught and locked up. That kind of dangerous."

"Sometimes," Bachelor said. "That happens sometimes. Not very often."

"And will I get training?"

"Yes. But it'll all have to be done in secret. As far as anyone knows, you'll still be the girl you always were. Woman, I mean."

"Yes. You mean woman."

She looked upwards again, as if the answer to her questions sat hidden among leaves. And then she looked at John Bachelor.

"Okay," she said.

"Okay?"

"I'll do it. I'll be your spy."

"Good," he said, and then, as if trying to convince himself, he said it again. "Good."

It was three months later that Jackson Lamb made an unaccustomed field trip. Hertfordshire was his destination: he'd received advance word of a wholesale spirits outlet going down the tubes, and had hopes of picking up a case or two of scotch at knockdown prices.

It was a long journey to make on the off-chance, so he went on a work day, and made River Cartwright drive.

"This is official business?"

"It's the secret service, Cartwright. Not everything we do is officially sanctioned."

Two hours later, with a satisfied Lamb in the back seat, and two cases of Famous Grouse in the boot, they were heading back towards the capital.

Three hours later, with a rather more disgruntled Lamb in the back seat, they were still heading back towards the capital.

"This is supposed to be a short cut?"

"I never claimed it was a short cut," River said. "I explained it was a diversion. A lorry shed its load on the—were you actually listening?"

"Blah blah motorway, blah blah road closure," Lamb said. "If I'd known it was a magical mystery tour, I might have paid attention. Where are we?"

"Just coming out of St. Albans. And you're not smoking that."

Lamb sighed. In return for River driving him, buying lunch and not having the damn radio on, Lamb had agreed not to smoke in the car, and was starting to wonder how he'd let himself be bested. "Turn in here," he said.

"A cemetery?"

"Does it have a No Smoking sign?"

River parked just beyond the stone gateway.

Lamb got out of the car and lit a cigarette. The cemetery was basic, a recent development; had no Gothic-looking statuary, and was essentially a lawn with dividing hedges and headstones. A wide path led to the far end, which was awaiting occupants, and here and there were standpipes where visitors could fill watering cans, with which to tend the plots of their beloveds. Lamb, who carried his dead round with him, didn't spend a lot of time in graveyards. This one didn't seem busy, but perhaps Wednesday afternoons were a slack period.

St. Albans was ringing a bell, though. He sorted through his mental files, and came up with the name Dieter Hess. Who'd run a ghost network from here, and had now joined one of his own.

Wondering if Hess was nearby, and to give himself time to smoke more, Lamb wandered up the path. The only other human in sight was an elderly woman sitting on a bench, possibly planning ahead. At the far end he counted down a row of newer headstones. Sure enough, third along was Dieter Hess's; a simple stone with just his name and dates. A lot of story crammed between two numbers.

Lamb regarded the stone. A ghost network. The lengths some people go to for a few extra quid, he thought; but knew, too, that the money hadn't been all of it. The reason they called it The Game was that there were always those ready to play, even if that meant switching sides. Ideology, too, was just another excuse.

But now the old boy was buried, and no harm done. At least,

Lamb hoped there was no harm done . . . He didn't trust dying messages, and Hess's posthumous list fell under that heading. When something was hidden, but not so well that it couldn't be found, the possibility existed that that had been the intention. And if a ghost network consisted of nine shut-ins and one living breathing young woman, well: a suspicious mind might think that resembled bait.

He dropped his cigarette and ground it underfoot. It was too much of a stretch, he conceded. Would have meant that the hypothetical Hans, far from being Dieter Hess's dupe, was truly cunning: paying Hess simply to hide a coded list under his carpet, knowing that when he pegged out, his flat would be steam-cleaned—when a spy passes, his cupboards need clearing out. So the tenth name would come into the hands of the Service, and maybe—just maybe—its owner, already in the employ of the BND, would be adopted by MI5.

And what looked like a ready-made double would become, in fact, a triple.

But plots need willing players. Lamb could accept that a young woman with a sense of adventure might let herself be recruited by a foreign service in her teens, but didn't think John Bachelor had the nous to play his part, and re-recruit her in turn; or, come to that, that Diana Taverner would give him the green light to do so. Taverner was ambitious, but she wasn't stupid. Too bad for Hans, then. Sometimes you put a lot of effort into schemes that never paid off. Everyone had days like that, though today—thinking of the booty in the boot—wasn't one of Lamb's.

An atavistic impulse had him bend over, find a pebble, and place it on Hess's headstone.

One old spook to another, he thought, then headed back to the car.

Later that same afternoon, Hannah Weiss made her way home by tube. It had been a good day. Her probation at BIS was over; her supervisor had given her two thumbs up, and let her know that great things were expected of her. This could mean anything, of course; that a lifetime of key performance indicators and quarterly assessments lay ahead; or that her career would stretch down Whitehall's corridors, far into an unimaginable distance. "Great things" could mean Cabinet level. It wasn't impossible. She had influential support, after all, even if it had to remain covert. This was the life she had chosen.

She changed at Piccadilly, and found herself standing on a platform next to a middle-aged man in a white raincoat. He carried a rolled-up copy of *Private Eye*. When the train arrived they stepped on board together, and were crammed into a corner of the carriage. The train pulled away, and she found herself leaning against his arm.

For upwards of a minute, the train rattled and lurched through the darkness. And then, just as it began to slow, and the next station hauled into sight, she felt him shift so that his lips were above her ear.

"Wir sind alle sehr stolz auf dich, Hannah," he said. Then the train halted, the doors opened, and he was gone.

We're all very proud of you.

A fresh crowd enveloped Hannah Weiss. Deep inside its beating heart, she hugged secret knowledge to herself.

THE
MARYLEBONE
DROP
. . .

Seasoned Park watchers later said that the affair really began in Fischer's, that beloved "café and konditorei" that bestows a touch of early twentieth-century Vienna on the foothills of twenty-first-century Marylebone High Street; its warm interior, its spring yellows and glazed browns, a welcome refuge from the winter-drizzled pavements. The more callow of their brethren preferred to believe that it started, as all things must, at Regent's Park, but then the new generation had been trained to think itself at the constant heart of events, while the older knew that Spook Street, like Watling Street, runs backwards and forwards in time. The meeting at the Park might well have occurred earlier than the drop on Marylebone High, but that was a detail only, and when the time came for the whole business to be black-ribboned and consigned to the archive, nobody would care that a strip-lit office with functional furniture had been where the starting pistol was fired. No, once the facts were safely recorded, they'd print the legend instead. And legends thrive on local colour.

So Fischer's was the starting point; as good a place as any, and better than most. To quote from its website, "The menu includes an extensive choice of cured fish, salads, schnitzels, sausages, *brötchen* and sandwiches, *strudels*, biscuits, ice cream coupes, hot chocolates and coffees with traditional *tortes mit schlag.*" How could that not set the heart racing, with its enticing umlauts, its brazen italics, its artfully roman "coupes"? Solomon Dortmund can never pick up its menu without feeling that life—even one as long as his—holds some consolations; can never put it down again without inner turmoil having raged.

Today, he has settled upon a hot chocolate—he breakfasted late, so has no need for anything substantial, but various errands having placed him in the neighbourhood, it would be unthinkable to pass Fischer's without dropping in. And his appearance is instantly celebrated: he is greeted by name by a friendly young waiter, he is guided to a table, he is assured that his chocolate has so nearly arrived that he might as well be dabbing a napkin to his lips already. To all of which Solomon, being one of those heroes whom life's cruelties have rendered gentle, responds with a kind smile. Secure at his table, he surveys the congregation: sparse today, but other people, however few in number, always command Solomon's interest, for Solomon is a people-watcher, always has been, always will be. His life having included many people who disappeared too soon, he is attentive to those who remain within sight, which today embraced an elderly pair sitting beneath the clock, and whose conversation, he feels, will mirror that device's progress, being equally regular, equally familiar, equally unlikely to surprise; three intense young men, heavily bearded, discussing politics (he hopes), or at least literature, or chess; and a pair of women in their forties who are absorbed in something one of them has summoned up on her telephone. Solomon nods benevolently. His own telephone is black, with a

rotary dial, and lives on a table, but he is one of those rare crea-
tures who recognises that even those technological developments
in which he himself has neither interest nor investment might
yet be of value to others, and he is perfectly content to allow them
to indulge themselves. Such contemplation happily consumes the
time needed to prepare his chocolate, for here comes the waiter
already, and soon all is neatly arranged in front of him: cup, saucer, spoon, napkin; the elements of ritual as important as the
beverage itself. Solomon Dortmund, eyes closed, takes a sip, and
for one tiny moment is transported to his childhood. Few who
knew him then would recognise him now. That robust child, the
roly-poly infant, is now stooped and out of synch with the world.
In his black coat and antique homburg, whiskers sprouting from
every visible orifice, he resembles an academic whose subject has
been rendered otiose. A figure of fun to those who don't know
him, and he is aware of that, and regards it as one of life's better
jokes. He takes another sip. This is not heaven; this is not per-
fection. But it is a small moment of pleasure in a world more
commonly disposed to pain, and is to be treasured.

Sated for the moment, he resumes his inspection of the room.
To his left, by the window, is a young blonde woman, and Solomon allows his gaze to linger on her, for this young woman is
very attractive, in today's idiom; *beautiful* in Solomon's own, for
Solomon is too old to pay heed to the ebb and flow of linguistic
fashion, and he knows beauty when he sees it. The young woman
is sorting through correspondence, which gives Solomon a little
flush of pleasure, for who today, young or old, sorts through correspondence? Ninety percent of what drops through his own
letterbox is junk; the other ten percent mere notifications of one

sort or another: meter readings, interest rates; nothing requiring a response. But this young lady has a number of envelopes in front of her; brown envelopes of the size codified as C5 (Solomon Dortmund knows his stationery). Job applications? He dabs his lips with his napkin. He enjoys these little excursions into the lives of others, the raising of unanswerable questions. He has solved, or reconciled himself to, all the puzzles his own life is likely to throw at him. Other peoples' remain a source of fascination. Glimpses of their occupations are overheard prayers; doors left ajar on mysterious existences.

He returns to his chocolate, slowing down his intake, because endings should never be hurried. Once more, he surveys the room. The young woman has gathered her things together; is standing, preparing to leave. A man enters, his attention on his mobile phone. Through the momentarily open door intrude the mid-morning sounds of Marylebone High: a passing taxi, a skirl of laughter, the rumble of London. And Solomon can see what is about to happen as surely as if he were reading the scene on a page; the brief moment of impact, the startled *oomph* from the young lady, an equally surprised *ungh* from the man, a scattering of envelopes, the sudden monopoly of attention. It takes less time to happen than it does to recount. And then the man, fully recovered, is apologising; the young woman assuring him that the fault is as much hers as his (this is not true); the envelopes are gathered up while the young lady pats at herself, confirming that she still has everything she ought to have; the bag slung over her shoulder, the scarf around her neck. It is done. The stack of envelopes is returned to her with a smile, a nod; there would have been a doffing of a hat, had the props department supplied a hat. A moment later, the man is at a table, busying himself with the buttons on his coat; the young woman is at the door, is through it, is gone. Marylebone High Street has swallowed her up. The morning continues in its unhurried way.

And Solomon Dortmund finishes his chocolate, and at length rises and settles his bill, a scrupulous ten percent added in coins. To anyone watching as he heads for the outside world, he is no more than old-fashioned clothing on a sticklike frame; a judgement he would accept without demur. But under the hat, under the coat, under the wealth of whiskers, Solomon carries the memory of tradecraft in his bones, and those bones are rattled now by more than the winter wind.

"John," he says to himself as he steps onto the pavement. "I must speak to John."

And then he too dissolves into London's mass.

Meanwhile—or some time earlier, by the pedant's clock; the previous week, or the one before that—there was a meeting in Regent's Park. A strip-lit office, as mentioned, with functional furniture and carpet tiles, each replaceable square foot a forgettable colour and texture. The table commanding most of the floorspace had two saucer-sized holes carved into it, through which cables could be threaded when hardware needed plugging in, and along one wall was a whiteboard which, to Diana Taverner's certain knowledge, had never been used, but which nevertheless mutely declared itself the room's focal point. The chairs were H&S-approved, but only to the extent that each could hold an adult's weight; long-term occupation of any would result in backache. So far, so good, she thought. The head of the Limitations Committee was expected, and Lady Di liked to lean austeritywards on such occasions, Oliver Nash having made something of a circus, on his last visit, of harumphing at whatever he deemed unnecessary extravagance. His singling out of a print on her wall, a perfectly modest John Piper, still rankled. Today, then, the only hint of luxury was the plate of pastries neatly placed between the table's two utility holes. Raisin-studded, chocolate-sprinkled, icing-sugar frosted, the patisseries might have been assembled for a weekend supplement photo-shoot. A pile of napkins sat next to them. On a smaller table in the corner was a pot of filter coffee and a stack of takeaway cups. It had taken her ten minutes to get it all just right.

She had rinsed her hands in the nearby bathroom; stuffed the box the pastries came in into the nearest cupboard. By the time she heard the lift arrive, by the time the door opened, she was in one of the dreadful chairs; a notebook in front of her, a pen, still capped, lying in the ridge between its open pages.

"Diana. Ravishing as always."

"Oliver. Have you lost weight?"

It was an open secret that Nash had been attempting one diet or another for some time; long enough, indeed, for the cruel suggestion to be made that if he'd attempted them sequentially instead of all at once, one of them might have proved effective.

The look he gave her was not entirely free of suspicion. "I might have," he said.

"Oh, I'm positive. But please, sit. Sit. I've poured you a coffee."

He did so. "Rather spartan accommodation."

"Needs must, Oliver. We save the larger rooms for group sessions. Less wear and tear, and saves on heating, of course. I must apologise for this, by the way." She gestured at, without looking towards, the plate of pastries. "They're for the departmental gathering, I can't think why they've been brought in here. Somebody got their wires crossed."

"Hmph. Stretching the budget a little, wouldn't you say?"

"Oh, out of my own pocket. A little treat for the boys and girls on the hub. They work so hard."

"We're all very grateful."

His sandy hair had thinned in the last months, as if in mockery of his attempts to diminish himself elsewhere, but his chins remained prominent. Fastidiously avoiding looking at the plate of pastries, he placed his hands on his paunch and fixed his gaze on Diana. "How's the ship? Come through choppy seas lately, haven't we?"

"If we'd wanted a quiet life, we'd have joined the fire brigade."

"Well, so long as we're all having fun." He seemed to realise that the placement of his hands emphasised the roundness of his stomach and shifted them to the tabletop, a more dynamic posture. "So. Snow White." He raised an eyebrow. "By the way, have I mentioned—"

"Everybody's mentioned."

"—what a ridiculous codename that is?"

"They're randomly assigned."

"I mean, what if it had been Goldilocks, for God's sake?"

"We might have had to re-roll the dice. But as things stand, we live with it."

"Do you ever feel that we've become slaves to the processes? Rather than their existing to facilitate our objectives?"

He had always been one for the arch observation, even when the observation in question was of unadorned banality.

"Let's save that for Wants and Needs, shall we?" she said, meaning the bi-monthly inter-departmental catch-up most people termed Whines & Niggles. "Snow White. You've received the request. There's no difficulty, surely?"

But Oliver Nash preferred being in the driving seat, and would take whatever damn route he chose.

"If memory serves," he said, "and it usually does, she was recruited by an older chap."

"John Bachelor."

"But here she is being handled by a new boy. How'd that come about?"

"It was felt that Bachelor wasn't up to the job."

"Why?"

"Because he wasn't up to the job."

"Ah. Got on your wrong side, did he?"

"I have no wrong sides, Oliver. I just find the occasional thorn in one, that's all."

Not that he had been particularly thorny, John Bachelor, since that would have required more character than he possessed. He was, rather, an also-ran; constantly sidelined throughout his career; ultimately parked on the milk round, the name given to the after-care service provided to pensioned-off assets. Bachelor's remit—which, in the last round of cuts, had been downgraded to "irregular"—involved ensuring that his charges remained secure, that no passes had been made in their direction; increasingly, that they were still alive and in possession of their marbles. They were Cold War foot-soldiers, for the most part, who had risked their younger lives pilfering secrets for the West, and were eking out what time remained to them on Service pensions. A dying breed, in every sense.

But they had careers, or at least activities, to look back on with pride. John Bachelor, on the other hand, had little more than a scrapbook full of service-station receipts and the memory of a lone triumph: the recruitment of Snow White.

"And this new chap—Pynne? Richard Pynne?"

"He's not that new."

"Bet that name gave him sleepless nights as a boy."

"Luckily the Service isn't your old prep school. He'll be along in a moment. And—forgive me, I can't resist. I had to skip breakfast."

She helped herself to an almond croissant, took a dainty nibble from one end, and placed it carefully on a napkin.

"An extra five minutes on the treadmill," she said.

There was a knock on the door, and Richard Pynne appeared.

"You two haven't met," Taverner said. "Oliver Nash, Chair of Limitations, and one of the great and the good, as you won't need me to tell you, Richard. Oliver, this is Richard Pynne. Richard was Cambridge, I'm afraid, but you'll just have to forgive him."

"No great rivalry between Cambridge and the LSE, Diana, as I'm sure you remember all too well." Without getting up, he extended a hand, and Pynne shook it.

"A pleasure, sir."

"Help yourself to a pastry, Richard. Oliver was about to ask for a rundown on Snow White's request."

"Do you want me to . . ."

"In your own time."

Pynne sat. He was a large young man, and had dealt with a rapidly receding hairline by shaving his head from his teenage years; this, combined with thick-framed spectacles, lent him a geeky look which wasn't aided by his somewhat hesitant manner of speech. But he had a fully working brain, had scored highly on the agent-running scenarios put together across the river, and Snow White was a home-soil operation: low risk. Di Taverner didn't play favourites. She'd been known, though, to back winners. If Pynne handled his first joe without mishap he might find himself elevated above shift manager on the hub, his current role.

"Snow White's been having problems at BIS," he began.

"The Department for Business, Innovation and Skills," proclaimed Nash. "And I'd have a lot more confidence in its ability to handle all or any of those things if it could decide whether or not it was using a comma. What kind of problems?"

"Personnel."

"Personal?"

"*Onn*el," stressed Pynne. "Though it covers both, I suppose."

Nash looked at the pastries and sighed. "We'd better start at the beginning, I suppose."

In the beginning, Snow White—Hannah Weiss—was a civil servant, a fast-track graduate; indistinguishable from any other promising young thing hacking out a career in Whitehall's jungle, except that she'd been recruited at a young age by the BND—the Bundesnachrichtendienst; the German intelligence service. It was always useful to have agents in place, even when the spied-upon was nominally an ally. Especially when fault-lines were appearing the length and breadth of Europe. So far so what, as one of Pynne's generation might have ventured; this kind of low-level game-playing was part of the territory, and rarely resulted in more than the odd black eye, a bloodied nose. But this game was different. Hannah's "recruitment," it transpired, had been carried out without her awareness or consent: she had been no more than a name on a list fraudulently compiled by one Dieter Hess, himself a superannuated asset, one of the pensioners on John Bachelor's milk round. Hess, a shakedown of his cupboards had revealed after his death, had been supplementing his income by running a phantom network, his list consisting of shut-ins and lockaways, for each of whom the BND had been shelling out a small but regular income. Hannah Weiss alone had been living flesh, and unaware of her role in Hess's scheme. She was the one warm body in a league of ghosts.

It was John Bachelor who had uncovered Hess's deception, and Bachelor who'd come up with the idea of recruiting Hannah, then about to embark on her career in the Civil Service, and allowing the BND to continue thinking her its creature. It had been a bright idea, even Taverner allowed; the one creative spark of Bachelor's dimly lit career, but even then, the flint had been pure desperation. In the absence of his injurytime coup, Bachelor's neck would have been on the block. As it was, he'd scraped up enough credibility to hang onto his job, and Hannah Weiss, whom the BND thought in its employ, had been recruited by the Service, which, in return for low-grade Whitehall gossip, was building up a picture of how the BND ran its agents in the field.

Because it was always useful to have agents in place, even when the spied-upon was nominally an ally . . .

"Snow White's been doing well at BIS, but she feels, and I agree, that it's time for her to move on. There are offices where she'd be more valuable to the BND, which would mean, in return, that we'd get a peek at their more high-level practices. The more value they place on her, the more resources they'll expend."

"Yes, we get the basic picture," said Nash. He shot a look at Diana, who was taking another bite from her croissant, and seemed, in that moment, to be utterly transported. "But I thought we didn't want to get too ambitious. Maintain a solid career profile. We turn her into a shooting star, and put her in Number Ten or whatever, the BND'll smell a rat."

"Yes. But there've been, like I say, personnel problems, and this gives us an iron-clad reason for a switch."

"Tell."

"Snow White's manager has developed something of a crush on her."

"Oh, god."

"Late night phone calls, unwanted gifts, constant demands for one-on-one meetings which turn inappropriate. It's an unhappy situation."

"I can imagine. But this manager, can't he be—"

"She."

"Ah. Well, regardless, can't she be dealt with in-house? It's hardly unprecedented."

Diana Taverner said, "She could be. But, as Richard says, it provides us with an opportunity for a shuffling exercise. And we're not suggesting Snow White be moved to Number Ten. There is, though, one particular Minister whose office is expanding rapidly."

"The Brexit Secretary, I suppose."

"Precisely. A move there would be perfectly logical, given Snow White's background. German speakers are at a premium, I'd have thought."

Oliver Nash pressed a finger to his chin. "The Civil Service don't like it when we stir their pot."

"But there's a reason they're called servants."

"Not the most diplomatic of arguments." He looked at Pynne. "This suggestion came from Snow White herself?"

"She's keen to move. It's that or make an official complaint."

"Which would be a black mark against her," Diana said.

"Surely not," said Nash, with heavy sarcasm. His gaze shifted from one to the other, but snagged on the plate of pastries. It was to this he finally spoke: "Well, I suppose it'll all look part of the general churn. Tell her to make a formal transfer application. It'll be approved."

"Thank you, sir."

"Do take one of these, Richard. They're best fresh."

Richard Pynne thanked her too, took a raisin pastry, and left the room.

"There," said Lady Di. "Nice to get something done without umpteen follow-up meetings." She made a note in her book, then closed it. "So good of you to make the time."

"I hope young Pynne isn't taking a gamble with our Snow White just to cheer his CV up. Making himself look good is one thing. But if he blows her usefulness in the process, that'll be down to you."

"It's all down to me, Oliver. Always is. You know that."

"Yes, well. Sometimes it's better to stick than twist. There are dissenting voices, you know. An op like this, misinforming a friendly service, well, I know it comes under the heading fun and games, but it still costs. And that's without considering the blowback if the wheels come off. We rely on the BND's cooperation with counter-terrorism. All pulling together. What'll it look like if they find we've been yanking their chain?"

"They keep secrets, we keep secrets. That, as you put it, is where the fun and games comes in. And let's not forget the only reason we have Snow White is that the BND thought they were running a network on our soil. What's sauce for the goose goes well with the schnitzel, don't you think? More coffee?"

"I shouldn't."

But he pushed his cup towards her anyway.

Lady Di took it, crossed to the table in the corner, and poured him another cup. When she turned, he was reaching for a pastry.

She made sure not to be smiling on her return.

Solomon Dortmund said: "It was a drop."

"Well, I'm sure something was dropped—"

"It was a *drop*."

When he was excited, Solomon's Teutonic roots showed. This was partly, John Bachelor thought, a matter of his accent hardening; partly a whole-body shift, as if the ancient figure, balancing a bone china teacup on a bone china saucer and not looking much more robust than either, had developed a sudden steeliness within. He was, like most of those in Bachelor's care, an ambassador from another era, one in which hardship was familiar to young and old alike, and in which certainty was not relinquished lightly. Solomon knew what he knew. He knew he had seen a drop.

"She was a young thing, twenty-two, twenty-three."

John Bachelor mentally added ten years.

"Blonde and very pretty."

Of course, because all young women were very pretty. Even the plain were pretty to the old, their youth a dazzling distraction.

"And he was a spook, John."

"You recognised him?"

"The type."

"But not the actual person."

"I'm telling you, I know what I saw."

He had seen a drop.

Bachelor sighed, without making much attempt to hide it. He had much to sigh about. An icy wind was chasing up and down the nearby Edgware Road, where frost patterned the pavements. His left shoe was letting in damp, and before long would be letting in everything else: the cold, the rain, the inevitable snow. His overcoat was thinner than the weather required; it was ten-fifteen, and already he wanted a drink. Not needed, he noted gratefully, but wanted. He did not have the shakes, and he was not hungover. But he wanted a drink.

"Solly," he said. "This was Fischer's, on a Tuesday morning. It's a popular place, with a lot of traffic. Don't you think it possible that what you thought you saw was just some accidental interaction?"

"I don't think I saw anything," the old man said.

Result.

But Bachelor's hopes were no sooner formed than destroyed:

"I *know*. She passed him an envelope. She dropped a pile, he scooped them up. But one went into his coat pocket."

"A manila envelope."

"A manila envelope, yes. This is an important detail? Because you say it—"

"I'm just trying to establish the facts."

"—you say it as if it were an outlandish item for anyone to be in possession of, on a Tuesday morning. A manila envelope, yes. C5 size. You are familiar with the dimensions?"

Solomon held his hands just so.

"I'm familiar with the dimensions, yes."

"Good. It was a drop, John."

In trade terms, a passing on of information, instructions, *product*, in such a manner as to make it seem that nothing had occurred.

Bachelor had things to do; he had an agenda. Top of which was sorting his life out. Next was ensuring he had somewhere to sleep that night. It was likely that the first item would be held over indefinitely, but it was imperative that the second receive his full and immediate attention. And yet, if the milk round had taught John Bachelor anything, it was that when an old asset got his teeth into something, he wasn't going to let go until a dental mould had been cast.

"Okay," he said. "Okay. Have you a sheet of paper I can use? And a pen?"

"They don't supply you with these things?"

Bachelor had no idea whether they did or not. "They give us pens, but they're actually blowpipes. They're rubbish for writing with."

Solomon chuckled, because he was getting what he wanted, and rummaged in a drawer for a small notebook and a biro. "You can keep these," he said. "That way you will have a full record of your investigation."

I'm not an investigator, I'm a nursemaid. But they were past that point. "Young, blonde, very pretty." He wrote those words down. On the page, they looked strangely unconvincing. "Anything else?"

Solomon considered. "She was nicely dressed."

"Nicely dressed" went on a new line.

"And she was drinking tea."

After a brief internal struggle, Bachelor added this to his list.

Solomon shrugged. "By the time I knew to pay attention, she was already out of the door."

"What about the man?"

"He was about fifty, I would say, with brown hair greying at the temples. Clean-shaven. No spectacles. He wore a camel-hair coat over a dark suit, red tie. Patterned, with stripes. Black brogues, yellow socks. I noticed them particularly, John. A man who wears yellow socks is capable of anything."

"I've often thought so," Bachelor said, but only because Solomon was clearly awaiting a response.

"He ordered coffee and a slice of torte. He was right-handed, John. He held the fork in his right hand."

"Right-handed," Bachelor said, making the appropriate note in his book. The clock on the kitchen wall was making long-suffering progress towards twenty past the hour: with a bit of luck, he thought, he'd have grown old and died and be in his coffin by the time the half-hour struck.

"And he was reading the *Wall Street Journal*."

"He brought that with him?"

"No, he found it on a nearby seat."

"The one the girl had been using?"

"No."

"You're sure about that? Think carefully. It could be a crucial detail."

"I think you are playing the satirist now, John."

"Maybe a bit." He looked the older man in the eye. "Things like this don't happen any more. Drops in cafés? Once upon a time, sure, but nowadays? It's the twenty-first century." He'd nearly said the twentieth. "People don't do drops, they don't carry swordsticks."

"You think, instead, they deliver information by drone, or just text it to each other?" Solomon Dortmund shook his elderly head. "Or send it by email perhaps, so some teenager in Korea can post it on Twitter? No, John. There's a reason why people say the old ways are the best. It's because the old ways are the best."

"You're enjoying this, aren't you?"

"Enjoy? No. I am doing my duty, that is all."

"And what do you want me to do about it?"

Solomon shrugged. "Do, don't do, that is up to you. I was an asset, yes? That is the term you use. Well, maybe I'm not so useful any more, but I know what I saw and I've told you what I know. In the old days, that was enough. I pass the information on." He actually made a passing motion here, as if handing an invisible baby back to its mother. "What happens to it afterwards, that was never my concern."

Bachelor said, "Well, thanks for the notebook. It will come in handy."

"You haven't asked me if there is anything else."

"I'm sorry, Solomon. Was there anything else?"

"Yes. The man's name is Peter Kahlmann."

"...Ah."

"Perhaps this information will help you trace him?"

"It can't hurt," said Bachelor, opening the notebook again.

The previous night had been unsatisfactory, to say the least; had been spent on a sofa not long enough, and not comfortable. His current lodgings were reaching the end of their natural lease, which is to say that after one week in the bed of the flat's owner—a former lover—he had spent two in the sitting room, and now the knell had been sounded. On arriving the previous evening, he had found his battered suitcase packed and ready, and it had only been by dint of special pleading, and reference to past shared happinesses—slight and long ago—that he had engineered one final sleepover, not that sleep had made an appearance. When dawn arrived, reluctantly poking its way past the curtains, Bachelor had greeted it with the spirit a condemned man might his breakfast: at least the wait was over, though there was nothing agreeable about what happened next.

And all that had brought him to this point: none of that was pretty either. Especially not the decision to cash in his pension and allow his former brother-in-law to invest the capital—no risk, no gain, John; have to speculate to accumulate—a move intended to secure his financial future, which had been successful, but only in the sense that there was a certain security in knowing one's financial future was unlikely to waver from its present circumstance. And he had to give this much to the former brother-in-law: he'd finished the job his sister had started. When the lease on Bachelor's "studio flat"—yeah, right; put a bucket in the corner of a bedsit, and you could claim it was *en suite*—had come up for renewal last month, he'd been unable to scrape together the fees the letting company required for the burdensome task of doing sweet fuck all. And that was that. How could he possibly be homeless? He worked for Her Majesty's government. And just to put the icing on the cupcake, his job involved making sure that one-time foreign assets had a place to lay their head, and a cup of sweet tea waiting when they opened their eyes again. They called it the milk round. It might have been a better career choice being an actual fucking milkman, and that was taking into account that nobody had milk delivered any more. At least he'd have got to keep the apron; something to use as a pillow at night.

He was in a pub having these thoughts, having drunk the large scotch he hadn't needed but wanted, and now working on a second he hadn't thought he wanted but turned out to need. In front of him was the notebook Solomon had given him, and on a fresh page he was making a list of possible next moves. There were no other ex-lovers to be tapped up, not if he valued his genitals. *Hotel*, he'd already crossed out. His credit cards had been thrashed to within an inch of their lives; they'd combust in the daylight like vampires. *Estate agents* he'd also scored through. The amount of capital you needed to set yourself up in a flat, a bedsit, a vacant stretch of corridor in London, was so far beyond a joke it had reached the other side and become funny again. How did anyone manage this? There was a good reason, he now understood, why unhappy marriages survived, and it was this: an unhappy marriage at least had two people supporting it. Once you cut yourself loose, disinvested from the marital property, you could either look forward to a life way down on the first rung or move to, I don't know, the fucking North.

But let's not get too wrapped up in self-pity, John. Worse comes
to worst, you can sleep in your car.

Bachelor sighed and made inroads on his drink. At the top of
this downward spiral was work, and the downgrading of his role
to "irregular," which was HR for part-time. A three-day week,
with concomitant drop in salary: You won't mind, will you, John?
Look on it as a toe in the waters of retirement . . . He'd be better
off being one of his own charges. Take Solomon Dortmund.
Dortmund was a million years old, sure, and had seen rough times,
and it wasn't like Bachelor begrudged him safe harbour, but still:
he had that little flat, and a pension to keep him in coffee and
cake. There'd been a moment an hour ago when he'd nearly asked
Solomon the favour: a place to kip for a night or two. Just until
he worked out something permanent. But he was glad he hadn't.
Not that he thought the old man would have refused him. But
Bachelor couldn't have borne his pity.

Feisty old bugger, though.

"I waited until he'd left," Solomon had said. "There is always
something to do on the High Street. You know the marvelous
bookshop?"

"Everyone does."

"And then I returned and had a word with the waiter. They all
know me there."

"And they knew your man? By name?"

"He is a regular. Once or twice, he has made a booking. So yes,
the waiter knew his name just as he knew mine."

"And was happy to tell you?"

"I said I thought I recognised him, but too late to say hello. A
nephew of an old friend I was anxious to be in touch with."

Solomon had given an odd little smile, half pride, half regret. "It is not difficult to pretend to be a confused old man. A harmless, confused old man."

Bachelor had said, "You're a piece of work, Solly. Okay, I'll raise this back at the Park. See what they can do with the name."

And now he flicked back a page and looked again: Peter Kahlmann. German-sounding. It meant nothing, and the thought of turning up at Regent's Park and asking for a trace to be run was kind of funny; beyond satire, actually. John Bachelor wasn't welcome round Regent's Park. Along with the irregular status went a degree of autonomy; which meant, in essence, that nobody gave a damn about his work. The milk round had a built-in obsolescence; five years, give or take, and his charges would be in their graves. For now, he made a written report once a month, unless an emergency happened—death or hospitalisation—and kept well clear until summoned. And this non-status was largely down to the Hannah Weiss affair.

Hannah should have been a turning point. He'd recruited her, for God's sake; had made what might have been a career-ending fiasco a small but nonetheless decorative coup, giving the Park a channel into the BND: a friendly Service, sure, but you didn't have to be in John Bachelor's straits to understand what friendship was worth when the chips were down. And given all that had happened since—Brexit, he meant—Christ: that young lady was worth her weight in rubies. And it had all been down to him, his idea, his tradecraft, so when he'd learned he wouldn't be running her—seriously, John? Agent-running? You don't think that's a little out of your league?—he'd got shirty, he supposed; had become a little boisterous. Truth be told, he might have had a drink or two. Anyway, long story short, he'd been escorted from the premises, and when the Dogs escorted you from Regent's Park, trust this: you knew you'd been escorted. He might have lost his job altogether if they could have been bothered to find a replacement. As it was, the one morsel he'd picked up on the grapevine was that Snow White, which was what they were calling her now, had been farmed out to Lady Di's latest favourite: one Richard Pynne, if you could believe that. Dick the Prick. You had to wonder what some parents thought they were doing.

Bachelor yawned, his broken night catching up with him. Through the pub window he could see it trying to snow; the air had a pent-up solid grey weight to it, like a vault. If he had to spend the night in the car, currently Plan A by default, there was a strong likelihood he'd freeze to death, and while he'd heard there were worse ways to go, he didn't want to run a consumer test. Perhaps he should rethink approaching Solomon . . . Pity was tough to bear, but grief would be worse, even if he weren't around to witness it. But if so, he'd have to either come up with a story as to why he'd got nowhere tracing Peter Kahlmann or, in fact, try tracing Peter Kahlmann. It occurred to him that of the two options, the latter required less effort. He checked his watch. Still shy of noon, which gave him a little wiggle room. Okay, he thought. Let's try tracing Peter Kahlmann. If he'd got nowhere by three, he'd apply himself to more urgent matters.

And he did, as it happened, have an idea where to start.

A coffee shop just off Piccadilly Circus: a posh one where they gave you a chocolate with your coffee, but placed it too close to your cup, so it half-melted before reaching the table.

Hannah Weiss didn't mind. There was something decadent about melting chocolate; the way it coated your tongue. Just so long as you didn't get it on your fingers or clothes.

Richard Pynne said, "So it'll go through like you asked. Make your transfer application. You don't have to mention the stalking thing. It'll be expedited end of next week at the latest."

"That's great, Richard. Thank you."

She'd enjoyed working at BIS, but it was time for a change. If Richard hadn't come through, "the stalking thing," as he'd put it, would probably have done the trick, but it was as well she hadn't had to go down that route. Julia, her line manager, would be horrified at the accusation; though of all the people who'd inevitably become involved, Julia would be easiest to convince of her own guilt. There was a certain kind of PC mindset which was never far away from eating itself. But more problematic would be being noticed for the wrong thing. Like all large organisations, the Civil Service hoisted flags about how its staff should report wrongdoing, but if you actually did so, your card was marked for life. It was hard not to feel aggrieved about that, even if the reported wrongdoing was fabricated.

Pynne said, "I actually had a pastry earlier. Not sure I want a chocolate now."

Because he was expecting her to, she said, "Well, if you don't ...."

He grinned and turned his saucer round so the chocolate was nearest her. Using finger and thumb, she popped it into her mouth whole. Richard watched the process, his grin flickering.

"You're okay with us meeting here?"

"Sure. I'll have to be back in the office in twenty minutes though."

"That's okay. I just wanted to pass on the good news."

They were of an age, or at least, he wasn't so much older that it looked unusual, the pair of them meeting for coffee. Nobody observing would have to make up a story to fit; they were just pals, that was all. He'd suggested, of course—back when they were building this legend—that he be an ex-boyfriend; still close, maybe on/off. And she'd given it genuine thought, but only for the half-second it took to reject it. The alacrity with which he'd agreed that it wasn't, after all, a great idea had amused her, but she'd taken care to keep that hidden. On paper he was her handler, and it was all round best if he thought that was the case in the real world too.

She supposed, if she were more important to the Park, they'd have given her someone with more experience; a father figure, someone like the man who'd recruited her in the first place. Pynne, though, was learning the game as much as she was; they were each other's starter partners, or that was the idea. A fun-and-games op; blowing smoke in a friendly Agency's eyes, just to show they could, though European Rules had changed in the years since Hannah's recruitment, and if nobody was expecting hostilities to break out, a certain amount of tetchiness was on the cards. So maybe her value to the Park was on an upward trajectory, but even so, she wouldn't be assigned a new handler now. It didn't really matter. The fact was, Hannah Weiss had been playing this game for a lot longer than Richard Pynne. And the handler the BND had matched her with had a lot more field savvy; but then, he knew Hannah was a triple, working for the BND, while the Park thought she was a double, working for the Park.

Maybe everyone would sit down and have a good laugh about all of this one day, but for the moment, it suited her real bosses that she be transferred to the office handling Brexit negotiations. It wasn't the world's biggest secret that Britain had been handling these discussions with the grace and aplomb of a rabbit hiding a magician in its hat, but, on the slim chance that somebody had a masterplan up their sleeve, the BND wouldn't have minded a peek.

"So . . . Everything else all right?"

Hannah sipped her coffee, looked Richard Pynne directly in the eye, and said, "Yes. Yes, all fine."

He nodded, as if he'd just managed a successful debriefing. It was hard not to compare his treatment of her with that of Martin, who sometimes insisted on clandestine handovers in public places—the old ways are the best, Hannah; you have to learn how to do things the hard way; this is how we do a *drop*, Hannah; learn this now, it may someday save your life—and other times spirited her away for the evening; one of the brasher clubs round Covent Garden, where up-and-coming media types mingle with new-breed business whizzkids. Those evenings, they'd drink champagne cocktails, like a September/May romance in the making, and his interrogation of her life was a lot less timid than Richard Pynne's. What about lovers, Hannah; fucking anybody useful? You don't have to say if you don't want to. I'll find out anyway. But she didn't mind telling him. When they were together, she didn't have to hide who she was. And not hiding who she was included letting him know how much she enjoyed hiding who she was; how much she enjoyed playing these games in public. Because that's what it was, so far; a fun-and-games op in one of the world's big cities. How could she not be enjoying herself?

"But don't ever forget, Hannah, that if they catch you, they'll put you in prison. That's when the fun stops, are you receiving me?"

Loud and clear, Martin. Loud and clear.

Now she said to Richard Pynne, "I'll put my application in this afternoon. The sooner the better, yes?"

"Good girl."

She finished her coffee, and smiled sweetly. "Richard? Don't get carried away. I'm not your good girl."

"Sorry. Sorry—"

"Richard? You have to learn when I'm teasing."

"Sorry—"

And she left him there, to settle their bill; not looking back from the cold pavement to his blurred face behind the plate glass window, like a woman who's just told her Labrador to stay, and won't test his mettle by flashing him kindness.

At Regent's Park the weather, to no one's surprise, was much the same as elsewhere in London; the skies sea-grey, the air chill, and packed with the promise of snow.

John Bachelor was having conversation with a guardian of the gate, who in this particular instance was seated at a desk in the lobby. "You're not expected," she was telling him, something he was already aware of.

"I know," he said. "That's what 'without appointment' means. But I'm not meeting with anyone, I just need to do some research."

"You should still book in ahead."

He swallowed the responses which, in a better life, he'd have had the freedom to deliver, and managed a watery smile. "I know,

I know. Mea culpa. But my plans for the day have gone skew-whiff, and this is the one chance I have at redeeming the hour."

His plans for the day had obviously involved shaving and putting a clean shirt on, the woman's non-spoken reply spelled out. Because those things hadn't happened either. But she ran his name and ID card through her scanner anyway, and evidently didn't come up with any kill-or-capture-on-sight instructions. "It says you're in good standing," she said, with a touch too much scepticism for Bachelor's liking. "But I'd rather see your name on the roster."

All or nothing.

"You want me to give Diana a ring?" He produced his mobile phone. "Sorry, I mean Ms. Taverner. I could call her and she can put you straight."

For a horrible second he thought she was about to call his bluff, but the moment passed; gave him a cheery wave, he liked to think, on its way through the door. She did something on her keyboard, and a printer buzzed. Retrieving its product, peeling a label from the sheet, she clipped it onto a lanyard. "That's a two-hour pass," she told him. "One second over, I send in the Dogs."

"Thank you."

"Have a nice visit."

Seriously, he thought, passing through the detectors and heading for the staircase; seriously: Checkpoint Charlie must have been more fun, back in the old days. Not that he'd actually been there. On the other hand he knew what it was, and wouldn't mistake it for a Twitter handle.

He took the lift and headed for the library. He didn't have an appointment, it was true, because an appointment would have appeared on someone's calendar, and anything documented in the Park carried the potential for blowback of one sort or another. Bachelor's standing might be "good," as the guardian of the gate had reluctantly verified, but "good" simply meant he wasn't currently on a kill-list. If he actually did bump into Di Taverner, she might have him dropped down a lift shaft just for the practice. So no, no actual appointment, but he had rung ahead and made contact with one of the locals; asked if they could have a quick chat, off the books. In the library. If the local was around, that was.

He was.

They still called it the library, but there weren't books here any longer, only desks with cables for charging laptops. Bachelor settled in the corner furthest from the door, draped his coat on a chair, then went and fetched a cup of coffee from the dispenser, on his way back suffering a glimpse of a future that awaited him, one in which he haunted waiting rooms and libraries, anywhere he might sit in the warmth for ten minutes before being asked to move on. How had it come to this? What had happened to his life? He made a panicky noise out loud, a peculiar little *eck*-sound, which he immediately repeated consciously, turning it into a cough halfway through. But there was only one other person in the room, a middle-aged woman focused on her screen; she had earplugs in, and didn't glance his way.

At his table, he warmed his hands on the plastic cup. He didn't have his laptop—he'd left it in his car; a disciplinary offence, come to think of it—so opened his notebook and pretended to study his own words of wisdom. He must have looked like an illustration of how he felt: an analogue man in a digital world. No wonder it was leaving him behind so quickly. But others managed.

Look at Solomon. Bachelor thought again of that cosy flat, its busy bookshelves, the active chessboard indicating Solomon's continuing engagement in struggle, even an artificial one, played out with himself. By any current reckoning, Solomon was of no account; part of the last century's flotsam, unless it was jetsam; discarded by a now-unified state, washed up onto an island that had lately reasserted its insularity. But he still felt himself part of the game, enough to alert Bachelor that he'd thought he'd seen a drop. No, Bachelor corrected himself; Solly *knew* what he'd seen. He might have been wrong, but that was barely relevant. Solomon knew.

The name Peter Kahlmann stared up at Bachelor from the notebook in front of him.

So okay, it was true that he had designs on Solomon's sofa; on having somewhere to sleep that wasn't the back seat of his own car. But that didn't mean he couldn't pursue the trail in front of him to the best of his careworn abilities—he wasn't, when you got down to it, acting under false pretences. He was, in fact, acting under genuine pretences, and if in some eyes that might seem worse, it was the best he could manage in the circumstances.

"Bachelor?"

He started, alarmed that he'd been found out.

"It is you, right?"

And he admitted that indeed it was.

"Alec?" was how Bachelor had greeted him the first time they met. "Do I detect a touch of Scots?"

"It's Lech," Alec said. "And no, I'm not one of the Scottish Wicinskis. But good catch."

So yes, Alec Wicinski, born Lech, to parents themselves UK citizens, but both offspring of Poles who'd settled here during the war; named by his mother for the hero of the hour, Lech Wałęsa, which proved such a burden to the young Lech throughout a turbulent school career that he reinvented himself at University: Alec, good proper name, nothing off the wall about it. He'd since come to semi-regret the change, and now answered to both, depending on who was addressing him. That he had two names—two covers, both real—amused him. Made him feel more a spy than his Service card did.

Which stated, when run through a scanner, that Alec Wicinski was an analyst, Ops division, which meant he worked on the hub, except for those rare occasions when he sat in the back of a van, watching other people kick doors down. Afterwards, he'd be who you went to to find out why the door hadn't come off its hinges first kick, or where the stuff you'd expected to find behind it might be now. Where John Bachelor had encountered him had been at the funeral of an ancient asset, who'd been a friend of Alec's grandfather, unless he'd been the grandfather of Alec's friend. Bachelor was hazy on the details, having launched himself wholeheartedly into the inevitable wake, but he'd made a point of scratching Wicinski's name on the wall of his memory cave. You never knew when a contact at the Park would come in handy.

Alec sat, and shook his head when Bachelor suggested coffee. "You have a name that might interest me?"

"It came through one of my people," Bachelor told him. Having people lent him weight, he thought. "Might be something, might be nothing."

"Are we currently in a movie?"

"...What?"

"It just sounds like movie dialogue, that's all. 'Might be something, might be nothing.' I process information, John. It is John, right?" It is. "So, all information's either useful or it's not. But none of it's nothing. What's the name?"

"Peter Kahlmann," Bachelor said.

"And what's the context?"

Bachelor said, "One of my people, I look after retired assets, I think I told you that, one of my people thought he saw him making a drop. Or taking a drop, rather."

"A drop?"

"An exchange of some sort. A package. An envelope. Done surreptitiously in a public place."

"Sounds kind of old school."

"That's what I thought."

"I didn't know they even did that any more. Whoever they are." Alec scratched his head. He had thick dark curls. "And even if they did, that doesn't make it our business. Could be anything. Could be drugs."

"A lot of drug money goes places where it becomes our business," Bachelor said.

"Yeah, I know. Just thinking out loud. Who's the asset?"

"An old boy, one of our pensioners."

"Behind the curtain?"

"Back in the day, yes."

Alec nodded. The eyes behind his glasses were dark, but lively. "And where did he see what he says he saw? And where did the name come from?"

Bachelor ran through it all, start to finish. He didn't hide what he thought was possible: that Solomon Dortmund, who was sharp but ancient, might have witnessed an innocent stumble. But he didn't hide, either, that Solomon had seen such games played for real; that he'd played them himself, in places where, when you were caught, they didn't just make you sit out the next round.

"So why aren't you going through channels?" Alec said, when he'd finished.

"... Channels?"

"If this is real, and not just an old man's mistake, it should go on the record. You know how this works. There's a reason we keep intel on file. It's so we can see the bigger picture. This Kahlmann, somewhere down the line, if he turns out to be planning an acid-attack on the PM's hairdresser, I don't want to be the one sticking my hand up and saying, oh yeah, we had a line on him, but it didn't go through channels so nobody noticed."

Bachelor, freewheeling, said, "If it's a mistake, it's a mark against Solly. And you're right, he's an old man. They decide he's being a nuisance, they might pack him off to one of those homes they have, where you're not allowed more possessions than'll fit in your locker, and everyone gathers in the home room for an afternoon sing-song. It'd kill him."

"But if he's seeing things that don't really happen, maybe one of those places is where he ought to be."

"Do you have parents, Alec?"

"Please. Don't play that card."

"It's the only one I've got."

Alec Wicinski scowled, then stared for a moment or two at Bachelor's coffee cup. Then said, "Okay, here's what I'll do. I'll run the name through the records, see if it rings any bells. And if it does I'll let you know, and then you can take it through official channels, okay?"

"Thanks, Alec."

"But don't tell anyone I made a pass at it first. We're not supposed do favours. Not even for people we don't actually know, but just bumped into at a funeral."

"Hell of a funeral, though," Bachelor said.

Alec grinned. "It was," he said. "It was a hell of a funeral."

Afterwards, Bachelor lingered in the library, drinking two more cups of coffee, then—inevitably—had to take himself off to find the nearest toilet. And as he did so, he had that sense of foreboding again; a glimpse of a life spent looking for facilities he could use. Brushing his teeth in car park lavatories. Lurking near department store bathrooms, trying to look like a customer.

For the first ever time, it struck him: if this was what he had to look forward to, should he maybe just bow out?

It wasn't a moment of illumination; more a taking-on-board of something found at the back of his mind. Not *the* answer, necessarily, because something might turn up, but still: a way out of his current predicament; a means of avoiding the humiliations piling up ahead, like a roadblock designed by Kafka. He could simply pull the switch. The thought didn't fill him with a sense of triumph, but the fact that it didn't fill him with dread struck the deeper chord. It was said that people who talked about killing themselves never actually did so. And he wondered if those people who did had had moments similar to this one; whether their first inkling that that big word, suicide, had specific relevance to themselves arrived not hand-in-hand with calamity but during an ordinary day; and whether it had felt to them, as it did to him, like opening an envelope addressed to The Occupier, and finding their own name on the letter within.

And then he shuddered and filed such thoughts away, though he knew that a seal had been broken, and that he'd be forced to dip into this dark jar again in the future, probably at night.

There was a bathroom down the corridor. After he'd peed, while he was washing his hands, someone else entered, and Bachelor spoke almost without intending to. "Do they still have showers on this floor? I pulled an all-nighter. I could really do with cleaning up."

"Next floor down," he was told.

"Thanks."

Next floor down was easily found. The building's geography was coming back to him as he wandered: showers, yes, and wasn't this where the bunking-down rooms were, where staff could crash when they were under the hammer? In the shower room were cupboards with towels, and even overnight kits: toothpaste, toothbrush, soap. He stayed under water as hot as he could manage until his skin grew lobster-pink. Then brushed his teeth and dressed again.

He was working on automatic now. It barely constituted a plan. Back in the corridor he made his way towards the bedrooms. None were in use. He chose one, let himself in, and locked the door behind him. The room wasn't much bigger than the single bed it contained, but that was all he was interested in. He undressed again, climbed into the bed, and when he flipped the light switch, the room became totally dark; a chamber deaf to noise and blind to light. For the first time in weeks, Bachelor felt alone and completely secure. Within minutes he slept, and dreamed about nothing.

It didn't do to be a man of habit, so Martin Kreutzmer wasn't: varying the routes he took to work; shuffling the bars he frequented, and the shops he patronised with no discernible brand loyalty. Some days he wore a suit; others, he dressed like a student. But he contained multitudes, obviously—he was a handler, an agent-runner, and handlers are all things to all joes—so it wasn't surprising that some of his identities took a less stringent attitude: an identity hardly counted as such if it couldn't be broken down into lists. Likes/dislikes, favourite haunts, top ten movies. So when he was being Peter Kahlmann, he did the things Peter Kahlmann liked to do, one of which was visit Fischer's every so often, because even agent runners enjoy a taste of the homeland now and again. He'd barely sat, barely glanced at the menu, when the waiter was asking him, "Did your uncle's friend get in touch?"

"... I'm sorry?"

"Mr. Dortmund. One of our regulars, I'm surprised you've not crossed paths before. Though you're not usually here in the mornings, like he is."

"Could you start at the beginning, please?"

Afterwards, he enjoyed his coffee break, to all outward appearance unbothered by the exchange: Yes, now he remembered; old Mr. Dortmund—Solly, that was it—had indeed been in touch, and yes, it was lovely to hear from someone who'd known Uncle Hans in the Old Days. Not many of that generation left. And yes, thank you, a slice of that delicious torte: What harm could it do? He gazed benignly round, and cursed inwardly. What had he done to attract the attention of an old man? There was only one answer: the drop. If the old man had noticed this, he must have been in the game himself. And if he'd taken it upon himself to establish Martin's—Peter's—identity, maybe he still was. Maybe he still was.

Martin blamed himself. Here on friendly ground—more or less—his duties were mostly administrative, and the bulk of his time was spent schmoozing compatriot bankers and business-men, who thought him something to do with the Embassy. Hannah Weiss was his only active agent, and yes, he'd made a game of his dealings with her, partly so she could learn how things were done properly; partly because he got bored other-wise. Lately, though, the ground had been shifting. European boundaries were being resurrected; the collapse of the Union couldn't be ruled out. There were those who said it couldn't happen, and those who couldn't believe it hadn't happened yet, and as far as Martin was aware, similar groups of people had said similar things about the Wall, both when it went up and when it came down again. It wasn't like the Cold War was about to be redeclared. But still, Hannah's value as an agent could only increase in the future. It was time to stop playing games.

As for the here and now, the report she'd passed him, here in Fischer's, indicated that all was going to plan. Her move from BIS to the Brexit Secretary's office was in the bag. With that jump, her value to the BND would increase fivefold; no longer an amusing sideline, she'd be a genuine source of useful data. But even if that weren't so, he chided himself, he remained at fault for putting her in harm's way. Even amusing sidelines had to be taken seriously. Practising old-school spycraft on the streets of London was one thing; getting spotted doing it was another. Hannah's career to date might have been little more than a joke one Service was playing on another, but they wouldn't simply waggle a finger in her face if she was caught. And whoever this Solomon Dortmund was, he looked set to make that happen, if he hadn't done so already.

Caught by sudden urgency, Martin Kreutzmer paid and left. In the old days, he'd have had to head back to his office and set research wheels in motion; track this fox Dortmund to his den. But these days you could do all that on the move, which is exactly what Martin did, striding along the High Street, coat collar up against the wind; one glove dangling by a fingertip from his teeth as he squeezed information from his phone.

Back in the Park, Alec Wicinski was doing much the same thing.

Dark curly hair; glasses half the time; a need to shave twice a day, though needs didn't always must in his case. Alec was a tie-wearer, a reader, and a walker; not one for hill and field or coastal path, but a pounder of city streets, his usual cure for the bouts of insomnia that plagued him being to march through London after-hours. His fiancée, Sara, joked that she'd picked him up on a street corner in the middle of the night. They'd actually met through a mutual friend, the old-fashioned way. Alec once worked out that they were the only engaged couple he knew who hadn't met online, and still wasn't sure whether to be surprised by that, and if so, why.

Alec, as noted, was an analyst, and oppo research his special-ist subject, "oppo" being granted broad definition these days.

The lines were wavier than they used to be, old rivalries nearer the surface, and anyone who wasn't spying for us was spying on us. That, at least, was the motto on the hub, where whistleblowing was the worst of crimes. There was something about an enemy pretending to be a friend, or a friend pretending to be an enemy, that could be lived with; but that either kind could pretend to have a conscience was a play too far. The boys and girls on the hub knew things could get murky, and that dirty truths had to be buried deep to keep the soil fertile; dragging them to the surface did nobody good. Lech understood this, and any dirty truths he uncovered that he was unhappy about he shelved in an attic corner of his mind, alongside his memories of his grandfathers' generation; those who'd fled Poland before the occupation, and fought their war under foreign skies. Back then, there was no doubting who the enemy was. Things were black or they were white, and even when they weren't—when there was shading round the edges—you acted as if they were, because that was what life during wartime was like, especially when your country was overrun. You'd picked your side. You didn't get to dictate strategy.

Those foreign skies were his own now, but his Polish extraction—at least, he'd always assumed that's what it was, though maybe it was some individual quirk all his own—kept history fresher in his mind than most of his colleagues managed. And whereas the general attitude was that right would ultimately triumph, something in Lech's bones sang of doom, or whispered along with the chorus: he was in his job to prevent bad things happening, but couldn't entirely suppress the fear that sooner or later he'd fail, that they'd all fail, that their home skies would look down on cataclysm. His grandfathers had taught him this much:

that if you expected things to get worse, history would generally see you all right. Not that he'd be thanked for broadcasting this round the office.

For the moment, though, he did what he could.

Peter Kahlmann. Alec had a few spelling variations up his sleeve, but that was the version he entered first, running a multiple-site search on a number of Service engines: foreign operatives, British civilians, persons of interest of any nationality. The breadth meant he couldn't expect a response any time soon, so he let his laptop get on with it, while he busied himself with a report on a recent op in the Midlands—seventeen arrests, and an armed assault on Birmingham International scotched at the planning stage. Preventing bad things happening: one for our side, he thought, and suppressed the inevitable comeback from his mental gremlin, *Nobody wins all the time.*

Outside, it was starting to snow.

The flat was off Edgware Road, in a pleasant block with railinged-off basement areas, almost all of which contained an army of terracotta pots with small, neatly sculpted evergreens standing sentry. Upper storeys boasted windowboxes on most of the sills. At this time of year, they were little more than a gardener's memento mori; the odd scrappy fighter among them battling the winter, but most standing fallow, waiting the bad months out. As if in vindication of their decision, it started to snow as Martin Kreutzmer approached; big chunky flakes drifting lazily down, the way Christmas card artists prefer, and a nice change from the dirty sleet London usually conjured up.

Outwardly, the block maintained the appearance of a row of

houses, each with its own front door up a flight of stone steps. Sets of doorbells were fixed to the brickwork, labelled by name, and Martin had no trouble finding the one he was after: No. 36, Flat 5. He looked up and down the road. There were few people, and the only moving traffic was out of sight: shunting up and down Edgware Road. All he was doing, he told himself, was checking out the opposition. There remained the possibility that Solomon Dortmund was exactly who he said he was: a friend of Martin's uncle. Except Martin didn't have any uncles, and even if he did, they wouldn't have any friends. So maybe Solomon Dortmund was in play, which meant Martin had to find out who was pulling his strings. For his own part, he was fireproof: the worst the British Secret Service could do to him was purse its lips in his direction. But if Hannah was blown, he'd have to put her on the next flight out of the country.

First things first: Martin rang the bell. Old people respond to doorbells; ingrained politeness, combined with a sense of need: the need to show visitors they were up and dressed, mobile, *compos mentis*. It was possible he was projecting. Any-way, Solomon Dortmund didn't answer his bell, meaning the odds were he was out, which gave Martin a whole new set of options: act as if the worst had happened, and pull Hannah's rip-cord, or carry on digging in case the whole thing turned out to be an old man's brainfart. When in doubt, he thought, secure your joe; that was the bedrock of agent-running. Back home they'd throw their hands up and ask if he was getting scaredy-cat in age, but screw that: they weren't the ones who'd be carted off in a Black Maria if it all went wrong. He wasn't about to gamble Hannah's future just to keep the bean counters happy, so he was pulling the cord, and that was the decision he'd come to as the door opened and an old woman emerged, a dog in her arms, a shopping basket looped through one of them too. "You are *such* a nuisance," she was saying, and Martin could only presume she was addressing the dog. Confirmation arrived when she looked him directly in the eye. "He is *such* a nuisance."

"But a fine fellow all the same," he told her. "Let me get that for you." Meaning the door, which he held while she made her slow way through: dog, shopping basket, a walking stick too, it turned out. "Can I see you down the steps?"

"That would be kind."

"Let me just fix this," he said. "Don't want to have to disturb anyone again." He lay his gloves down to prevent the door shutting and then, to forestall any interrogation as to who he was visiting, and what the nature of his business was, kept up an unbroken commentary on dogs he had known while helping his companion to the pavement: was he one for chasing squirrels? Martin himself had heard that terriers were the very devil for squirrels; had known one personally, hand on heart, that had learned to climb trees. Sweetest dog in the world, that quirk apart. Would rescue ducklings, and escort lost fledglings back to their nests, but squirrels: that dog had an issue with squirrels. By the time all was done, and she was heading off towards Marks & Spencer, Martin had almost convinced himself he'd known her years, such was the degree of fondness with which she took her leave. Dear boy. He headed back up the steps, retrieved his gloves, and closed the door behind him. Solomon Dortmund: Flat 5. Two flights up.

Must be a game old bird right enough, Martin thought, as

proud of his command of English idiom as he was of his ability to get up the stairs without losing breath. He'd found no
images of Solomon Dortmund on his quick trawl through the
ether, but the one in his mind had the old man a robin: bright
of eye and twice as perky, hopping up and down these stairs
twice a day, for all he was eighty. Ninety? And here was his
door, and Martin rapped on it, and again there was no response.
This wasn't great tradecraft, but sometimes you rode your luck.
Plan an operation, and it took you weeks. Grab an opportunity,
and you could be back in your foxhole by teatime, mission
accomplished. It was a good solid door, and a top-hole lock.
There were spies out there, good and bad, who could find their
way through a locked door, but Martin Kreutzmer wasn't one
of them. He'd read a few books, though. He ran a hand along
the top of the doorframe and found nothing, then bent to the
welcome mat. Who kept a welcome mat outside their front
door? An old person. Or maybe just a hospitable person, he
amended, and lifted the mat and found the spare key carefully
taped to the underside. Solomon, Solomon, he thought. Thank
you for that. He heard a noise downstairs and froze, but the
noise—a door opening and closing—was followed by its own
echo: someone going out onto the street. He looked at the key.
Yes or no? He'd not have a better chance. Three minutes tops,
he told himself. Just to find out who this geezer—this robin—
thinks he is.

   And he let himself into the flat.

And here was the snow they'd been expecting, thought Solomon;
a few little flurries to start with, to make everyone sentimental

about how pretty London looked with its edges rounded, and then more intently, more seriously; this was snow with a job to do, snow that would cause everything to grind to a halt: buses and taxis, the underground, the people, the shops, the law, the government. All these years gone by, and he still didn't know what it was with the British and snow. Pull on your boots, wear gloves, spread a little salt and put shovels in the hands of the right people: What was so difficult about that? But no, let any kind of weather turn up looking grim and the country went into shock. But ah well, he thought; ah well, at least he'd had the sense to notice which way the wind was blowing. So here he was, loaded shopping bags in each hand, and if the snow meant he was confined to his flat for a week, while the oafs on the Council ran round like headless chickens, wondering what the white stuff was and how to make it go away again, at least he wouldn't be wondering where his next tin of sardines was coming from, or be forced to re-use coffee grounds. That had happened before.

He had to put all his bags down to find his doorkeys. They were never in the pocket you'd put them in; that was something else a long life had taught him, that keys were determined to drive you out of your mind, but ah, here they were, and he could perhaps fish them out without removing his gloves, but no, that wasn't going to happen: off come the gloves, Solomon. Off come the gloves, as if he were about to enter battle, when in fact his day's campaign was over: he had his shopping, he had his keys—yes, there they were, plain as daylight in his hand—and now all he had to do was carry this shopping up two flights of stairs and he could settle down in his chair while the outside world did its worst.

The door was open, the shopping bags lugged over the threshold, the door was closed again, the light was on. Solomon felt dizzy when this was completed, and was breathing hard. Nonsense to suggest that a little exertion was too much for him; but on the other hand, on the other hand. He had outlived everyone he had ever loved, and while he viewed a number of those still breathing with affection, he wouldn't miss them when he was gone as much as he'd delight in the company of those he'd be joining. And it was often the case, he reflected, that you had such thoughts at the bottom of a staircase. Once you'd reached the top, there were more immediate things to dwell on, such as the contents of his shopping bags. Tins of sardines and necessary pints of milk apart, a few treats had been included. An old man doesn't need chocolate. But an old man has every right to a few things he doesn't need, when the snow outside is falling hard, and no telling when he'd next make it to Fischer's. The dizziness passed, and he chuckled. What were a few more flights of stairs? His life so far, he'd long lost count of how many stairs he'd climbed. Everyone did, after the first few.

But here he was now, up both flights, and his front door awaiting him. Again, there was the problem with the keys, which turned up in the wrong pocket, second time of looking. A sorry business, this growing older every day. But moments later he was home; in his own warm flat where all his possessions waited, his comfortable chair, his small library, his slippers, his life. He closed the door, and would have taken his bags through to the kitchen had something not struck him: not a thought, not a sound, a smell; a stranger's smell—there had been, possibly still was, someone in his flat who should not be there; someone who

carried, as Solomon did, his own odour: sweat, soap, all the unde-
finables we muster along the way. Solomon's heart was
hammering now; his breathing rapid. Were they still here? The
door had been locked, was unbroken; a skilled burglar could enter
through a window, but not without being seen from the street,
surely, at this time of day? He sniffed deliberately, but the smell
had been erased by odours from his shopping bags: the fresh
bread, the fruit, the minced lamb, the cheese—the cheese? Was
that what had snagged his attention, the urgent clamouring of a
goat's cheese? He reached out for the nearest shopping bag and
raised it head-high, sniffed again. Ha! Goat's cheese! He had
heard many tales of old men frightened by their shadows, but
this—this!—he would not be living this down soon, even if it
remained his closely guarded secret, which it would. It would.

Solomon carried the bags to the kitchen then returned to the
door, removed his coat and hung it on the stand. Hat too. He'd
not be leaving again in a hurry; he could see through the window
the snow drawing crazy patterns in the air. The streets would be
thickly carpeted soon. He removed his shoes, and headed for the
bedroom. Cheese was on his mind. That smell of cheese, already
occupying the entire flat. In his bedroom he sat and, before putting his slippers on, cradled each foot for a while. Even through
his socks he could feel the miles these extremities had carried
him; travels carved into skin which didn't even feel like skin any
more; felt like a thick plastic covering, onto which various lumps
and ridges had been moulded. The body's journey, written on
itself. He planted both feet on the floor and stood, and felt again
that wash of dizziness he'd suffered at the foot of the stairs.
Careful, Solomon. He reached out for support, and found the

handle of the wardrobe door: that was better. Thumping heart, the smell of cheese. A shiver down his back. He should put something warm on, make some tea. There was a cardigan in the wardrobe, so he opened the door and a shape loomed out, sudden and dangerous. Something burst inside old Solomon, though the shape was only briefly there; it had gone, stepped past him, was through the door before Solomon had finished his journey. This had started many years before, very far away, and ended where the floor began. For a moment or two he lingered on the threshold of himself, but the possibility of rejoining his loved ones proved too beguiling to resist, so Solly stepped across whatever the boundary was, and closed the world behind him.

It was much later that Alec Wicinski checked his laptop for search results: he'd become caught up in several matters, each more urgent than a name-chase for an acquaintance. He wanted to get home: travel was going to be a bitch, with tube lines down because of the snow (why? Why did snow affect the underground?) and while he never minded walking, he didn't have shoes for the weather. He texted Sara, confirming their dinner date, filled out his time sheets, then called up the search engines he'd set in motion and scanned the hits: six Peter Kahlmanns, the length and breadth of Europe. Which didn't mean there weren't more, and—allowing for fake IDs—didn't mean there weren't fewer, but it did mean there were six that fell within the parameters of the chosen engines. And this wouldn't have been more than a passing observation were it not for something that rang a bad bell: loud and bastard clear.

One of the Peter Kahlmanns was flagged.

Flagging could have meant any number of things. It could have meant Peter Kahlmann was a friendly, an asset, a joe even; could have meant he was on a watch-list; could have meant he had diplomatic status, and was to be immediately released if he turned up under a hooker's bed during a raid. But what it most definitely meant was, Alec would need a cast-iron reason for having looked him up in the first place. Running a search on a flagged target was like stepping on a tripwire: hard to tell whether you'd done any damage until you lifted your foot again. Everything might be okay, and the world go on as normal. Or you might find your leg blown to kingdom come. Life was full of surprises.

What was certain was that his favour for John Bachelor wasn't a secret any more. When you ran up a flag, someone in the Park saluted.

He cursed under his breath, then closed all the engines down, not even bothering to examine the particular Peter Kahlmann who'd taken the starring role in his extracurricular trawl. Some things it was better not to know. The bright side was that if Alec had stepped into anything especially messy, he'd not be finding out about it now; he'd have been hauled away and given the treatment the minute he'd fed the name into the system. So with any luck it was a procedural mis-step, no more; one he'd answer for to Richard Pynne, his unlovable shift-manager, come their end of the week catch-up, but not one that had capsized an op. He hoped to God not, anyway. Nothing to do now but cross fingers and hope.

As for Bachelor, he could go whistle. There were favours you did for friends, and there were risks you took for family: Bachelor wasn't the latter and barely qualified as the former. The best

Bachelor could hope for was that Alec didn't come looking for him. To point out the error of his ways.

He sighed, powered down and left. Outside, the snow was coming thick and hard: London didn't usually get like this, but when it did, it didn't mess about. It took him two hours to get home, and he missed his date with Sara by a mile. Worse things could happen. Still, that sense of history that Alec carried with him was flickering like a faulty lamp; reminding him that if you expected everything to go tits up, you'd rarely go far wrong.

He'd been woken late evening by a pounding on the door, and a sickening awareness that the Dogs had tracked him down. The pass the dragon at the gate had allowed him had expired hours ago. The place might be in lockdown by now, every corner turned inside out in the hunt for an irregular; a part-time milkman out-staying his welcome.

But you know what, John? That was the best sleep I've had in weeks. As he clambered out of bed, pulled his trousers on, opened the door, Bachelor felt, if not entirely refreshed, at least no worse than when he'd lain down, which was a significant improvement on recent events.

The Dog in question was called Welles, and was new to Bachelor. Time was, he'd kept up with the ground staff at the Park, for the sensible reason that you never knew when you might need a favour, but that was a big ask when you were part-time, and unwelcome on the premises.

"Man, you're in trouble."

"Yeah, yeah. I've been there before."

Except this time, it didn't seem such hostile territory. Welles, after delivering the requisite bollocking, gave him a pitying look and said, "What happened, your wife kick you out?"

As it happened, yes. A while back, but as it could reasonably be seen as the starting pistol on his current circumstances, Bachelor did his best to look sheepish and nod.

"It's a skeleton crew tonight. London's at a standstill because of the snow, and most were let go early. If anyone needs the bed, I'll be back to kick you out. But for now, get your head down. I'll clear it at the desk."

"Thanks. I appreciate that."

"Just don't do it again."

So he climbed out of his trousers once more, and back into bed, and slept another eight hours, after which he really did feel like a new man; a man who wasn't afraid of what the day might hold. Riding his luck, he showered again, then went to the library and drank two cups of free coffee before leaving the building. The guardian of the gate, a new one, barely batted an eye as he turned in his pass. And then he was out in the world again, and it was a winter wonderland.

It always felt like that, first sight. Pour a couple of tons of snow onto the city streets, and that was all you could see: clean white brightness, all of London's sins forgiven, but it didn't take long for reality to seep through. There wasn't much traffic, but what there was had ploughed the snow, pushing oily puddles of slush into the gutters, and the pavements were punctuated with yellow patches and small piles of filth where London's dogs had relieved themselves. By nightfall, once everything had iced over, romance would have given way to treachery, and every step you took, you'd be worried you'd end up flat on your back. But it was nice to have your philosophy borne out by the facts, thought John Bachelor, as he stood on a snowbound pavement and wondered what to do with his day.

His car was in a long-term near King's Cross, his suitcase in its boot, and this was as much of an address as he currently boasted. But an epic sleep and two showers had set him up well, even if his circumstances had witnessed no improvement over-night. He checked his phone for messages—to see if Alec, Lech, had got back to him—but he was all out of charge. Even that didn't depress him unduly. The snow had provided a time out; nothing would happen for the next little while, which provided him with an alibi of sorts. He could make his way to Solomon's, cadge some breakfast, tell him everything was in hand; that meanwhile, the snow made it impossible for him to get home to Potters Bar, and would it be possible to kip on his sofa? It was a soft way in. He wouldn't have to confess the car crash his life had become. Tomorrow, things would either look different again, or they wouldn't. Either way, he'd have had twenty-four hours to think things over, and at Solly's he was sure of a constant supply of coffee, maybe a good red wine towards the close of play.

So he walked. There were others on the streets, of course, some finding pleasure in the new white world; others plodding grimly through it as if looking forward to the next. On Edgware Road a car had crumpled into a lamp post, attracting an audience, and further along a snowball fight had broken out, apparently good-humoured, but it was early yet. When he reached Solomon's Bachelor rang the bell, but got no answer. He'd grown cold; his overcoat, too thin yesterday, definitely wasn't up to the mark today. He could hang around waiting for Solly to return, or see if he

could get a neighbour to buzz him in. This dilemma didn't occupy
him long, and on the third time of trying he was inside the building; soon after that, was on bended knee outside Solomon's door,
retrieving the spare key. So far so good. He let himself in, called
out but got no answer, so went to the kitchen to put the kettle
on. Solomon wouldn't mind. Solomon had European manners.
There was a stoppered bottle of red on the counter, and Solly
wouldn't mind this either, Bachelor decided, pouring a quick glass.
It wrapped itself around him like a shroud. He missed this: having a kitchen, having things in it, helping himself to them when
he desired. The kettle boiled and switched itself off. Before
seeing to it Bachelor removed his coat and went to hang it up,
which was when he noticed Solly's bedroom door hanging open.
His heart sank. Doors, in Solomon's world, were kept closed.
He took a step towards it, then changed his mind; returned to
the kitchen, where he poured another, larger glass of wine. He
drank it, soaking in the peace and quiet; the muffled quality of
the snowed-on city. And then he went to discover the body of
his friend.

No drops this time. No clever footwork. He needed to talk to
Hannah, in person; no coded messages, no dead-letter she-
nanigans. All the fun and games of running an op on foreign
soil: Martin had enjoyed teaching Hannah the old ways, but
everything had become less funny once the old man dropped
dead in front of him. He hadn't meant to scare the bastard;
had meant to be long gone before he arrived home, but you
couldn't plan for the cosmic fuck-up, and nobody expected to
find himself hiding in a wardrobe. He'd left the flat as

invisibly as he could, taping the spare key under the mat; had vanished into a whitening world which erased his footsteps behind him. And had kept both ears on the news ever since, and both eyes on the internet. But nothing yet about a body in a flat off Edgware Road. Which meant either that the body hadn't been found, or that it had been found and was being dangled from a tree in a clearing, while hunters waited in the undergrowth.

So he met Hannah at Liverpool Street Station the following morning, in the bookshop, browsing the thriller section. No surreptitious chat, just a surprised "Gosh, fancy you being here," then a wander into the crowd, thinner than usual because of the snow. The floor was slick with dirty footprints, and the tannoy's announcements were mostly of cancelled trains.

"It's best you don't know why I'm asking," Martin said, "but have any wires been tripped?"

"Something odd happened."

"Tell me."

She told him: Dick the Prick had mentioned his name, on the phone, the previous evening. "Is there any reason why someone would be running a search on your handler?"

"You're my handler, Richard. Is this line secure, by the way?"

"It's fine. And yeah, sure, I'm your . . . handler, but I meant the other one, you know? The one you're only pretending to . . ."

"Pretending to report to."

"Yeah."

"No reason I can think of," she'd told him. "Why?"

She'd asked the question, though the answer was obvious: because someone had done precisely that. Run a search.

Peter Kahlmann was harmless, as far as the Park was concerned; a mediocrity the BND were using to run Hannah, their unimportant mole in an unexciting branch of the British Civil Service. And Peter Kahlmann would carry a little weight if leaned on; Peter Kahlmann wouldn't break at the first hint of pressure. But Peter Kahlmann wasn't indestructible, and if the Park chose to test his strength, he'd splinter and crack eventually, and there—peeping out from the broken shell—would be Martin Kreutzmer, and Martin Kreutzmer was a much more interesting character than Peter Kahlmann. For a start, Martin Kreutzmer wouldn't be running an unimportant mole like Hannah Weiss, which meant that the Park's double agent might require a little more attention herself.

Richard Pynne had said, "So he hasn't said or done anything funny lately? He doesn't suspect that you're not what you claim to be?"

Every triple has moments like this: when they have to consider, for a moment, who and what they claim to be. It largely depends on who they're talking to at the time.

But Hannah had just said, "Nothing's changed. It's not like he's a big deal or anything. I think he regards running me as a chore he's been lumbered with."

And now, in Liverpool Street, Martin said to her: "Good. That's good."

It wasn't good, but you never tell a joe the ground just got swampy.

He asked her to talk while he thought, and she launched into a work anecdote while they paced the station, stepping round or breaking through the queues forming at coffee stands. She was good at this, he registered, even as his mind chewed over other fodder. Whether she'd had this story up her sleeve, whether it had actually happened, whether she was improvising: didn't matter, she delivered it like a natural. And it washed through her while they marched, providing cover for his pondering.

Martin hadn't wanted the old man to die, but these things happened. And if Solomon Dortmund hadn't died then, he'd have died at the first opportunity; the next time a shock was delivered to his door—a backfiring motorbike, a peal of thunder, a telephone, a doorbell. So what mattered now was whether anything could put Martin on the scene. Because he'd thought himself bulletproof, here in bumbling old Blighty, but if the Park got wind that a BND operative had been present when a Service asset died, there'd be retribution. How harsh this might be he wouldn't want to guess, nor would he want to be there when guessing became unnecessary.

And Hannah needed to be secured too. His own position might be in jeopardy, but Hannah's safety was paramount—the joe always came first.

He said, "How far would Pynne stick his neck out for you?"

"Richard? Pretty far, I think."

"And if that wasn't far enough?"

Hannah thought about it, surveying the morose crowds of winter travellers. "I could get him to stick it out further."

"Let's hope it doesn't come to that. But do what you have to."

"What do you need?"

"Find out who ran the search on Peter Kahlmann."

She hugged him, made a loud goodbye; turned to wave when she was ten yards off, and he stood there watching her go: an uncle, a family friend, an innocent colleague, with a rolled-up newspaper under his arm.

The ground was swampy, but once he had the name of whoever had been checking his cover story out, he'd know what to do. If it had rung Pynne's bells, it must have come from within Regent's Park, but Pynne himself obviously didn't know why it had happened. Which might mean it had come from up the ladder, above Pynne's head, which probably meant game over: that Martin and Hannah would have to up sticks. But if it was someone lower down—someone who'd wandered off reservation on their lonesome—well. There might be other ways of solving the problem. Martin was old school, and rarely indulged in dirty work, but there were others within reach, a phone call away, who had different skills, different talents. They could turn a man's life upside down without laying a finger on him. If that happened to you, you'd quickly forget whatever extracurricular games you'd been playing. You'd be too busy trying to plug the leaks you'd sprung, and hoping the damage wasn't permanent.

He left Liverpool Street, noting that the sky overhead was still a grey vault, and the air still bit back when you breathed it. There'd be more of this weather before there was less. He wasn't entirely sure the English language would bear that construction, but it sounded right in his head, and there was no one around to correct him.

John Bachelor sat for a while, drinking the wine, deciding he might as well eat. Solomon had been shopping; there were bags of food in the kitchen, still awaiting unpacking. Fresh bread, cheese; chocolately treats. Tins of sardines. There was no point letting it go to waste. And nothing he could do right now about reporting Solly's death: his phone was still uncharged, and his charger was in his car. There was a department to ring in these circumstances, and a telephone in the flat, but Bachelor didn't know the number by heart, couldn't read it on his powerless phone, and tracking it down would mean talking to half a dozen suspicious civil servants. No, he'd sit a while before putting it all in motion: the necessary investigation, the endless reports, the winding down of Solomon's afterlife—his Service pension, his flat.

He went to take another look at the body. There were no signs of violence, and it was clear from the shopping that Solly had not been in the flat long when he died. Bachelor, not a doctor, reached the obvious conclusion: Solly had over-exerted himself doing an emergency shop, and this was the result. It was sad but it must have been quick, and among other things meant that Bachelor no longer felt obliged to indulge Solomon's final whimsy. The drop, the *pas de deux* Solomon thought he'd seen in Fischer's, had been nothing more than an ancient asset's final glimpse down the twists of Spook Street. Even if Bachelor put it on file, there'd be no follow-up; it would be dismissed as an old man's fantasy. Alec, if he'd run Kahlmann's name through the databases yet, had done so as a favour to Bachelor; he wasn't putting it through channels. So the drop could be quietly dropped, which meant that Solomon's passing would cause no more a ruffle than a passing pigeon. All Bachelor needed to do was write up today's one-sided visit, sign his name, and attend the funeral.

A stray thought wafted past, and whispered in his ear.

He dismissed it and made a cheese sandwich; ate looking down from Solomon's window to the muffled street below. It was warm inside; heating was paid by direct debit, from a Service account, and as this had been set up in the days before austerity—when people were valued for what they had done, rather than dismissed out of hand for being no longer capable of doing it—it was a generous monthly sum, ensuring Solomon need never grow cold. Like everything else to do with Bachelor's charges, the process was automatic and unquestioned. That was one thing about the Civil Service: once it decided to do something, it carried on doing it. It would march on, indestructible, and sooner or later would probably inherit the earth, though when it did, it wouldn't do anything with it that it hadn't already been doing for centuries.

His sandwich eaten, Bachelor remained where he was, mulling options. As usual, there weren't many available. But for now, at least—warm and comfortable—he was in no hurry to exercise choice; he'd just sit for a bit and watch the snow. In the other room lay Solomon Dortmund, but that was okay. The old man had learned patience in life, and there was no reason why this virtue should abandon him now.

The snow lingered for days, hardening to ice on the pavements, the better to keep a grip, and though traffic reasserted itself eventually, it did so with a chastened air, reminded of its place in the great chain of being: the car was king of the road, but only while the weather allowed. Shops that had been closed opened up, and opportunist roadside vending vans moved on. In Regent's Park, the hub had maintained its quiet buzz throughout the hiatus, but the surrounding offices were only just coming back to life, proving what Alec Wicinski and his colleagues had long known: that actual work continues untroubled, regardless of management's presence. As for Alec himself, he hadn't turned up that morning, causing troubled glances among the boys and girls of the hub. Unexplained absence was a cause of concern in their world.

In her office, Lady Di was grilling Richard Pynne.

"When did it come to light?"

"During yesterday evening's sweep."

"And there'd been no previous hint of . . . anything?"

Pynne shook his head.

He hadn't been at the Park lately, frozen lines having made his commute near-impossible, but he'd bravely struggled into town to meet Snow White the evening before last. He'd worried when he got her call, an emergency-only code, and had spent the expensive cab ride picturing any manner of calamity. In his imagination, she was being hauled into a cellar by disgruntled BND operatives. So to find her fine—perky, even—was more than a relief; it was cause for celebration.

"I'm sorry, Richard. I got a case of the frights. But I'm okay now."

"It happens." Their hug went on longer than he'd expected. "Joes in the field, you're allowed to get the frights. That's what I'm here for. To make them go away again."

Instead of coffee and a chocolate, they'd snuggled down in a bar off Wardour Street, and at her suggestion he'd ordered tequila slammers. Just the thing to chase the jitters away. And a legitimate expense, almost certainly.

Inevitably, things had become hazy towards the end. She'd asked, he remembered, about what he'd said the previous day; those mysterious questions concerning Peter Kahlmann, and he'd explained, fuzzily, that he couldn't go into details; that a flag had been raised because someone on the hub had run a search on Kahlmann, and no, he couldn't tell her who. Clashified information. She'd laughed: You sound like James Bond. *On Her Majeshty's Shecret Shervish.* He'd laughed too: I preferred Roger Moore. It had been a crazy evening. Crazy. But he was almost certain he'd not mentioned Alec Wicinski by name. Which would have meant nothing to Hannah anyway.

So yesterday he'd stayed off work using snow as an excuse, but the truth was he'd got home so loaded, he'd barely been able to crawl out of bed in the morning. His first few hours had been spent cradled over the toilet. Touch of flu, he'd phoned in: yeah yeah yeah. And then, come evening, when he was just about upright again, the results of the weekly remote sweep of the boys' and girls' laptops came in.

Which is when the problem with Wicinski came to light.

Pynne said, "The laptop's been in Alec's sole possession. The download took place outside office hours, but that's neither here nor . . . Thing is, he's claiming not to know anything about it, but he would, wouldn't he? And if anyone else gained access to his machine, that in itself's a disciplinary offence. These things are beyond classified. That's the first thing they tell you when you're given one."

This hadn't prevented their being left in cabs or on trains, but that wasn't the issue right now.

Di Taverner said, "And the download's illegal?"

"Child porn," said Pynne. "It's . . . they're saying it's pretty disgusting."

"Yes, the clue's in the name." She glanced towards the hub, and half a dozen faces turned quickly away. Sighing, she reached for the switch that frosted her glass wall. "Could it have been planted remotely?"

"IT says yes, technically, but it would require serious, state of the art intervention. Another Service might have the wherewithal to hack into one of our laptops and dump that stuff there from a distance, but it's not something a kid's done in his bedroom. And that being so, why would they? Why would another Service want to frame Wicinski?"

"What's he working on?"

"Nothing to put anyone's back up."

"You're sure?"

Pynne was sure, or at least, he was sure that was the answer he wanted to give. Coincidences happened, everyone knew that. Had he mentioned Alec's name to Snow White? He was pretty certain not. Besides, Alec was on his team, his name cropped up all the time. Alec this and Alec that. That was the nature of being a manager: your team was always on your radar.

"Where is he now?"

"Dogs."

Through the frosted wall came the dim suggestion of movement. That would also be the Dogs, here to ransack Lech Wicinski's workstation and dismantle his hardware. His locker would have been turned out by now too. Either more evidence of his moral corruption would be found, or he'd be shown to have buried it completely—this slip-up aside, that is.

"I can believe he gets off on that stuff," she said. "Everyone has a dark side. What I don't understand is why he'd download it onto our laptop."

Pynne didn't know either. But he said, "If you get away with something for long enough, you start to think you're too clever to be caught."

"So he's been doing it for a while?"

There were any number of pitfalls here, chief among them that he'd be called to account for not having rumbled Wicinski's predilections earlier. "There've been no indications of aberrant behaviour. He's always passed the psych tests. But . . ."

"But if it wasn't possible to disguise the urge, we'd all know who the paedophiles were," she finished. "Jesus, Richard."

It crossed his mind to offer comfort, but he wisely kept his mouth shut.

She said, "He'll have to go on suspension. While the Dogs do whatever they need to do."

Pynne said, "It's a criminal offence. Shouldn't we pass it to the Met?"

"And enjoy another season of spook-bashing? I don't think so. Things are bad enough without gifting the tabloids their head-lines. No, we'll handle this in-house. If he's got any sense, he'll come clean without letting the whole thing drag on too long." She defrosted the window. "And then it'll be just how we like it. Everything out in the open."

He could rarely tell, with Lady Di, where the irony stopped.

She shifted gear. "How's Snow White coming along?"

"Fine," he said. "Her transfer's come through. She starts in the Brexit office Monday."

"And it's all going smoothly? The two of you?"

"Yes."

"Good. It's not an easy business, running an agent. Even on

friendly soil. If this continues to go well, we'll think about expanding your brief. But I'll need to be sure you're up to it."

"Thank you." He stood to go, but paused at the door. "What'll happen to him? Alec?"

"If he turns out guilty?"

He nodded.

She said, "Well, we can't sack him. Not without inviting attendant publicity. But he can't stay here, obviously. Not that he'd want to, now his secret's out in the open." She reached for her laptop, tapped in her password. "Just as well we've somewhere we can put him."

"Oh," said Pynne.

"Yes," said Diana Taverner. "Man's got a nasty kink. Slough House should be right up his street."

And the snow stays where it is, and the weather doesn't turn, and the streets remain cold, and the days are dark from dawn to dusk. In different parts of London, different people feel different things. Alec Wicinski is mostly numb, dumbfounded by the speed with which his life has spiralled into hell, while Martin Kreutzmer has the sense of having narrowly avoided disaster, and can now see a clear path ahead, leading steadily upwards. Hannah has started in her new role, where it is apparent she will have access to information useful to the folk back home; together, the pair look set to enjoy many a triumph. And it's a pleasure to hoodwink another Service, especially when that Service thinks it's hoodwinking you. Contemplating the last few days, Martin gives silent thanks to the BND's sneaker team, who can walk through the Park's firewalls, and leave packages in laptops the way couriers leave parcels in dustbins—without notice, and undetected—but if he spares a thought for the poor bastard on the receiving end, it's a brief one. Martin has been playing this game a long time, and knows that, like those of politicians, all spies' lives end in failure. The best among them fade away with no one having suspected their true calling; for others, the end comes sooner, and that is all. It is part of the game. He lights a rare cigar and wonders what his next move will be. There's no hurry. The game lasts forever.

As for John Bachelor, he spends a lot of time at Solomon's window, looking down on what once were Solomon's streets. Solomon himself has been taken away, of course. An ambulance removed the body; a police officer came and took notes. Bachelor faked nothing, just described what had happened: he'd arrived to check on the old man, and the old man didn't come to the door. There was a spare key taped under the mat . . . His cover held up. There is an actual company, existing on paper, by which he is employed to visit the elderly and infirm, ensuring their needs are catered for, their lives secure and intact; the sort of service once provided free by society, before the 1980s happened. There'll be a funeral next week. He's called the numbers in Solomon's address book, kept by the phone. He's booked a room in a pub, and will put money behind the bar.

But he hasn't informed the Park. That stray thought that wafted past him, the same hour he found Solomon's body, returned, and returned again, and somehow clarified into intention. He has not informed Regent's Park that Solomon Dortmund is dead. So Solomon's pension will continue to be paid, and Solomon's flat will continue to be warm. It will only be for a short while, he tells himself; just until he has found his feet again, and it's not precisely corruption—is it?—more administrative streamlining. He's a free-floating irregular, poorly paid and unsupervised; if he chooses to keep his reports free of burdensome detail, that is up to him. It's not like anyone else is keeping an eye on his milk round. And he will do his job better, be more alert to his charges' needs, if he isn't worrying about his own life circumstances; if he has somewhere to lay his head at night.

It occurs to him that he never heard back from Alec Wicinski, but that's a detail that has ceased to matter, and it won't bother him long.

And meanwhile the streetlights come on, and the view from the window thickens and slows. He remains where he is for a while, fascinated by the world he is no longer locked out in. There are no guarantees, he knows; his stratagem could be discovered at any time, and then he'll be for the high jump. Right now, though, John Bachelor is warm, he is fed; there is wine in Solomon's larder. In a minute, he'll go pour himself a glass. But for now he'll sit and watch the quiet snow.

THE CATCH

· · ·

They came for him at dawn, just as he'd feared they would. But instead of using the Big Red Key so beloved of SWAT teams—the miniature battering ram that reduces a front door to matchsticks—they entered in civilised fashion, and when he opened his eyes they were in his bedroom, one regarding him as if he were a carving on a tomb, and the other examining a photograph on the dressing table that showed Solomon Dortmund when young, a mere fifty or so, holding hands with a woman the same age, and whose quiet smile for the camera could pull a drowning man ashore. Surrounding this photograph were a pair of beloved relics: a hairbrush and a small velvet drawstring bag, an inch square, containing three baby teeth and an adult molar. This was disturbing, but when you appropriate a man's life without his blessing, you leave his family treasures where you find them.

"Two minutes, John. You'll be on the pavement in two minutes."

"Could you make it five?" His voice was scratchy, and badly dubbed. "I could do with—"

"Two minutes. Richard here will keep you company."

And then it was just John Bachelor and this man Richard, a large, shaven-headed thirtysomething with thick-framed spectacles, who gazed at him unsmiling. It seemed unlikely that they would arrive at an odd-couple friendship in the time allowed.

When he shifted, a sour smell escaped from the blankets.

"You couldn't pass me my trousers?"

Richard patently regarded this as either rhetorical enquiry or statement of fact.

There is a peculiar humiliation in dressing in front of a hostile stranger, particularly when one's body is an increasingly rackety collection of limbs attached to a soft, baggy frame, and one's clothing a medley of items purchased at bargain prices. Bachelor's corduroy trousers were shiny at the knee, and his shirt had a faint spray of blood on the collar. His own, it's important to note. Even so, it was a relief not to be standing in his briefs in front of someone whose own physical decline, if already etched in outline beneath his dark blue suit, had yet to be framed and hung for all to see.

Squeezing his feet into socks produced the kind of hyperventilation that running up stairs once triggered.

He stood up. "I need to, ah . . ."

Richard affected incomprehension.

"To piss, man. I need to piss."

John could see him thinking about it—actually thinking about it. When did we grow so hard? He was too young to be former-Stasi.

"It's your two minutes," he said at last. "But leave the door open."

Of course. In case John used the precious moments to retrieve the handgun from the toilet cistern, or assemble the miniature helicopter secreted beneath the floorboards.

It was an old man's bathroom, with an old man's shaving gear on a shelf, an old man's mirror on the wall, and an old man's reflection residing there, so Bachelor ignored it, raised the toilet lid and pissed. Lately, he had been dosing himself with Solly Dortmund's sleeping tablets, a large number of which he had found in the medicine cabinet housing that same mirror. Solly Solly Solly. Old men have trouble sleeping, and medication was an obvious recourse. But if he had been pre-scribed pills, why were they still here? Solly had been a hoarder, but to collect sleeping pills spoke of building himself an escape hatch, equivalent to a handgun in a cistern, or a miniature helicopter. In the end, of course, he had needed neither, which meant that his trove remained intact for John to plunder. Which, in turn, meant side effects: John's urine had acquired a metallic odour, and he wondered now if it were drifting out through the open door, assaulting Richard's nostrils. He hoped not, and at the same time tried to convince himself of the upside to the worst happening: that he need no longer await its appear-ance.

"Time's up."

I know, John thought.

He'd known it for a while.

They took him not to Regent's Park, the home of the Service, but to Marylebone High Street. Richard drove. The other man sat in the back with John. He looked to be in his fifties, a man with some years' secret experience behind him, and not unused to collecting the wayward and conveying them somewhere like this: an empty office above London's favourite bookshop, its white walls newly decorated, its carpet squares not yet bedded in, so that the joins could be seen crisscrossing the floor, as if marking out a board game. For the players, there were two chairs, dining-room variety. There were no blinds, and light streamed through the windows while the city yawned. It was all very—John strained, momentarily, for the precise word. It was all very alarming. If they'd been thugs, he'd have known he was in for a kicking. But they were suits, which suggested a more vicious outcome. In other circumstances, he'd have been wondering what he'd done to deserve this. As it was, he knew full well.

"Sit there."

Not an invitation.

He took the chair indicated, and the older man sat in the other, a clean metre or so between them. The younger man took station by the door. There could be no mistaking this for anything but what it was: the interrogation of a wrongdoer. It would be sweeter, quicker, if he simply confessed and saved everyone time. Whatever it is you think I've done, I've done it. Can we go home now? Though he had, of course, no home to go to. A fact which lay at the heart of what it was he'd done.

"So, John. John Bachelor."

"That's me."

"Yes, John. We know it's you, John. Otherwise we'd look a right pair of nanas, wouldn't we, collecting someone who *isn't* John Bachelor this bright summer morning. So you're who you are, and we're us. Richard there, you already know his name. And I'm Edward. Eddie to my friends. Very much Edward to you."

"Edward it is."

Edward sighed. "I recognise that you're eager to cooperate, John, and that's going to save a lot of inconvenience. But don't waste breath on things that don't need saying. Which is a polite way, John, of telling you not to speak except to answer questions." He clasped his hands. "If you want to hear a less polite way of being told that, go ahead with the irrelevant interruptions. Clear enough?"

John nodded.

"Nods aren't going to cut it, John. When I ask a direct question, I'm going to need to hear words coming out of your mouth. So once again, was that clear enough?"

"It was."

"That's better." Edward smiled, though not in a realistic way. Edward, thought John, was less of a suit than he appeared. Edward might have put on jacket and tie at some ungodly hour this morning, but that was as far as it went.

Edward unclasped his hands. Even at this distance, John was getting a hint of a fragrance he'd first detected in the car; a robust, peppery smell, from a soap that doubtless came in masculine packaging. He imagined waxed paper wrapping a weighty disc, its surface embossed with an heraldic design. All of this was offset by his awareness of his own body odour, never alluring first thing in the morning, and worsened by fear and interrupted sleep. His stomach churned repeatedly. His chin felt rubbery. His whole body, when you got down to it, was a sad disappointment. But Edward was speaking again:

"Before we start, there's something you should know. When an action like the one we are currently undertaking is mandated, a certain amount of administration occurs. Acceptable limits are signed off on. Mission parameters defined. What

I'm saying, John, is that the worst-case scenario has been budgeted for, so I'm not looking at reputational damage if things turn sour this morning. Nor is Richard. I thought it might help if you were in possession of that information. There's no need to acknowledge your understanding. You don't get to sign a waiver or anything. What happens, happens."

John thought, All this, really? He'd been expecting some kind of bureaucratic retribution, but this melodrama? An empty office, a sinister warning? And yet it was working, because he was scared.

Edward nodded, confident his words had hit home. He tugged at his lapels, straightening his suit jacket. "So let's get down to business, shall we? Benny Manors, John. What can you tell me about Benny Manors?"

Well, okay. He hadn't been expecting that.

John Bachelor was Service, had been all his adult life. So by any fair calculation, he ought to have been comfortably settled by now: not a Desk, obviously—reaching Desk level required drive, ambition, contacts, dress sense and at least a glimmer of sociopathy—but enjoying cubicle status and a pension. Instead, he was on the margin; downgraded last year to "irregular," which meant part-time, with an accompanying reduction in salary. When he'd complained to HR, the rebuff had been comprehensive. If the Service operated a zero-hours contract, it ran, that's the level he'd have been pegged at, so he might as well stop trying to make waves. Even making ripples was above his pay grade. They were barely aware, to be frank, that he was in the pool at all. Putting the phone down after this illuminating chat, he'd felt as if everything had become a little looser: the buttons on his cuffs, his shoelaces, his sense of self. What made it worse was its inevitability. His life trajectory resembled one of those puzzles in the Saturday papers: *What is the next number in this sequence?* He'd been counting down to zero for years.

And it was salutary how a few poor choices could scuttle you, information it would have been useful to have had at the outset. There had been a house once, he remembered that much, and he was pretty sure it was still standing, and that his ex-wife still enjoyed the breakfast bar, the bedroom extension and the patio that had been intended to both improve their quality of life and increase the property's value. The latter had almost certainly happened—he'd never heard of a property in London *losing* value, short of it burning down—but was no longer of direct relevance to him, a matter that, for the avoidance of doubt, had been clarified in a courtroom. There'd been a pension too, until he'd taken advantage of the drawdown opportunity to bury a huge chunk of it in his former brother-in-law's foolproof investment opportunity, a mirage of such IMAX proportions that he genuinely couldn't recall the details of the product at its heart. Skateboards for mermaids? Feline Zimmer frames? Some such fucking thing. And meanwhile here he was, wrong side of sixty, catering to the Service's has-beens. A milkman.

"Milkman" was a term of contempt, of course. Agents were joes; desk jockeys were suits. They were different ways of fighting the same battles, and while each had been known to look down on the other, like characters inhabiting the same Escher staircase, they shared a commonality neither would deny; a sense of purpose. A milkman, though, had failed to make a mark in either endeavour, and could be trusted to do no more than his weekly round:

touching base with the pensioners and the walking wounded; those who'd served behind whatever lines had been drawn in their day, and now required support in their evening. Not that all were elderly, or, if the truth mattered, entirely honourable. Solomon Dortmund, though, had been a jewel. Had it ever occurred to Solly to view John Bachelor with disdain, it was a thought he'd have smothered in its cradle.

And so, in the way these things have of occurring, John had been living for the last eight months in Solomon Dortmund's apartment, two flights up in a proud brick building off the Edgware Road. It wasn't large, but it was comfortable. Solly's choice of pictures hung on the walls, and Solly's umbrella lived in a stand by the front door. And Solomon had died of a heart attack in the bedroom, and John had done right by him, he was morally certain of that—arranged the funeral, invited the old man's comrades, put money behind the bar. Had spent an evening in the company of strangers, all of whom remembered Solly fondly, and all of whom had wondered who he, Bachelor, was, precisely? Not a relative, surely. That "surely" contained a wealth of ethnic certainties. So no, John wasn't a relative; was, rather, the son of a man with whom Solly had done business in the long-ago. The nature of this business was left vague, and those who had known that Solly, for all his gentle manners and kind habits, had once performed certain services for a certain Service, had nodded wisely, and left it at that. And afterwards John had returned to the flat, Solly's keys in his pocket, Solly's umbrella in his hand.

It had been a hard winter, with inches of snow even in London, and it had been a relief to find himself behind a closed door, the weather locked out in the cold. Relief has a way of becoming habit. The tasks John performed after Solly's departure had not included informing his department that Mr. Dortmund was no longer on the planet, and it was surprising how easy it was for a bureaucracy to overlook such trivia. Left to its own devices the Civil Service is a *perpetuum mobile*, and accordingly the arrangements for Solly's well-being remained in place: his bills paid, his pension gathering dust in his bank account. John never laid a finger on Solly's money, obviously. That would have been wrong, and difficult. But John laid his head on Solly's pillows, and laid his body down on Solly's bed; he rested his feet on Solly's coffee table while planting his arse on Solly's sofa, and he cleaned out Solly's fridge and pantry without his conscience uttering one chirp. He was doing no harm. It was this or sleep in his car: who could afford London rents on a three-day-week salary? And he'd run out of friends among the living. So it was Solly's generosity he relied on, and Solly's roof that sheltered him through the rest of that hard winter, and a wet spring, and a record-breaking summer. If there was a downside, it was the anxiety that fizzed in the background like white noise. Unbroken luck was an unknown factor in John's life, and waiting for the fracture to happen wore at his nerves. Hence his use of Solly's sleeping pills.

This, or most of it, provided a wealth of explanations for his current situation: sitting on this chair in this room, with Edward being fierce at him.

Benny Manors, though, had never entered his mental picture.

"Benny Manors, John. What can you tell me about Benny Manors?"

Bringing him back to the present.

"Benny, well, Benny," he said. "What can I say? Benny's one of mine."

"We know, John. Sole purpose of visit, as they say at passport control. Little more detail, eh?"

John searched what others might refer to as their mental database, or perhaps Rolodex, if they were of a certain generation. For John, it was more akin to opening an ancient filing cabinet he'd long stopped keeping in alphabetical order. Some of the papers were scribbles on envelopes. Benny Manors. That was a name he'd shoved to the back, in the hope he'd not have to deal with it again.

"Because I've been looking through your Ts and Cs, John. That an abbreviation you're familiar with? Doesn't mean tits and cooze, if you were wondering. No, it means terms and conditions. As in, of employment. You remember that, John, the job you do? The one you're paid for? Remind me what they call you?"

"I'm a retirement needs evaluation counsellor—"

"You're a milkman, John."

John nodded.

"And what your Ts and Cs very eloquently state is that, in that role, you make contact with your clients, bare minimum, once a month. Which is handy for me, as I'm keen on having a word with one of those clients, the aforementioned Benny Manors, and on account of the terms and conditions of your employment, I'm in the happy position of knowing I'm talking to someone who's had contact with Benny in the last four weeks. Bare minimum. Meaning that within the next two minutes I'm going to have a much clearer picture of our Benny's current whereabouts than I do now. So that's nice for me, isn't it, John? Nice knowing I have you to paint that picture for me."

It must indeed have been nice for him, living in that state of certainty, though it was a little less comfortable for John Bachelor. Because John hadn't laid eyes on Benny Manors in well over two years.

It was one of those things, one of those moments. You meet someone and right there, in the first flush of new acquaintance— forget about taking time to be sure; sometimes you can feel it in your marrow, no hesitation—right there, in that first moment, you think: well, this isn't going to fucking work, is it?

He'd already had Benny Manors's history down pat. Say what you like about John Bachelor, but he did his job, or at least, turned up prepared to do his job. It was only after that preliminary stage that things might go wrong, as with, for example, Benny Manors. So yes, he had Benny's number, and it wasn't what you'd call prime. Because Benny was a louse and Benny was a chancer. One of those who definitely fell within the category "not entirely honourable." What Benny had been, when you got down to it, was a crook. Breaking and entering, though he'd discovered a sideline when a venture into a likely looking property had yielded an interesting collection of Polaroids among the loose cash and petty jewellery, Polaroids Benny had amused himself with a time or two before it occurred to him that while the starring role of Old Man in a Nappy had evidently been taken by the gentleman occupier of the recently burgled house, the two young women supporting his act were definitely not his wife. And thus Benny had learned that some stolen property enjoys a cash value above and beyond what it might reach down the local, because the elderly gentleman proved expensively keen to reacquire possession of his souvenirs rather than have them, say, appear on the internet. It was Benny's pleasure to make the old man's dream come true. Well, his latest dream. Going by the evidence, earlier versions had already been taken care of.

So that was Benny Manors, and that became his career: housebreaking a speciality, but with an eye for the unusual item. Careers have been built on lesser talents—soap stars, presidents, novelists—and he might have happily continued his course without interruption had he not come to the attention of a Service talent spotter. Every so often Regent's Park found itself in need of an amateur, largely to avoid any fallout should the situation at issue turn unexpectedly professional. So, Benny Manors having dropped onto its radar as a snapper-up of unconsidered truffles, the Service pressganged him into carrying out an after-hours excursion into the premises of a certain Eastern European gentleman resident in Knightsbridge, whose diplomatic status technically put him off-limits, but whose private life remained of surpassing interest regardless. Anyway, long story short, the situation did in fact turn unexpectedly professional, with the result that Benny Manors, in what turned out to be the briefest Secret Service career since George Lazenby's, rather than acquiring any useful information acquired a permanent limp instead, courtesy of the Eastern European gentleman's domestic help, which was rather more energetic than the average Knightsbridge household required. Benny, and what remained of his left leg, were deposited in a dumpster just outside the postcode. This was felt by Regent's Park to be coincidence rather than deliberate slight, but who knew?

Anyway, never let it be said that the Service turns its back on those wounded in its employ, even when the employ is unofficial, and especially when the wounded suggests appealing to the court of public opinion, or Twitter, as it's now known. Which is how Benny Manors came to be on John Bachelor's books: not exactly a retiree, and not exactly a shining example of one who's given all for his nation's benefit, but a man with a limp nevertheless, which he hadn't had before the Service came into his life. It took all sorts, John supposed.

And that first meeting had been at a pub near King's Cross, he thought—he remembered the occasion, but it wasn't like he'd be treasuring it on his deathbed or anything. So let's say King's Cross, and let's say the usual dark panelling and Fuller's beer-mats, the usual door to the gents as easy to negotiate as a tiger trap. Benny let John buy the drinks, because that was the way of the world. And Benny let John explain what their relationship was going to be before sinking that ship before it left harbour.

"Once a month? No no no. No no no no."

Seven nos. Even allowing for the double negative, he was definitely giving this the thumbs down.

At this time Benny would have been late forties. No longer as lithe as he'd been in his youth—who is?—but given that much of his particular youth had been spent worming through windows technically too small for him, he'd had a higher bar to fall from than most. So he wasn't in terrible shape, damaged leg apart—it had required metal pins, several of them; he was a special case at airports, Benny Manors—but all in all, he wasn't too bad a picture of a late-forties man, also allowing for this being his choice of meeting place, mid-afternoon. *Homo saloon-barensis.* He had wiry gingerish hair and a two-day stubble. And his suit was classier than the pub they were in, not to mention the beer he was drinking—Newcastle Brown Ale? John hadn't been aware anyone actually drank that. He thought the bottles were just kept handy in case a fight broke out.

He followed up his Lear-like string of negatives with an unnecessary clarification. "Once a month isn't going to work for me."

"I don't make the rules."

"See, that's the sort of thing that gets said by people who spend their sorry little lives doing exactly what they're told."

John Bachelor's life at the time wasn't as sorry as it would become—he was still on a full-time salary—and he didn't enjoy the description.

"What exactly is your problem, Benny? What makes it such a chore to have a quick face-to-face round about pay day?"

"Did I say it was a chore?"

"You're not making it sound like a pleasure."

Benny was drinking straight from the bottle. He took a good long pull without taking his eyes off John, then said, "This leg I'm carrying round. I didn't break it climbing out a window. I had it shattered, bespoke-like. By two bastards doing an impression of a pair of brick walls."

His accent was plain and unvarnished, but *bastards* had a flatness to it. His file hadn't included deep background—Benny Manors was evidently unforthcoming with his personal information, possibly an occupational wariness—and he hadn't been important enough to warrant legwork, if you didn't include the job carried out on his actual limb. So John didn't know but wondered if Manors wasn't city-born at all, but hailed from up country. Would explain his choice of drink. But he was still talking:

"So the way I see it is this. You pay the compensation as agreed, and you stay out of my line of sight. That clear enough?"

"If I don't see you, you don't get the money, Benny. It's as simple as that."

"Yeah, right, but, that's not actually simple at all, is it? What that is is downright complicated. Because I don't plan to spend the rest of my natural being wherever you want me to be once a month simply to collect what's owing to me. The dosh goes straight into my account, right? It's not like you're carrying round an envelope full of fivers."

There had been a time when that was precisely what milkmen did—carried round bags of money. But this way of doing things, reliant as it was on the honesty of all parties, had been brought to an end back when Michael Jackson was King of Pop.

"So there's no actual reason for me to have to be anywhere, is there?"

John Bachelor wasn't used to this attitude. Most of his clients were glad of the company: a friendly face, some kind words. The opportunity to talk about the old days, when they'd done whatever they'd done that had brought them into his ambit. Mostly, this had involved acts of courage rather than petty burglary. Mostly, they were better men and women than Benny Manors. Snap judgement, but this didn't seem an uphill battle.

It occurred to him that he didn't want to spend the rest of his own natural having this conversation once a month.

"So what I suggest," Benny was saying, "is that you just turn in your monthly report saying yes, all's well, Benny's fine. And instead of us actually having a meeting, you can have a lie-in. How does that sound?"

"Again, Benny, what's your problem? It's ten minutes out of your busy schedule. Which, let's face it, must have gaps in it these days. I mean, it's put a crimp in your burglary career, right? Having a leg like an overcooked noodle."

When he got up from the floor the barman was already in Benny's face, telling him to bugger off sharpish, no mistake. Benny was shaking his head, not disputing the marching orders, but ruing the punch he'd delivered. A little more precision, John's teeth might have made a pretty necklace. As it was, he simply had a bloodied nose.

"Misunderstanding," said John. "Just a misunderstanding." He made to pick up his stool.

"Don't you worry, sir, I'll see to that."

He cleaned himself up in the gents, assured the barman there was no need to trouble the police, and left. It was brighter outside than he'd been expecting, or maybe that was just his head ringing unnecessary changes. When was the last time he'd been hit? Must have been at school. On the other hand the next time might be on the cards already, because here was Benny Manors again. But he had his palms showing, indicating he wasn't about to throw another punch. The limpy git.

"You asked for that," was what he said.

Actually, he might have had a point.

"But I'll tell you how I plan to make it up."

And he did.

"So tell me, John, where's our Benny? And what's our Benny up to?"

"Well," John said, and toyed with the possibility of leaving it at that. Looked at philosophically, while Edward's questions remained unanswered, the possibility of John's being able to answer them remained alive, as did John's future and, indeed, John himself. Not that he seriously thought these two were going to kill him. On the other hand, if Edward didn't look precisely like someone who'd killed people before, he did look like someone who'd received news of other people having been killed with perfect equanimity. Which was enough of a prompt to allow John to get to the end of a sentence: "Well, he moves around a bit."

"He does, does he? I'm assuming you mean residentially speaking, John. Because the information I have regarding Benny Manors is that his mobility is seriously compromised. Not about to launch into a rumba without warning, is he?"

"He doesn't like to be tied down," said John. "Feels the need for flexibility."

"Again, I would cite the construction work done on his leg. Except I suspect you're going to tell me you're speaking metaphorically, aren't you? You're going to tell me Benny Manors fancies himself a free spirit, just one Volkswagen camper van short of a trip to Kathmandu."

"Well . . ."

"Or put another way, what you're telling me, John, is that the address currently on file for Benny Manors—the file you're in charge of keeping up to date, I don't need to remind you, except it seems I do—that address is not actually his address, which would explain why he's not there now, and hasn't been for some considerable time. Would I be right in summing up the situation in that fashion, John?"

"...Yes."

Edward sighed.

John said, "It's a delicate business, looking after the Service's old-timers. I have to take into account their needs, their situations, their psychological—"

"Bullshit."

Well, precisely, thought John. Their psychological bullshit.

"Benny Manors isn't some traumatised asset still having nightmares about his weeks behind the Wall. He's a small-time housebreaker and blackmail artiste who, if he hadn't had his leg smashed up on a one-night stand for the Park, would almost certainly have had his dick caught in someone else's mousetrap by now, except that way we wouldn't be paying for his cornflakes. So when he told you about his *needs*, you should have told him about his obligations. Among which was keeping the Service informed of his whereabouts. And that would be you, John. In this very minor instance, you represent the Service."

From over by the door, a snorting noise reminded John that Richard was still in the room.

"And yet, you have fucked up. Fucked up, John. And while that is nothing new in your long and unillustrious career, it puts me in an embarrassing situation, and that, let me make clear, *is* something new. And to make it even more humiliating, I now find myself in the demeaning position of looking to you to extricate myself from this embarrassment."

"...Yes."

"You still haven't got the hang of this, have you? That wasn't a question."

Edward leaned back, which struck John as mildly dangerous.

These chairs weren't made for cavalier posturing. But mostly what he was thinking was, this wasn't as bad as he'd feared. If he was required to do something, that meant being allowed to walk out of this room in order to do it. Moreover, whatever this was about, it wasn't about Solly. It wasn't about him living in dead Solly's Service flat, which—the shock of a dawn collection notwithstanding—was far more crucial to John's well-being than any minor fuck-up he might have made regarding Benny bloody Manors. Because if the Solly business came up he not only wouldn't have the flat any more, he wouldn't have a job either. And this wasn't a world waiting with open arms to find future prospects for John Bachelors. It was a world waiting to crush them under its unforgiving heel.

"So, let's start with the confession. Because there's always a confession, John, we both know that. Let's start with why you let Benny Manors wander away like a kid at a fairground, without ever putting it on a report."

He could have lied, but John Bachelor had told enough lies in his life to know when one was likely to haul him out of the mud and when one would step on his head. So he told the truth: about that first meeting in King's Cross, which had ended with Benny punching him in the face and him falling off his stool with a bloody nose. And about what Benny had said when he'd joined him outside in the sunshine; about how he planned to make it up.

"And this would be money, wouldn't it, John?"

"Yes."

"Because it always comes down to money with a certain type of citizen."

John couldn't immediately tell whether the type in question was Benny or himself. He supposed, though, that it didn't really matter in the circumstances.

What Benny had suggested was that they arrive at a little understanding. The understanding would be in the nature of fifty quid a month, payable the day after Benny's monthly stipend reached his bank account.

"I'm getting paid to keep quiet, when it comes down to it," Benny had said. "And now you're being paid for exactly the same thing. And this way I get to keep my privacy intact. More secure, see? And as you're in charge of my welfare, that should suit you down to the ground."

"I'm supposed to file a report."

"Well, there's nothing to stop you doing that, is there? I mean, how detailed do these reports get?"

Details, well. John had details down to a fine art. "Nothing to report" was a not uncommon entry.

"Can't stand here all day, John."

And so he'd said yes, and that was how it started, and pretty much how it finished too. *Going to need your bank details, John. Not like I'll be turning up on your doorstep once a month with the cash. Whole idea is, I get to do my own thing here.*

Edward was shaking his head in disbelief by the time it got to this part. "John Bachelor," he said. "John Bachelor. You would have lasted exactly two seconds in the field. Any field. Walk into a fucking *corn*field, you'd last two seconds."

Richard spoke for the first time. "He made one payment only, didn't he?"

John nodded, then remembered his instructions. "Yes."

"And then you were on record as having received money from him, and after that he didn't have to pay you sod all."

"The art of the bribe, John," Edward said. "Once you've made your catch, you can keep the rest of the bait for yourself. And you're telling us you've had no contact with Benny Manors since?"

"... That's right."

Another sigh.

He could hear traffic building up; cars and taxis ferrying people to their places of work. The cafés up and down the High Street would be welcoming breakfast customers, and the homeless in the doorways would be stirring, knowing they'd be moved on soon. The day, which was going to be a hot one, was starting to flex its muscles. John had forgotten what he'd had planned for the day ahead. Everything looked different now.

Edward was staring at him, and he had the sense that there was unspoken communication going on between him and Richard. As if they were checking cues, awaiting a prompt. Whether it arrived John couldn't tell, but Edward began talking at last, and it went on for a while.

"Now, I'm going to explain the facts of life to you, John. I'm aware that some of them may have come to your attention in the past, but it's always good to have a refresher, isn't it? And the important thing you have to remember is, your balls are in a vice. And I'm operating the vice, John. And if I ever decide to take a rest from operating that vice, which I won't, but if I ever do, young Richard there is going to step in for me while I do whatever it is I've decided is more important than operating the vice in which your balls are trapped, and he is going to operate that vice in my stead, and let me tell you something about Richard, John,

Richard is a disappointed man. About ten minutes ago in our terms, which translates to half a year or so in young Richard's, he was very much the rising star. Diana Taverner's favourite son type of thing. Man most likely to. Instead of which he found himself stepping into the most enormous pile of shit, as a result of which he is no longer anybody's favourite son, and is in fact as popular at Regent's Park as a red-headed orphan. This close to Slough House he came. This close." The helpful gesture illustrating this was a thumb and a finger, so close to touching no daylight slipped through. "The only reason he was spared that fate is Lady Di wanted to deny Jackson Lamb the fun of dismembering him. But that lucky escape aside, Richard's disappointment is a real and living thing, John. What you might call organic. So Richard finds himself in the position of having to feed that disappointment, John, feed it so that it doesn't devour him instead, and what he likes to feed it is anybody he can. Which right here and right now, John, would be you. Let me know that you're keeping up."

"... Yes."

"Good. So this is what's going to happen, John. You are going to find Benny Manors for us, and you're going to hold him in place until we come and collect him, and that is going to happen swiftly. Otherwise you are going to discover what a vice round your balls feels like, and you're not going to be discovering that while hiding away in a cosy little flat off the Edgware, John. Because yes, John, we're aware you've been living in a dead man's trousers. Using a dead man's electricity and gas and water, and for all we know hocking a dead man's treasures in order to satisfy whatever unnatural cravings keep you awake at night. Porn or booze, John, I don't care which.

All I care about is you finding Benny Manors, failure to do which will turn my full attention to the clamping properties of this vice we're discussing. For example, I might decide to take a closer look at whatever caused Solomon Dortmund to have a heart attack last winter, and without wanting to give away spoilers, John, I'm very likely to decide that it was you. I mean, it's the old *cui bono*, isn't it? Who profited from Solomon's demise? That would be the man who's taken over his life and trappings."

So much for this not being as bad as it might be, thought John.

"In summary, I really wouldn't want to be your balls, John. Neither one of them. But on the upside, your way out of this mess is clear, yes? You simply do what you're told." He stood abruptly, and the chair toppled onto the carpet with a muffled thud. "Richard here will be in touch soonest. Check on your progress. We'll give you a couple of days, John." He cracked his knuckles. "A couple of days. Then I'll start getting irritable. And you don't want that."

The list of things John didn't want had grown exponentially this morning, but he could agree that Edward growing irritable was likely to be included. It didn't seem worth corroborating this, though, so he didn't waste his breath on a reply.

As they watched him weave up Marylebone High Street, looking not all that different from others starting to appear on the streets now—those who had places to go and things to do—Richard said to Edward: "I think we motivated him."

"That was never going to be the problem. Someone as shit-scared as Bachelor's easy to motivate. No, the major difficulty is the usual one when you're using shoddy tools. Are they up to the job? Or will they fall apart in your hands?"

And as he was watched doing his weaving, John Bachelor thought: whatever's going on here involves several layers of fuckery. He was a milkman, for god's sake. If they wanted to put the frighteners on him, all they had to do was threaten to sack him. So there was something going on here, more than appeared on the surface. Not that that altered things much. Whichever way you looked at it, he was going to have to find Benny Manors.

Biggest puzzle of all, though, was: How come they couldn't do this by themselves?

First thing first, he had a drink. Early doors by anyone's reckoning, but sometimes you skip the niceties. Back in Solly's flat, sitting by the window, he watched the morning get a grip on itself while he drank an inch of peach brandy, discovered at the back of Solly's sideboard and saved for an emergency. The first gulp burned the way the first gulp does any time of day, though the peach flavour added a hint of breakfast. Good to maintain a schedule. And while he was doing that he ran through his mental records on Benny Manors, which took zero minutes. It wasn't as if he knew the man's haunts or habits; they'd had exactly one meeting, and that hadn't gone well. And if Edward and Richard hadn't managed to find him with the Park's resources at their disposal: well. Why did they expect him to accomplish what they couldn't?

In this whole sorry mess, he was holding only one card that he could see.

He knew who Richard was.

Because their stories had collided in the past. Or brushed

against each other, rather, the way a pass might be made at a railway station: information delivered, received, in the briefest of exchanges: an envelope swapped, a password muttered. So he knew this much: that Richard's name was Richard Pynne, inevitably demoticised to Dick the Prick. And how he knew him was, Dick the Prick had stolen what should have been the crowning jewel of John's career.

For once, just once, he'd had a glimpse of the limelight. After the death of one of his older clients, a list had come into John's possession, a list of supposed sleeper agents. The details were probably written down somewhere, but the upshot was that John himself—John Bachelor, milkman—recruited an agent, Hannah Weiss. Not a high-flying operative, no Red Sparrow, no Modesty Blaise, but a mole of sorts, allowing the Service a glimpse into the workings of its German counterpart: not a bad day's work, if he said so himself. And he did say so himself, but to little avail; Hannah was taken away from him and placed in the care of one Richard Pynne, Lady Di's favourite and a noted high-flyer, who for some reason was thought a better choice to run a minor domestic op than clapped-out John Bachelor, who'd never done anything more complicated than carry bags and tell bedtime stories to ancient spooks.

Funny thing was, he'd heard rumours since that the whole operation, small beans as it was, had gone tits up, with young Hannah turning out not to be a double at all, but a triple; not so much allowing the Service a glimpse of the workings of its German counterpart, but the precise inverse. Which meant Richard had in fact done him a favour, even if it hadn't felt like that at the time. London Rules: always be a fair distance from a fuck-up.

And if it had been a rumour when he'd first heard it, it had obviously calcified into fact since, for here was Richard, so far from the seat of power that he was manning the door while someone bigger and crustier than he was put the screws on that clapped-out milkman.

You could call it karma. Or just one of life's *fuck you*s.

The brandy was gone. He contemplated a second glass, but experience suggested that a second had a way of becoming a fifth, so instead booted up his cranky Service laptop and accessed his client files. There Benny was, in all his muted glory: the history of his brief career in the Service, the slightly longer history of his previous known activities, the address in Wandsworth which was clearly no longer current, his bank details . . . bank details? The man was out there with a bank account, money going in, money coming out, and those clowns couldn't find him with the whole of the Hub at their disposal? Unless it wasn't. That possibility had been nagging at him from the start, when they took him to a vacant safe house instead of the Park. Unless this pair were on a frolic of their own. So he considered that for a while, and came to the alarming conclusion that it made little difference. Even if they were off-reservation, that didn't render their threats harmless. They knew about the flat. They knew enough to screw him up badly.

And unless he could think of a way of getting round that, he had no choice but to find Benny Manors.

So he hit the pubs round King's Cross. What else was he going to do? He asked about his old friend Benny, had Benny been in?, and received blank looks. One place he was convinced had been the pub where it started: this was where he'd been sitting when

Benny punched him in the face. There was the door to the gents it had been a struggle to navigate. But he had the same sensation an hour or so later somewhere else, and besides, what difference did it make? Nobody had heard of Benny here, there, or any of the places in between. They weren't establishments where one punch thrown several years back was still talked about. There'd been punches since. They blurred together.

And another problem was, going into a pub and asking questions, it was de rigueur to buy a drink.

Drunks and pigeons: there are homing instincts. In fact—one of the random thoughts that flitted through John Bachelor's brain at two in the morning, when it occurred to him that he was back at Solly's, with no recollection of getting there—in fact, it would be interesting to get a pigeon drunk, to see whether this improved its homeward flight time. But that thought only lasted as long as it took him to crawl into bed, where the ceiling rotated like a fan in a black-and-white movie. He hadn't found Benny Manors; hadn't even found anyone pretending they knew Benny Manors. If Benny Manors had suggested King's Cross as a convenient meeting place, it was only because Benny Manors hadn't wanted John to know where a really convenient meeting place might be, such as wherever it was Benny Manors actually hung out. And as things stood, the only pointer he had to Benny's whereabouts was that, on their one and only encounter to date, the man had been drinking Newcastle Brown Ale. That notion circled John's head in the opposite direction to the ceiling, making him nauseous. He was too old for this. And even when he'd been young enough for this, it had lacked what you might call glamour. He slept at last, or managed a kind of sleep, which felt more like a ride on a broken Ferris wheel. When he regained consciousness, he felt abandoned rather than rested. And the usual morning stocktake yielded no happy balance: he'd spent nigh on a week's salary greasing conversational wheels, and his mouth felt like a ferret's timeshare.

He stumbled to the shower. It was still early, way too early, but the glimmer of an idea had broken on him while he was riding that wheel, and although its only real attraction lay in the absence of any alternative, there was a slight possibility that its light might guide him home. He was probably still drunk, after all. And it would be foolish not to take advantage of the fact.

So not long afterwards he was loitering near a gym in north London, head pounding, eyes bloodshot, but upright, showered and dressed, which, given that it wasn't yet half seven, suggested from a distance that he was a productive member of society. More productive members had jobs to do: while he waited, a van dumped bundles of newspapers outside a shop, their headlines variations on the same theme, that the waves made by the recent suicide of an American billionaire in his prison cell were still breaking shore this side of the Atlantic. The man had been a sex trafficker, and a well-connected one. A particular connection was mentioned by name in 48-point font. Not a happy day at the Palace, John surmised.

He was spared further contemplation of this odious pairing by the appearance of the woman he'd been hoping for.

She emerged from the gym with the air of one for whom the world has been on hold while she'd been otherwise occupied, a gym

bag over her shoulder, her hair tied back. She was wearing sunglasses, possibly to avoid being recognised, but more likely because
it was already bright, already warm. John wished he were wearing
shades himself. At the very least, they'd have helped disguise his
bleary appearance. But too late now. She'd already spotted him.

"John Bachelor," she said, making little attempt to hide her
contempt.

"It's important."

"It had bloody better be."

She was all in black: black sweats, a black hoodie. Only her
trainers offered colour: black too, but with a crimson band.
Her hair was wet, and though she was still recognisably Diana
Taverner—Lady Di—First Desk of Regent's Park, he'd never
seen her looking like this before: like someone who had a life.
He suspected few people had. He wondered how many of them
dared boast of the experience.

"How did you know to find me here?"

This was disingenuous. She liked it known that she did a
ninety-minute early morning workout three times a week, and this
was the most expensive place near her private residence. So he'd
got lucky that this was one of those mornings, but everyone
deserves the occasional break.

All he said was, "I didn't. Not really."

"Do I need to press a button?"

Which she'd have in a pocket, and would bring the Dogs
running. That was all he needed, second morning in a row: to be
tossed into someone else's vehicle and taken somewhere he didn't
want to go. "No. Please don't."

She pushed her sunglasses up her nose. It was an oddly

endearing moment, which was not something he'd ever expected in her company.

"There's something you need to know about," he said.

For a second or two, it seemed she'd dispute this. To inform him that it was unlikely he'd ever be in a position where there was something he knew that she didn't, yet. He remembered their being in a pub together once, at a wake for a dead colleague, and she'd outlined his role in life, the full ambit of his responsibilities. *It's hardly* Tinker Tailor, *John. You wipe their noses, feed their cats, and make sure they're not blowing their pensions on internet poker.* The kind of summation he might have made himself, though he'd have pretended there was humour in it. But instead of heading down that road again, she said, "Okay, you've got my attention. For twenty seconds. Let's hear what your problem is, and then I'll decide whether it's worth this gross intrusion of my privacy."

"I'm being played."

She rolled her eyes. "You're being 'played'? *You're* being played? Seriously, John, that's a three-word sentence, and it's only the middle one isn't ridiculous. Who do you think is trying to play you? An amateur percussionist?"

"One of them's Richard Pynne."

And this landed, he could tell.

She took a moment to change her bag from one hand to the other. "Pynne? What would Richard Pynne be doing on the streets? He was reassigned from Ops. I think he's in charge of the stationery cupboard now."

"And someone called Edward. Biggish guy. Fifties. Wearing a suit, but looks like he's done heavy lifting in his time."

"It's a big organisation. We could have any number of Edwards on the books."

But this name too had triggered recognition. He could tell.

"But here's me using up your twenty seconds. What were this pair after? Just the bullet points."

"They want me to find Benny Manors."

"Manors, Manors, Manors. Oh, Manors. Well, they went to the right person, I assume. He's on your round, isn't he?"

"Yes. Except . . ."

"Except what?" She halted, and John had walked a step on before he noticed and halted too. "Except you've mislaid him, yes?"

"He's not exactly one of my lock-ins."

"If he's on the payroll, he touches base. It's not a complicated principle."

"He hasn't always kept his appointments," John said.

"But when I check your records, and I will, I'll find the monthly reports all in order, right?"

"I keep clean records."

"I'm sure you do. Okay, leaving that aside, this pair, Pynne and this Edward, are looking for Benny Manors, and they come to you. What exactly do they have on you that makes them think you'll do their bidding?"

And here was the gamble.

Out in the sunshine he made his confession, trying to make it sound like an administrative oversight, one of those things that happens at work, the way a pad of Post-its might find its way into your briefcase. Everyone's wound up living in a dead colleague's flat, surely? That was the tone he was aiming for, all the while reminding himself that he had little alternative. Either he gave himself up, here and now, or someone else gave him up, soon. And at least this way he was bringing something to the table, besides his own misdeeds. At least this way he could spin it as gently as possible. And he could still tell himself he was halfway to getting away with it, until he clocked her expression.

There were rumours she'd turned a man to stone once, with the power of her stare. Except, John now realised, they weren't rumours, they were interdepartmental memos. He could feel his limbs solidifying. He'd never leave this spot: they'd have to fix a plaque to the pavement explaining who he'd been and warning people not to chain their bikes to him.

"You do realise," she said at last, "that I could sack you right now for what you've just told me."

"Yes, but . . ."

She waited. He'd sort of hoped she'd come up with a *but* all by herself.

"But I can make it right. This pair, they're up to something. I can help you find out what."

"And in return, I'll what? Forgive you your sins?"

"Maybe give me another chance."

"Jesus, John. How many second chances do you need? You've had more lives than a cartoon cat." She glanced at her gym bag, as if contemplating whacking him with it. If he was the cartoon cat she imagined, he'd go a funny shape on impact, before shaking himself back to normal. "Your time's more than up."

She meant the allotted twenty seconds, he hoped. But it was possible she was taking a longer view.

Taverner fell quiet. John had an urge to speak, to fill the silence with more apology, but had the sense not to. The hole he'd dug was deep enough. At last she said, "Pynne no longer has Hub privileges, which means he'd have to make a formal application to run a trace. So the reason they came to you is, they want to find Benny without anyone knowing they're trying to find Benny."

"Except me."

"Without anyone important knowing they're trying to find Benny," she amended. "Or maybe there's more to it. Manors, if memory serves, was a two-bit blackmail artiste before some idiot recruited him for an op. He's been feeding off the Service tit ever since. But if a pair of our own are looking for him, it's likely because he's reverted to type and has something on them. Black-mailers don't change their spots. So he's currently gone to ground, and they want the nearest thing to a friendly face to bring him into the open. And that would be you."

"I'm not sure Benny thinks of me as a friendly face."

"Well, that shows good judgement, but whether he likes you or not is beside the point. The fact is, he knows who you are. He's not going to fear the worst if you show up, he's just going to think his pension's at risk." She pursed her lips and thought some more. "Okay. If a couple of Park people are running rogue, I want to know why. So I'll tell you what I'll do, John. I'll find out where Benny Manors is. And then you find out what he knows that's so important to two of my agents."

"And what do I do if they come back before then?"

"I'm sure you'll think of something, John. When it comes to saving your own skin, you generally do."

• • •

Which was as much of a compliment as he was likely to receive from that quarter. Finding the nearest café, he drank a large Americano, black, while thinking about the peach brandy back in the flat. This didn't make him an alcoholic, he decided. The probability that he'd drink some once he got home did, though. It was another bright morning, everybody looking happier as a result, John Bachelor excepted. He didn't think he'd improved his situation. On the other hand, he'd prevented Edward and Richard from spoiling it first, so maybe that counted as a victory. Something to warm his cockles, when he ended up sleeping on a pavement.

And when he got home, Richard Pynne was in his sitting room, Solly's sitting room, holding a ceramic cat, plucked from Solly's collection of knick-knacks.

"You have a key," John said, redundantly.

"I have a key." He nodded towards the other chair. "Do sit."

John sat.

"You've been out early."

"Places to go, people to see. You know how it is."

"And is any of this activity connected with, ah, with the matter in hand?"

"With finding Benny Manors?"

Pynne nodded.

"Yes. Yes, it was."

"Good. So where is he?"

"I said it was connected," John said. "I didn't say I had a definitive answer yet."

"I'm here to remind you of the, of the *urgency* involved."

"Nobody said anything about it being urgent," John said.

"That was implicit in our interview."

"I know who you are," John said. "You're the one took over Hannah Weiss."

Pynne's face darkened. It made him look younger, somehow; not an angry man, but a sulky boy. He let the cat fall to the floor. The carpet was thick enough that this didn't matter. "That's none of your business."

"You're like me," said John. "Peaked early. You get used to it. You just have to not care that other people are doing so much better."

Pynne looked round. "I haven't sunk this low," he said. "An old man's flat. An old man's *life*. And none of it yours, not really."

"Can I offer you some peach brandy? It's surprisingly moreish."

"You need to focus on the task in hand," Pynne told him. "That's what I came to remind you. Where's Benny Manors? Everything else, that's background static. Find Benny Manors, and do it quickly. Or all this, crappy as it is, comes to an end."

"What did Benny do?" John wondered. "Or what did you do that he found out about?"

"Task in hand," Pynne repeated.

"You're not as threatening as Edward. You need to work on your menacing skills."

The younger man stood, and John's heart thumped faster. But all Pynne did was stoop and collect the cat. He put it back on its shelf, then stepped back to admire the collection as a whole, the bits and bobs that accumulate during the years spent standing still. "I don't need to be menacing," he said. "All I need do is make one phone call. And then you're back sleeping in your car. If they don't lock you up."

"I never slept in my car," John said, though he'd come close. And there'd been snow on the streets then, and would be again before long. The winters rolled round faster than they'd used to.

"Just find him." Pynne put a hand on his shoulder; took a brief grip on his collar. "You've got one more day."

And then he left, leaving the flat's front door wide open, so John had to follow after him and close it.

It seemed a childish form of aggravation.

But the whole encounter had lacked point. True, his heart had been thumping for a moment, but only because a large young man had got to his feet unexpectedly, and John—let's face it—wasn't built for confrontation. Still, though, why had Pynne bothered coming, if that was all he had to offer? He'd have mused on this more if his phone hadn't rung. Private number, the screen read. He was prepared for Taverner's voice before he answered.

"Your missing friend."

"Let me guess," he said.

Taverner paused.

John said, "He's in Newcastle, isn't he?"

". . . Where?"

"Newcastle upon Tyne."

"What the hell are you on about? No, he's not in Newcastle upon Tyne. He's in Seven Dials. Or that's where he's been using his plastic."

John wished he'd kept his mouth shut.

"Are you still there?"

"You don't have an actual address?"

"You're supposed to be a spook, John. A clapped-out, useless

one, true, but still a spook. Try to get in touch with what's left of
your ambition."

John Bachelor's main ambition was not to wind up homeless.

Di Taverner said, "Have you got a pen?"

"Sec."

He found one on the little hall table, next to Solly's landline,
which still rang occasionally. Cold calls; wrong numbers. There
was a neat little notepad too.

Lady Di read him a list of places where Benny Manors's credit
cards had been lately, and rang off without wishing him luck.

John Bachelor went to find the peach brandy. It had been a
long morning.

Oliver Nash was there when Di Taverner made that phone call. Head
of the Limitations Committee, he was a frequent presence at the
Park, above and beyond the regular meetings his role demanded;
was so much in evidence that one or two voices had been heard
wondering if he were nursing romantic feelings for Lady Di herself.
When these musings reached Taverner's ears, which they did with
an immediacy suggesting the use of either advanced surveillance
technology or the supernatural, she made it be known that random
executions were her preferred means of dealing with gossipmon-
gers. She was famous for many things, Diana Taverner, but not her
sense of humour. The wonderings ceased.

And anyway, Nash's romantic yearnings were directed less at
her than at the workings of the Park—a career bureaucrat, he
could still find hidden within himself the super-spy of his adolescent daydreams. And who was to say that hero wasn't still in
there? There was certainly space for him, with room left over for

an astronaut and an engine driver, Nash's ongoing diet having proved dogged rather than successful, like an English tennis player.

"So Bachelor came to you in person," he now said. "Something of a surprise?"

"Yes and no."

"That's how mediums and other charlatans work. Providing answers with maximum bandwidth."

She said, "We'd expected Pynne to be the one pointing him in the right direction. But Bachelor had other ideas, and doorstepped me instead."

"Resourceful type?"

"More the cowardly lion. It was a damage limitation exercise. He seems to think I was unaware of his living arrangements. But we always allow for a degree of improvisation."

Nash nodded, as if he knew full well the way operations were handled, but it didn't seem as if his heart were in it.

"Don't worry, Oliver. We'll get the desired result."

"It depends on what you class as desirable."

"Now now. Queen and country."

"I suppose so," he said. As always, he had his smartphone in his hand; as always, he couldn't conduct a conversation without it attracting his attention. At present, a morning headline filled his screen. The dead American sex trafficker. He shook his head. "Filthy business."

"That's often the way, I'm afraid."

"I have nieces," he said. "Teenagers. Young teens."

"Sometimes you have to focus on the bigger picture," she explained.

• • •

Seven Dials. He seemed to recall an Agatha Christie with that in the title, which suggested he might encounter the usual suspects in the usual places: spinsters in the kitchen, colonels in the bar. Maybe a vicar or two in the library. As it was, Monmouth Street was just another London thoroughfare, cheerful in the sunshine and grubby round the edges, and peopled by the usual young, the usual old, the former acting like they owned the place while the latter actually did. He'd made a list of the places where Benny Manors had paid bills, frequently enough that it could be assumed that this was his, well, manor. John Bachelor recognised the territorial instinct. With all the freedoms London offered, its natives tended to stick to their own warrens: local haunts, local habits. If Manors had drunk here last night, the night before, he'd drink here tonight, too.

Which meant John was early, but that was better than being late.

He could kill time any number of ways—there were shows to see, galleries to visit—but shows cost a fortune and galleries were full of art, so cafés and bars it was. The first was Italian: reasonable coffee, a stool by the window. Benny had been here last week for breakfast. It was only morning, but felt like evening already. John had been up hours. And had work scheduled that obviously wasn't going to happen, so spent twenty minutes on the phone while his coffee cooled, making apologetic calls to clients he wouldn't be seeing. He liked to think he made a difference to their lives— made them feel important, or at least, remember that they'd once been so—but the equanimity with which his absence was greeted caused him to wonder. On the other hand, little about his current situation didn't cause him to question something or other. If he remained in one place long enough, he'd doubt himself out of existence.

And there was money to think about; there was always money. He'd saved on rent these past eight months; on the other hand, what he'd saved on rent he'd spent on drink, to quell the anxiety caused by the means he'd adopted of saving rent. Life was a series of loops, each smaller than the last. He did sums on a scrap of paper: he wasn't carrying that much debt, if you didn't count the credit cards, but his bank balance didn't look healthy. Where did money go? If he could only answer that, he'd be free to live a happy, healthy life. Where did money go? All he did was eat and drink. He bought another coffee at London prices while he pondered. If he was kicked out of Solly's flat—when he was kicked out—best-case scenario, he'd be looking at a room in a multi-occupancy hovel, unless he could work his way round Diana Taverner first. She was the key. He had to work his way round Diana Taverner, which meant he had to be really, really lucky. He sipped his coffee, stared out of the window, and Benny Manors walked into the café and sat two stools along.

It was like being on a safari, or visiting a wildlife park, when you realise a lion has just wandered into view. First of all, don't scare it away.

Secondly, don't get eaten.

Instead of wasting time not believing what had just happened, John went with it, putting the scrap of paper in his pocket and gazing out of the window: sunshine and strangers, tourists and taxis. Meanwhile Benny had a newspaper and was turning to the back pages. Cricket. He hadn't looked John's way. And without his having placed an order, food was brought to him: scrambled egg and sausages. Definitely his regular breakfast haunt.

He ate unhurriedly, a man on his own timetable. John tried to match his carefree manner, addressing his coffee with what he hoped was insouciance, and thus slopping some onto his jacket. He fumbled for a napkin and dealt with the damage. By the time he'd finished, Benny Manors, instead of studying his paper, was staring at John, not bothering to hide his disdain. "That is one cack-handed approach to a cup of coffee."

"It just sort of splashed out."

"I'm trying to remember your name, and failing. But I know who you are."

"John. John Bachelor."

"Are you following me, John Bachelor?"

"I was here first."

"This morning, maybe." He also picked up a napkin, and dabbed his lips with it. "How worried should I be?"

John, nodding towards the paper, said, "About the Ashes? Very."

"I remember last time, I flattened you. You going for the double?"

"I just want to talk."

He seemed no older, John thought. Sure, it was only a couple of years, but they'd been the sort of years that can wreak damage—look what they'd done to the country, not to mention John himself—and Benny had weathered them like months in spring. He was wearing a cream linen jacket over a white shirt and blue chinos, and might have been about to head off to a relaxed office, a creative consultancy or whatever. With a bouncy castle in the lobby, roller skates in the corridors. As he hadn't seen him come in, John hadn't clocked how Benny was walking, whether the limp was better. But he didn't appear to be using a stick.

"So," Benny repeated softly. "Should I be worried?"

"Probably. But not about me."

"So how come you're the one who's here?"

"Maybe it's your lucky day."

Benny Manors said, "You don't look like anyone's idea of a lucky day." He glanced down at his plate, and speared half a sausage with his fork. "They called you a milkman, right?"

"Yes, well. There's a lot of jargon."

"But you were never important. Messenger boy type of thing. Despite your advancing years."

"Yes, well," John said again. He was going to have to work on his conversational stopgaps. "Reason I'm here, a couple of real spooks are looking for you, and they're doing it off the books. What that's about is anybody's guess, but it's unlikely to be because they had a sudden hankering to buy you scrambled eggs."

Benny gave an unamused smile. "Good job I can afford my own, then."

His phone rang.

Without taking his eyes off John, he answered it. The voice on the other end was a tinny whistle, but John could make out a name, almost: *It's Daisy.* Davy? No, Daisy.

Benny said, "Five minutes," and disconnected.

"Best guess," John said, "is that you're back to your old game. And that you've got hold of information you think is worth something."

"I'm trying to eat my breakfast."

"And I could walk away and let you. But that won't help you in the long run. These guys, the ones looking for you, they'll find you. Even I found you. How hard could it be?"

"I'm guessing you had help."

John blinked, which was probably a giveaway.

Benny returned to his breakfast.

John said, "Okay, I had help. And you know what? That emphasises that you're in a hole, Benny. Enough of one that you've got two spooks looking for you on their own time, and the Service putting a pin in you because they want to know what's going on. So I could walk out of here now, but all that would mean is, you'd lose your one contact on Spook Street. Your one chance to have someone to stand behind when things get complicated. Which they will do."

"Is that your hero speech?"

". . . I don't follow."

"It sounded like something you've been practising. A hero speech. You know, so everyone, or me anyway, will realise you're the good guy."

"I just don't want to be kicked out of my flat."

John hadn't realised he'd been about to say that. It revealed him as weak, as frightened. In some situations, that was the right move, but Benny Manors was a blackmailer, the last man on earth to be moved by someone else's predicament. Which made it strange, the look on his face now. He laid down his knife and fork. His mouth turned serious; his eyebrows clenched. "You're going to be kicked out of your flat?"

". . . It's possible."

"Boo fucking hoo."

He got working on his final sausage.

John nodded: yeah, okay. That was not unexpected. He had about an inch left in his coffee cup, and drained it, wondering what his next move should be. He didn't really have one. He could call Taverner; he could call Richard Pynne. He was leaning towards the latter: if Pynne and Edward were working this under the bridge, then chances were they planned harm to Benny Manors. Right now, that sounded good.

A young woman had entered the café and was standing behind Benny. He didn't look round when she spoke. "Stuffing your face again."

"But also working."

"Yeah, right. In what way exactly?"

Manors tilted his head towards John, without looking at him. "Told you they'd make contact."

The young woman turned John's way, regarded him speculatively. It was possible that she was not overwhelmingly impressed. "Him?"

"Regent's Park's finest," said Benny Manors, and laid his cutlery down again, this time on a clean plate. "You wanted proof. Here's your proof. They wouldn't be trying to stop me if they weren't worried."

John tried to look like he knew what was going on.

Mostly, though, he was just happy to learn that he wasn't the only one who was worried.

To say that the business with Hannah Weiss, when he'd found himself handling an agent who was spying on the Park rather than for it, still rankled with Richard Pynne was tantamount to suggesting that Tom might remain a little pissed off with Jerry. Before and after snaps of his career resembled those you'd get of a seventies kids' TV presenter pre- and post-Yewtree, and if he hadn't been exiled from the Park—assigned to Slough House, the spook equivalent of Devil's Island—he was *persona non grata* on the Hub, which was where the power plays went down and where he'd assumed his future would be spent. Richard had been Lady Di's go-to boy; she'd been grooming him for bigger things. So he'd foreseen a numbered desk there: a Second, at least. Instead, he was now taking up space in the press liaison office. Which meant that, sitting on a visitors' bench in the Park's central lobby as Diana Taverner approached, it was hard not to feel bitter about what might have been.

But hard, too, not to quell the spark of hope lately ignited. He'd fallen from grace but here he was all the same, chosen for an op, and who'd have had the sign-off on that but Lady Di herself? So maybe he'd done his penance, and was ready to be welcomed back into the fold.

"Richard."

"Ma'am."

"What have you got?"

He'd hoped for a *how's it going?*, a *good to see you*. But he could manage the business tone as well as anyone.

He said, "Bachelor's made contact."

"You're sure?"

"I tagged his collar. We know exactly where he is. And Manors's phone is in the same room. A café on Monmouth Street."

"Good."

She'd never been lavish with her praise, exactly, but the mono-syllable sounded niggardly to his ears nevertheless.

"And how did Entwhistle do?"

Entwhistle, who'd introduced himself to Bachelor as Edward, was ex-army and now one of the Dogs, the Service's internal police. A lot of recruitment was done from the armed forces. It was possible they enjoyed the prospect of coming the heavy with those known to the army as "the funny buggers."

"About how you'd expect," Richard told her. This didn't appear to be detailed enough, so he added, "He put the wind up Bachelor all right. But I could have done that myself."

"Of course you could."

"It's not like it would have been an uphill—"

"Richard, you're not without your talents, evidence to the contrary notwithstanding. But you're not hard-man material. I'm not saying you don't have the bulk. It's more that you lack the . . . gravitas."

"Ma'am."

"Entwhistle played his part, you played yours. I'm grateful for the assistance. I hope it didn't drag you away from anything important?"

Ha bloody ha.

"Then thank you."

She turned to go.

"Ma'am?"

"What is it?"

"Something you should know. Bachelor recognised me. My name, anyway. Entwhistle said too much, so Bachelor knows who I am."

She half turned back. "Yes, Richard. We wanted him to know who you are. Why do you think you were chosen for the job? Now, do carry on."

And then she really was away, out of the lobby and heading for the restricted areas, where Richard Pynne had once wandered freely but which were now closed to him, and thus looked like any other gated paradise.

After a minute or so, he made his way back to the press liaison room.

They'd left the café when an influx of tourists threatened their privacy, onto the street's morning sunshine, then round a corner and into a wine bar. It wasn't open for business, but Benny shouted a greeting to a man polishing the woodwork of the curved counter, and pointed to one of the booths against the far wall.

"Quiet business meet, Yol."

This seemed to be okay with Yol, or perhaps just so commonplace it wasn't worth taking issue with.

They settled themselves on a banquette.

"What kind of name is Yol?" John wanted to know, but Benny just stared at him, so he didn't pursue it.

Daisy appeared to be used to such encounters, or at any rate unfazed by them. She had hair that was probably normal really, but was currently feathered with strands of purple, or it might be indigo. Startling, either way. She looked a quarter John's age, and yet was old enough to have a career, which was also startling. It was a wonder his eyebrows weren't constantly raised these days: a perpetual state of mild shock. Hair apart, she looked the way all young people looked now, which was a lot healthier than young people had looked back when he was one. Maybe they had better role models. That or better drugs.

"You're a journalist, aren't you?" he asked her.

She seemed pleased he'd heard of her, though he hadn't really. It was just that he was starting to twig: Benny had got hold of some information. His usual recourse would have been to sell it back to whoever he'd stolen it from, but that evidently wasn't the profitable option here.

Daisy looked at Benny. "Fetch us some coffees, would you?"

"They're not serving yet."

"Or you could step over the road."

He cottoned on. "Be five minutes."

When he'd left, John said, "I didn't think people were called Daisy any more."

"It's making a comeback. Are you really a spy?"

"I'm a civil servant."

"That's a spy answer. Why did you come looking for Benny?"

"It's my job. Making sure he's all right."

"Why would he need someone doing that?"

"Injured in the line of duty," John said.

"His limp."

He nodded. "What kind of journalist are you?"

"How many kinds are there?"

"They're mostly columnists these days, aren't they?"

She said, "I'm the proper kind."

"For an actual newspaper? Or just one of those websites?"

"You're not a fan of the modern world?"

"It's not a fan of me."

"Can't think why." She gave him an appraising look: too appraising, really. He wasn't sure whether this was down to her being a journalist, or just being so bloody young. She said, "But no, I work for an actual newspaper."

She named it. It was indeed big, in the sense of being a household name.

"And what's your interest in Benny?" he said.

"He has a story."

John said, "Yes, well. Everyone's got one of those."

"But Benny's is big."

"So why haven't you published it?"

"There are details to be ironed out."

"Such as?"

"Well, Benny wants more money than my editor wants to give him. And my editor wants proof that it's actually true."

"Inconvenient things like that. What's the story?"

Daisy said, "Ah, you nearly had me there. I nearly gave it away."

"I thought when you people were working on a story with a witness like our Benny, you locked yourselves away in a motel or something. Lived on takeaways. Made sure nobody could poach your talent."

"I saw that film once. It was quite old, wasn't it?"

"Nobody's got the budget any more, have they?"

"Maybe sometimes. For a big enough story."

"And this isn't?"

"It is if it's true. But Benny has form. He approached us once before."

"Us?"

"The paper. Not me. It was before my time."

"And what was Benny selling then?"

"He didn't get around to saying. He had a story, he said. It involved spooks. That would be you lot."

John bowed his acknowledgement. Spooks would be his lot. Or that's what it might look to an outsider, anyway. As far as spooks were concerned, he was just a milkman. "So the story never got printed."

"The story never got printed."

And that would have been about how the Service recruited Benny for a black-books op, he thought. He must have worried he'd be left out in the cold, which was something that happened to spies, and sought an alternative form of payment just in case. Or else to encourage the Park to dig deeper. He didn't lack confidence, Benny Manors, that was for sure. A more circumspect character might have wondered how the Park would react to the squeeze being applied. But it had worked out for him in the end. And now here he was again, with another story to sell, only this time he seemed to really want to do it.

He said, "And now he's back."

"I was an intern at the time, but I was shadowing the journalist on the story. Dave Bateman?" She waited, but John offered no response. "Anyway, he's one of the best in the business, Dave. And he thought there was something there."

"Even though it never arrived."

"So when Benny turned up again, claiming he had another story, I thought, I want a piece of that."

"And Dave wasn't interested?"

"He's moved on."

Whether this was to a different paper or a different way of life entirely wasn't clear. John decided it didn't matter.

"So now you're talking to Benny. And your editor isn't sure."

Daisy said, "My editor doesn't trust Benny. Not after last time."

"And you do?"

"I think he's got a story." She put her elbow on the table, leaned her chin on her palm. "Your being here kind of proves that."

"In what way?"

"In a spy-ey way. You're here to tell me he's making it up, aren't you? That the evidence is faked."

"I don't even know what his story is, much less whether his evidence is shonky."

"So why were you looking for him?"

"Good question." He saw Benny entering with a takeaway cup in his hand. "He's being looked for, though. I can tell you that much. What's the story?"

She waggled a finger. "Uh-uh."

"But something big."

"Massive."

"Except your editor isn't buying it. In every sense."

Benny arrived and put the coffee in front of Daisy. "A latte. Just the way you like it."

"I take it black."

"Oh. Looks like it's mine, then." Retrieving the cup, he looked at John. "So. He's been explaining how unhappy MI5 is about you publishing my story. I told you the spooks would be coming out of the woodwork."

"You did," agreed Daisy. "On the other hand, this one doesn't have a clue what you're selling."

They both studied John. He felt like an art exhibit.

"In fact, I'm not convinced he's a spy. He doesn't look like one."

"The best don't," John suggested, though even he wasn't convinced himself.

"So you might have put him up to it."

Benny said, "Be reasonable. If I wanted someone who looked like a spy, I'd have picked someone else. Someone with a bit charisma."

I am still here, thought John. He said, "Look," and turned to Benny. "Like I said, there are people looking for you. Spooks, yes, but they're not on Park time, they've gone freelance. And whatever you've done, whatever you've got, my guess is they want to stop you. So your best bet is to come with me. You'd be safer at the Park."

Benny threw back his head and laughed.

"I mean it. I've spoken to First Desk there."

"First Desk?" asked Daisy.

"That's what they call the chief."

"Sounds like you got that from a book."

Benny was still laughing, adding theatre by producing a tissue and wiping his eyes.

"You've made your point," Daisy told him.

"I wasn't expecting that," Benny said. "I told you they'd try to stop us. And this is what they're up to. They're hoping I'll just trot along to the Park at John here's heels. Like a bloody puppy!"

He laughed some more: an over-long solo.

"So let me get this straight," John said, once Benny had more or less finished. "You"—meaning Daisy—"think he's using me to set you up. And you"—this being Benny—"think the Park's using me to set you up."

"And how does that make you feel?" Daisy wondered.

He shrugged. "At this stage, I'm pretty used to being used. But I have to tell you, I haven't a clue what it's all about."

"Hey, Yol," said Benny. "What time do you start serving?"

"Couple of hours."

"How about you make me a present of a bottle for now, then. And I'll make you a present of some money?"

"Not the way it works, Benny," Yol told him, but even as he was saying it he was reaching under the counter for a bottle of what John could only assume was Benny's regular tipple: a bottle of Greensand Ridge gin, it turned out. He'd evidently moved on from Brown Ale.

"And three glasses," said Daisy.

Daisy said, "My problem is, my editor's problem, you've got photos, you've got audio—you've got sound and vision, basically—but these things can be faked."

"Not by me."

"I'm not saying by you. I'm saying you're the one selling. And last time you came to us with a story, well. Story never happened, did it?"

The bottle was on its last legs, but the bar had opened for business now. So far, all this meant was the door had been propped open and the summer's afternoon had peeped in. It evidently hadn't liked what it had seen. Maybe the summer's evening would be more in the mood, and stop for a cocktail. Meanwhile it was just the three of them and Yol, who'd finished his polishing and was idling behind the bar. Yol, lolling. The words made a nice little circle in John's mind, and he admired their pirouette for a while before returning to the business at hand.

He still had no idea what story Benny was trying to sell, other than—as Benny had said more than twice—it was huge. Massive. Needed to be told.

"So why not slap it on the web?"

Benny rubbed finger and thumb together. "The old do-re-mi. Can't make money out of the internet."

"Nobody says 'do-re-mi.' And Amazon seems to manage."

Benny ignored him. "I'm not a citizen journalist."

"Thank God," said Daisy.

She had drunk less than the two men, possibly because she regarded this as working. Come to think of it, John was working too. Sort of.

He said, "Where did the stuff come from, anyway? The photos and what not?"

Benny just looked at him.

"Pick them up on the job, did you?" John turned to Daisy. "Benny used to be a burglar. Did he tell you that?"

"No," Daisy said. "He did not."

"Mended my ways, didn't I?" Benny asked.

"Can't scale the walls the way he once did, mind," John said. He slapped the banquette, having aimed for his own leg. He tried again. "Old war wound."

"In the service of my country."

Daisy said, "It's an honour, really. Just sitting in the same booth."

"I need a cigarette."

"And I need a . . ." John countered. He waved a hand in the vague direction of the toilets. "Pee."

He sat in a cubicle and called Di Taverner. There was unexpectedly good reception. But then maybe a lot of business calls were made from wine bar toilets: he wouldn't know.

"You're in a bar," she told him. "Surprise surprise."

"I'm in a bar because Benny's here," he said. "I've made contact."

"And what exactly is our Benny peddling that's causing such a fuss?"

"Yes, well, I'm still working on that."

She sighed emphatically enough that he could feel as well as hear it. "Do you remember what we said about second chances? Do you recall that part of our conversation?"

"It's in hand."

"Judging by the echo, it's not the only thing in hand. Next time you give me an update, be holding more than your dick, John. It makes you look needy."

Back at the booth, Benny's cigarette had speeded up his metabolism, or slowed it down: whichever was required to make him a notch drunker than he'd been. It seemed a good moment to divide the rest of the bottle and suggest a second. There was an out-there chance he'd be able to claim it on expenses, John thought, a flash of optimism that crashed and burned when he discovered the price. Accounts would assume he'd bought a car. When he returned to the table, Benny was saying, "So your editor'll just step on it, that what you're saying? Because there are other papers out there. Other editors."

"And they'll all know we passed on it, Benny. And they'll all know why."

"None of it's faked."

"So you keep saying. And what we've seen and heard looks good. But until you tell us how you came to have hold of it, we're not prepared to accept it as kosher. So please, Benny, if you want this story heard—and believe me, I do—then fill in the gaps, and we'll take it from there."

"You don't sound drunk," John complained.

"That's because I've not been drinking. I mean, seriously, John. It's barely lunchtime."

He could have sworn he'd filled her glass at least once. The possibility that she'd been pouring it on the floor filled him with expensive horror.

Daisy stood. "I'm going for some fresh air. And also, you know. Pop in to the office and that sort of thing. Why not think it over, Benny? Maybe John can help. Flesh out the details, and I'll run it past the paper one more time. But we're getting short of options, okay?"

Then she was gone.

Benny reached for the bottle.

"I should probably have got her to pay for that," said John. "Expenses."

Benny rolled his eyes. "Always a little behind the curve, eh, John?"

He shrugged.

They continued to drink.

And then it was late afternoon, and they weren't in the wine bar any more, but a nearby pub. There'd been some misunderstanding with Yol, John couldn't recall the details. It might have involved payment. Benny's limp didn't get in the way of a stand-up row, nor impede him when a swift departure was required. Practice,

John supposed. All of this, he was more spectator than participant. Didn't stop Yol catching him on the back of the head with a wet tea towel on his way out.

Anyway.

For reasons of economy they'd switched from gin to beer, which increased the traffic to and from the gents. Conversation had loosened up too, ranging from the quality of the bar snacks on offer to Benny fondly recalling their first meeting, when he'd punched John in the face.

"What was it you said?"

"Leg like an overcooked noodle," John remembered. "Not that it's slowed you down much."

"I still do holiday jobs, yeah."

". . . Like a student?"

"Keep up, mate. Do I look like a fucking student?" He didn't. "When the homeowners are on holiday, that's when I do a job. Less call for the speedy getaway."

"And that's how you found this story you're selling," said John.

Benny gave him a hard stare, blurred at the edges.

"The story Daisy thinks is important, but her editor doesn't believe."

"Yes he does. Just thinks it needs . . . nailing down."

"Because you stole it," John said. "Making things tricky from a legal point of view."

"Fag break."

This time, John followed him outside. There was a gaggle of smokers there, if that was the collective noun—a chokehold? Which sounded clever, though maybe wasn't. Benny begged a light then drew away, John following. The streets were busy, everyone enjoying a summer's evening: fun while it lasts. Tomorrow he'd feel more bruised than hungover, like he'd been dragged through a gravel pit. His mouth was numb and his pockets empty. He hated to think of the punishment he'd put his credit card through. But Benny was talking.

"Nice little score, that's all it was supposed to be."

A conversation in a pub: man who worked for a carpet-cleaning firm and had just that day completed a four-storey place in Hampstead. Family away for a fortnight. Some of the chemicals, you're best off being absent for a while.

Benny had laid a twenty on him before fading into the background.

"Some people," he said, "like the idea of getting their fingers a bit dirty. Too chickenshit to actually plunge their hands in."

Or just too law-abiding, John thought. A bit chatty down the boozer, but generally law-abiding.

"Thing is, the guy in the four-storey house? The family man? He was connected, right? Well connected. If you get my drift."

John didn't. Organised crime?

"Give you a clue, mate. A recently deceased gentleman."

John couldn't think of anyone who'd died since 2016. Nobody famous, anyway.

"Headlines?"

. . . The American, John remembered. The American billionaire. The American billionaire sex trafficker who suicided in his cell.

"Yeah, him." Benny sucked hard on his cigarette, as if he were trying to get the lit end into his mouth. "He lived over here half the time, didn't he? And that's who my man was connected to. Used to be invited to those house parties, the ones with happy endings guaranteed."

Happy endings for the fat rich men his age, thought John. Less happy for the teenage girls involved.

The beer and the gin were sloshing about inside him. He felt like a car wash.

He wasn't even sure he was still taking part in this conversation. Benny was doing all the talking.

"And of course, you know who else used to attend those parties."

John didn't.

Then he did.

Benny tapped the side of his nose with his finger. He seemed to have adopted most of his gestures from cheesy soap operas.

"H.R.H.," he said. "If you'll pardon the abbreviation."

The car wash was going into its lathering cycle. Cigarette smoke was drifting past John's face, crawling up his nose, into his mouth.

"And my man—Mr. Four-Storey—well, he had a few crafty souvenirs, didn't he?"

Audio and visual, John remembered.

"All on his laptop, handy as you like. Course, I fed that into a crusher first thing. Soon as I knew what I'd got hold of, I mean."

He put a hand in his pocket, and when he withdrew it was clutching a USB stick.

"Always with me," he said. "One and only copy."

John Bachelor turned and threw up into the gutter.

Benny stood next to him, a hand on his shoulder while he heaved.

"You're my milkman, John," he said. "Don't forget. You're here to make sure I'm all right."

"Oh God. What now?"

And here was Daisy back.

"John's been taken poorly," Benny said. "Must have been something he didn't bother to eat."

He felt better after being sick. Not brilliant, but better. And was capable of ambulatory motion—capable of constructing the phrase "ambulatory motion," even—because here he was, cutting through Holborn, the three of them like friends, Daisy one side, Benny Manors the other. Yes, friends. He hadn't had a day like this in as long as he could remember. Spending the sunshine getting wasted with his best mate, and staggering home shot to pieces. Jesus, he'd had a skinful. How much money had he got through? Best not think about that.

Daisy pulled on his arm as they reached a road. "Oi! Let's not walk under a bus, all right?"

Let's not.

He'd cleaned himself up in the loo before leaving the pub, and had managed a quick call to Di Taverner. Voicemail. So he'd left a message—nothing too revealing, but enough to let her know he'd completed his mission. And that Benny Manors carried his evidence, the *one and only copy*, on his person at all times. It was possible he'd mentioned Solly's flat, and their arrangement that he get to stay there. Anyway, that done, he'd returned to the bar to find Benny had bought another round, and it would have been rude not to drink it. Settled his stomach. That or the one after.

And now they were walking through Holborn, cutting down a back street, heading for a bus stop. And that feeling, the feeling of being with friends, wouldn't go away: it had been months, years, since he'd felt this companionship. Sure, there were clients. Mornings drinking weak tea with old men and women; hearing stories he'd heard before. Tales of courage as faded as the throws on their sofas. He didn't doubt their heroism, these wizened heroes; he just wondered what stories he'd have to tell when his time came, and whether there'd be anyone listening. Benny was saying something funny, and John hadn't caught it but laughed anyway, like friends do, and the large man who loomed out of nowhere didn't touch him hard, just rammed a forearm across his throat and the world went watery. He dropped to his knees so suddenly, something gave. And Daisy screamed, but not for long, and then she too was on the ground, everything about her out of focus. None of that took long. Benny, though; Benny was really being given the business. He was making the noises a punchbag makes. There must have been two of them, because someone was holding Benny up; he'd have been a puddle on the pavement otherwise. John stopped paying attention and threw up again. Then practised breathing. The men stopped hitting Benny and went away. More people came running towards them, shouting nothing coherent. And somewhere on the far side of London a siren was already wailing their way; would grow louder and louder until John couldn't hear it at all but was wrapped up inside it instead, a little lump of silence at the heart of a beating city.

He remained in bed for two days. Then his phone rang and wouldn't stop, and he had to crawl out to find it. Whatever they'd done to him at Casualty had stopped the pain for a while but not forever. It felt like his knee was bursting.

"You bastard. Thought that was clever, didn't you?"

". . . Benny?"

His voice was a scratchy old recording; one of those Victorian wax pressings that captured starched collars and indignation, but failed to convey much meaning.

"You bastard."

John managed to haul himself onto a chair. Here, once, Solly had sat, looking at the houses opposite and imagining the lives they held, all the different possibilities crammed into a terrace. His own possibilities had ended in the room John had just emerged from.

"They took my memory."

That's what he thought Benny said, and for a moment he revelled in the idea of the same thing happening to him. Total erasure. He could start again with a blank slate, make less of a mess of things this time.

Stick, though. Benny meant memory *stick*.

His one and only copy.

John said, "I didn't know . . ."

But he had really. Had known Lady Di Taverner would cause bad things to happen. You couldn't walk around with the kind of knowledge Benny had been carrying and not expect ramifications.

My man—Mr. Four-Storey—he had a few crafty souvenirs, didn't he?

H.R.H. If you'll pardon the abbreviation . . .

John remembered that feeling he'd had of being with friends, walking through Holborn with Benny and Daisy, and closed his eyes. Never friends. Never friends. They'd all wanted something from the others.

And then Benny was laughing: a manic chuckle. John pictured it escaping through broken teeth and swollen lips.

"You really thought that was it, didn't you? *The one and only.* You fucking idiot."

"...Benny?"

"Why'd you think I told you that? You think I wasn't expecting your pals to show up?"

"I didn't know, Benny. I didn't know they were coming."

"You keep telling yourself that."

"...How's Daisy?"

"How's Daisy? Daisy's battered, isn't she? Face like an overripe melon. Still, she's feeling better about things than you are."

"What do you mean, Benny? What do you mean?"

"Like I said, I was expecting your pals to show up. And that was the clincher, wasn't it? Daisy getting a battering too, that was the cherry on top." He paused, and John heard a fizzing sound, a cigarette being lit. "No editor in the world's gonna take that lying down, are they? Someone smashes your reporter's face in—*spook heavies* smash your reporter's face in—stands to reason you've a story on your hands. A real live breathing story. Your lot think they stole the proof when they took my memory stick." Another pause for inhalation. "But that was a copy, John. I'm not a fucking fool."

"That's why you kept me drinking."

"Well it wasn't for your company, was it?"

John shook his head, though he couldn't have said why.

"So it's a happy pay day for me, and fuck you, John Bachelor. I imagine your bosses are ready to dump on you good and hard."

He didn't want to ask why, because he suspected he already knew.

"Go look at the papers, John. All of them are running it now. Every last one."

"Benny—"

"Bye bye, milkman."

And Benny laughed again, that same broken chuckle, though there was genuine mirth in it, John could tell. And it continued bouncing round his head long after the call had ended.

Oliver Nash laid the newspapers out as if he were playing solitaire. Eleven front pages. Two broadsheets, the rest tabloid. The headlines on each were much the same, as was the photograph on all but one: a figure, naked from the waist up, turning away from the camera, a salacious grin shining on his teeth. The young woman he was reaching for was also topless, her frightened eyes gazing directly at the lens. The picture on the eleventh front page was of a woman in a bikini holding a lottery card. It was reassuring to know that some standards never wavered.

Nash said, "Well. This the sort of thing you were expecting?"

Lady Di scanned the display. It reminded her of similar situations, none of which had ended well for the subject of the photograph. Some heads rolled farther than others, of course. There was an historical precedent there which the broadsheets, at any rate, would no doubt cite in their editorials.

She said, "More or less."

He said, "The Palace has issued a denial in the strongest terms, of course. But then, it would, wouldn't it?"

"Of course."

"It's the worst crisis for the monarchy since the death of the princess."

"Yes, well, don't look at me. That was nothing to do with us."

He looked at his phone. "And the internet is going crazy. Calls for his immediate trial and imprisonment."

"The rule of law actually takes a little longer."

"Try telling that to our keyboard judiciary." He gave her a long stare. It was hard to tell whether it contained admiration. "I'm wondering whether you appreciate the scale of what you've done."

"What *I've* done?"

"The Park."

"I take instruction from our elected leaders. You know that. And Number Ten wanted this business dealt with once and for all."

He returned his gaze to the headline display. "Yes, I'm not sure this was the outcome the PM had in mind."

The PM had arguably weathered worse himself.

"And when do you pull the plug?" Nash asked.

"Twelve twenty-seven."

"Admirably precise."

"It's an operation, Oliver. We find it best to be precise. Aiming for there or thereabouts can prove woefully inadequate."

"And who gets it first?"

"The BBC."

"There's nothing like tradition, is there?"

"Well," said Lady Di. "Auntie does do these big occasions *so* well."

She glanced at her watch. Two and a half hours to go.

Nash removed one of the newspapers. "This one'll die in a ditch," he said.

"Probably."

"Shaky financial ground as it is," he said. "And once H.R.H. has sued its arse off, it'll be curtains." He shook his head. "You know, our national press has always been a guardian of our democracy. And here we are destroying its reputation for the sake of one of our, shall we say, less reputable figureheads."

She said, "It's not the first time I've green-lit an operation I'm not overwhelmingly proud of. It won't be the last. But look at the bigger picture. The Service hasn't enjoyed many favours from the present government. Any smile we can bring to its face, we'll be glad about when our budget's next considered. You of all people should think of that as good news."

"And democracy, anyway," Nash said, "isn't the PM's favourite institution." He dropped the paper. "He'll be glad to have this disappear from the news stands. Not exactly an admirer of his antics."

Diana said, "That paper bought the story from a known thief and blackmailer. Who, in turn, claims to have discovered those photographs, and the audio recordings, on a laptop stolen from a house belonging to an associate of a billionaire paedophile, an associate who does not in fact exist. The property our thief and blackmailer burgled is currently vacant, and has been for some time. And the evidence itself—the audio, the photographs—while extremely convincing, are fakes. And we can prove this because we have video footage of their being faked. Footage which everyone in the country will have seen a hundred times over by bedtime. On the BBC to start with, and then You-Tube or whatever." She steepled her fingers. "After which, all further rumours about H.R.H.'s involvement with a convicted sex trafficker will be stomped on by every newspaper proprietor in the country, not to mention every editor of every TV and radio news show in the land. Goodbye nudge-nudge headlines, good-bye sniggering comments on Radio Four panel shows."

"And the attack on the journalist?"

"She was on a drunken spree with Manors. Probably planning how they'd spend the loot."

"So our version is, she was involved from the start?"

"I think that's tidiest, don't you?"

Nash said, "Manors will know he was set up. The carpet cleaner he met in the pub, who pointed him at the target house. Obviously one of us. And John Bachelor, of course. Someone he actually recognised as a spook."

"He can know all he wants. Nobody will touch him with a bargepole. As for Bachelor, he didn't have a clue what was going on. He'd have found a way to mess it up if he did. But he owed the Service rent, and all he had to do was show his face, so Manors would think we were trying to shut his story down. Which, in turn, would corroborate the whole thing as far as the press was concerned. Job done."

"And yet, and yet," said Nash. He tapped the photograph of a leering H.R.H., or someone very like him, on the nearest front page. "Some mud'll stick."

"Enough's stuck already he could start his own farm. But a lot of people will think that him being innocent of this makes him innocent of everything else he's accused of. It's worked before."

"Oh, God in heaven! Who else have you—No. Don't tell me."

"I wasn't about to." She regarded him almost fondly. "I know it doesn't sit well. But if it makes you feel better, we'll expect certain assurances. As regards future behaviour."

"Assurances," repeated Oliver Nash. "Yes, that's a comfort, isn't it? Assurances."

"It's not nothing."

"Well, you consider the source, don't you?" said Nash. "From a man of honour, no. It wouldn't be nothing."

He stacked the papers into a pile, tucked them under his arm, and left the office.

And before the day dies John Bachelor, too, has caught up with events, or at least, has learned that events have moved on without him; has switched on Solomon Dortmund's funny little television set, with its rabbit-eared aerial, and switched it off again once the news has rolled past, over and over. It seems that the story Benny Manors was anxious to sell is just that: a story. It seems that writs are descending from on high, and that lawyers all over London are rubbing their hands in glee or running for cover. It seems that rumours that have slow-cooked for a decade or more have been plated and served, and found to be foul. And it seems that John himself was party to this feast, though on whose side, and hoping for what end, he remains unsure.

Perhaps the peach brandy will clarify matters. But for the moment all he has is a painful knee and a sore throat, and a mind that can't keep up with itself.

He wonders about Benny and Daisy, and how they will fare in the face of this reversal. (He will not have to wonder long.

Partners in slime will read one headline the following morning. *Devious pair plot to destroy Prince's reputation.* And Daisy's bruised and battered face will grace many pages, next to an old mugshot of Benny Manors, current whereabouts unknown.) Mostly, though, out of habit and fear, he wonders about his own situation, and how bad it will turn out to be. And again, he will not be left long in limbo: soon the phone will ring, and it will be Diana Taverner, or if not Lady Di, someone tasked by her with making a tiresome call. Is he John Bachelor? He is. Is he currently residing at blah blah, blah blah, blah blah? Yes, and yes, and yes. In which case, he is hereby informed that his presence at such address is illegal and unwarranted and shall cease forthwith. Keys to be surrendered. Absence to be swift and permanent.

As for his role in the Service, and its continuation or otherwise . . .

Well. He will find out soon enough.

Through the window the rest of London looms, large and devoid of welcome. The more he stares the darker it grows; and larger too, by the minute.

But at least there is still brandy in the bottle, he thinks.

Though in this, he is mistaken.

THE LAST
DEAD LETTER
. . .

Rules about access only took you so far. In St. Leonard's, a discreet brick establishment on a quiet close in Hampstead, they got you through the door courtesy of a concrete ramp, but after that you were on your own. The aisles were narrow, and the occasional memorial slab a hazard to cane- or Zimmer-users; the apparently random siting of a font might have been intended to force a congregation into a contraflow; and a set of railings sequestering an otherwise unremarkable example of twentieth-century stained glass jutted out a little far for those whose mobility was compromised, ensuring that, for a woman in a wheelchair, what might have been a quiet tour became a haymaker's outing. But St. Len's would not have been St. Len's if it offered itself for inspection without resistance. A notice in the porch suggested that mass was celebrated only irregularly, and locals knew that even these well-spaced events were invariably cancelled for illness or emergency. Funerals were the only reliable service, these more likely to be precipitated than postponed by such contingencies, and were strictly private affairs: family and friends; no hawkers, no tourists. Curtain twitching offered few clues. Those who arrived to pay their respects might have been a caravan of civil servants, some of whom had fallen on hard times. But Mrs. McConnell at Number 37 offered that she knew for a fact—had heard it from a friend on the council, whose son, a Metropolitan officer, had been assigned to take down number-plates of nearby cars during one of these funerals—that St. Leonard's was where they buried the spies. Those in the know, she claimed, called it the Spooks' Chapel. And if her neighbours dismissed this on the grounds, first, that surveillance techniques had long since outpaced a bobby with a notebook, and, second, that Mrs. McConnell's tales were famously taller than the hedge bordering St. Len's itself, this suited everyone perfectly, since neighbours invariably enjoy seeing through each other, and Mrs. McConnell, who in the long-ago had worked for the Intelligence Services, was well aware that a truth from an unreliable source is twice as effective as a rock-solid lie.

All of which Molly Doran knew, and none of which made her passage easier, but she was accustomed to difficult journeys, and her wheelchair was robust enough to inflict more damage than it suffered *en route*. Outside, behind the chapel, the grave-yard was a calm oasis in which visitors might forget a city lay mere streets away, and in here, too, such noises as filtered through were no more than light static on an old-time receiver. Molly apart, the building was empty. It was a bright cold day, and coloured light dropped in shafts onto benches and an uncovered altar.

She had come to rest by the west wall, which was studded with nameplates instead of windows, plaques to those not grand enough to occupy Hampstead's real estate, or whose remains were beyond the reach of mortal transport. Messy ends, as Jackson

Lamb had been known to remark, didn't lead to tidy burials, and there were bodies out in joe country that would never be found. So here their former owners were remembered, in a display informally known as The Last Dead Letter Drop, and if the names on the plaques weren't always accurate, the identities of those memorialised remained as true as they'd ever been. Few covers match those that shroud the dead. And if dates, too, were often fudged in the manner of a coy spinster, Molly Doran could read between lines like a harpist, and, for her, false facts often lit true pathways. There were stories here she'd followed through her archives, which lay below the pavements of Regent's Park, and she could tell a legend from a myth at a hundred paces—she always said "paces" when making this claim, staring hard at her interlocutor from the depths of her wheelchair, daring a furtive glance at her absent legs. Only Lamb had ever laughed, and she'd have been disappointed if he hadn't.

But not all stories laid themselves bare to her. Even for Molly Doran, some mysteries remained.

This section of wall contained seven plaques, ceiling to floor; the highest and lowest pair out of her reading range; the middle three dating back some years. In one of those curious jokes life plays, and death often chuckles along with, the upmost was for the name Huntley, and the one immediately below for a Palmer. The bottom-most, just below her eye level, read Gryff. One could easily mistake this for *Grief*, she supposed. For a while she remained there, the names dancing in front of her eyes. But maybe that was a trick of the light.

Behind her, a voice said, "No, don't get up."

She hadn't heard him enter, or approach across the clackety

floor, but she had long grown used to this: that he could move stealthily when he wanted, though to all appearances had the grace and flexibility of a fatberg.

"You came," she said.

"I pay my debts."

Because that was what this was. He owed her a favour, and here she would collect, in the process illuminating one of the mysteries that haunted her archive.

Now that he'd revealed his presence, Lamb apparently felt no further need for stealth. As she manoeuvred round to face him, he lowered himself onto the nearest bench with a groan suggesting that movement cost him pain. The odour of smoked cigarettes wafted towards her. His raincoat was shiny here and there, not with recent moisture but with well-established stains.

"Limbs giving you trouble?" she asked, with a hint of sarcasm.

"You don't know the half of it." He paused. "I said—"

"I get it."

"Because you've only got half the—"

"I said I get it."

"Jesus, what's eating you? From the ground up, I might add." He pulled a sorrowful face. "Sense of humour failure's the worst disability of all. You don't even get free parking."

"Finished?"

"Wish I was." Lamb looked around. "God, churches give me the creeps. So why am I here? Just to watch you pondering the mysteries of the whatever-the-bugger-it-is?"

"Ineffable."

"I thought that meant can't be fucked."

"There are probably theologians who'd agree. But let's not

waste time pretending you're duller than you look, Jackson. This is me you're talking to. Remember?"

"Hard to forget. It's like having a conversation with a demented armchair."

She came forward a few inches, effectively blocking any escape he might have attempted. "I've a story to tell."

"Oh, great. Jackabloodynory. Will it take long? Only I have plans."

"Plans? If you weren't here you'd be in Slough House, smoking and drinking."

"Like I said."

"Well, that'll have to wait." Her face was partly in shadow, so her messy cap of grey hair, her over-powdered skin, appeared two-tone. The effect should have been clownish, but somehow wasn't. "So make yourself comfortable."

Lamb took this as an invitation to fart, then stretched his legs under the bench in front of him. His collar was turned up, and he lowered his jaw to his chest. "And why exactly do I have to listen to this?"

"So you can tell me how it ends," Molly said, and began her story.

A long time ago, when we all lived in the shadow, most of human life could be found in Berlin, for Berlin was the Spooks' Zoo, and every agency in the world had, if not an official presence, at least a tame weasel or two lurking there. But it was a place where citizens and professionals alike could reinvent themselves, and not all those who checked their real names at the door were in the business. Some just liked the idea of being someone else, at least for a while. If it wasn't quite joe country, it was on the border, and more than a few passing souls never afterwards fitted back into their old lives. Travel's a way of finding yourself, it's said, but it's also a good way of getting lost.

("I saw this in a movie," grumbled Lamb. "Only they called it *Casablanca*."

"Hush now. I'm talking.")

There was a phrase at the time, describing Berlin's colours—*peacock shit*—because you had all these effervescent pinks and blues, these rainbow reds and greens, spraypainted onto cold grey concrete. There were party frocks for warehouse wear and glitterballs on bin lorries—the whole city was throwing a party; a rave-up in a wasteland, powered by whatever fuel was handy. Sex and drugs and rock and roll were all hard currency. But hardest of all was information.

So while young people danced and drugged themselves to oblivion in the shadow of the Wall, and made all kinds of music, most of which changed nothing, spies went about their business of soliciting betrayal: buying, stealing and seducing secrets from the innocent and the jaded alike. And some of these spies were young themselves, and some were old, and one was . . .

"Careful," said Lamb.

"Let's call him . . . Dominic Cross."

Cross wasn't young. He wasn't entirely old, either, but there's such a thing as joe years, which speed time up or slow it down, depending on your point of view. Minutes drag while glaciers form, and at the end of every hour you might have aged two, because that's how it was in the shadow of the Wall, especially on its wrong side. And Cross had spent time on the wrong side.

Because Cross ran a network, a crew of informers, thieves and traitors—of heroes, idealists and freedom lovers, in other words—who required constant comforts, of cash or company, and Cross was a singular man, a man who could settle a bar tab, soothe a mad dog and calm a frightened asset in the same two breaths. Often his presence alone was enough, because that was no small thing. There were more ways round the Wall than people realise, but all were dangerous. There was barbed wire and concrete; there were forged greasy papers; there were cavities built into the underbellies of trucks. There were long drives up-country to apparently unregarded areas, where a stretch of land you could cover on foot in five minutes could be a twenty-four-hour journey. And even when you just handed the right guard the right amount of money, like skipping a queue in a nightclub, you might have been buying a ticket to the underworld, and wouldn't know until your last minute. So Cross lived on his nerves so that his assets might keep theirs, and if, by a peacetime clock, he should have been approaching his prime, his organs were run ragged by tension; with the effort of keeping others calm while they put their lives at risk. So he was a drinker, which barely needs saying, and a smoker too, because this was Berlin. Most things a man could do to ruin himself he did, but only on his own time. When it came to keeping his network safe, he was concentration itself.

But you can only live so long on such terms. Booze and fags and dangerous journeys, and too many nights in bars: these things take their toll. Dominic had been in Berlin for eight years, and eight was at the edge of the envelope: the sticky bit. Field agents were burn-out material, and reckoned to be past their use-by anytime after six. Only the complicated nature of handing over a network to a newcomer kept them in place longer. Jittery assets didn't like new faces. And most assets were jittery. But sooner or later, and most likely sooner, Dominic Cross would have been airlifted out and put behind a desk in a safer city, where no doubt he'd have finished the job Berlin started, and drunk himself into early old age. But before any of that could happen something else happened instead, one of those awful things a spook wouldn't wish on his best friend.

Dominic fell in love.

"He was a good man, I think," said Molly. "At the time. For that place."

Lamb grunted.

"I mean, he was a cheat and a liar, and probably sold his soul several times over. But he always got a good price for it, and always brought his assets home before the roof fell in."

"Not always," said Lamb.

". . . No. Maybe not always."

"Get on with it."

It started in a bar, because when did anything start anywhere else? It was the winter of that particular year, one of the last spent in the shadow—though other shadows, God knows, would soon fall—and Dominic Cross was drinking near the station, not because he expected to catch a train but because you never knew. It was a workers' bar, with a low ceiling, tin-topped tables, and stools that warned you when you were nearing your limit, and Dominic had just lost at checkers against the blind pensioner who was a regular miracle there. Dominic had lost a small fortune trying to find out how he cheated, but was no nearer than ever as he shook hands with the old crook, and took his place at the counter. Gin was his tipple here, because everyone had habits and it was best to be everyone whenever possible, and while he was waiting he became aware of a small piece of theatre to his left: a blonde woman fishing in her bag, her expression a soliloquy. *I cannot find my purse. I cannot buy this drink.* It was a show he'd seen before, and had various endings, all of which left him out of pocket, but that didn't stop him buying a ticket. "I'll get that," he said to the bartender, which was the line written for him since before he'd got out of bed that morning, or any previous morning, come to that.

But as soon as he'd delivered it, it was capped.

"Ah—there you are!"

She produced a purse from the depths of the tote bag round her neck.

That had never happened before.

She smiled. "But you're kind. Let me get yours."

"No—really—"

"I insist."

Her purse snapped open, and a carousel of coins swarmed onto the counter. In the manner of barmen everywhere, the present example sorted those he required with an index finger, and swept them into his waiting palm.

"My name's Marta," she said. "What's yours?"

And the next part of that encounter was as inexplicable as the discovery of the purse, because one drink later Marta refused to allow him to repay the favour. Instead, she had looked at her watch, a chunky bootleg Timex with a Disney face, and told him it had been nice talking to him. And then kissed his cheek and slipped off her stool, made sure her purse was safe in her too-big bag, and walked out into the night. It was raining by then, and the windows were freckled with diamonds, which cast the street outside into a kaleidoscopic frenzy. She turned left, unless it was right, and vanished from view.

By the time the brief blast of cold air had swept its way around the room, the barman had already poured Dominic Cross a consolatory gin.

Lamb stirred. "Jesus. You're supposed to be an archivist, not Barbara bloody Cartland."

"And yet there you are, paying rapt attention."

"Only 'cause you're blocking my exit."

Perhaps in deliberate counterpoint to this observation, he farted again.

Molly didn't blink. "I've been wondering," she said, "what kind of woman might have proved so attractive to him. There's only one photo I ever saw. Dyed hair, dark roots. A little tacky."

"Said Coco the Clown."

"And her eyes looked hollow. Never a good sign." She glanced at Lamb, hoping for a reaction, but he had a hand down his trousers and was scratching his crotch while staring at the ceiling. "On the other hand, pictures don't reveal everything, do they?"

"Depends. I've seen a few could double up as X-rays."

"But she looked ordinary to me. I think mid-thirties, allowing her the benefit of the doubt."

"You don't have her birthdate? You're slipping."

"As you pointed out, I'm an archivist. Not an alchemist. I can't make something out of nothing. Everything I know about her is a detail invented by somebody else. Unless it wasn't, of course. Because that's the thing, Jackson. Maybe she really was who she claimed to be. And maybe she was shark bait. What do you think? All these years later?"

"I think you should hurry the fuck up," Lamb said. "Before the next funeral gets here."

Someone once called the spook trade a wilderness of mirrors, and that was never more true than in Berlin in those days, where, whichever direction you were facing, you always had to watch your back. So every working spook had a mirror-man, who wasn't quite a handler and wasn't quite a friend, and it was a mirror-man's job to take regular confession, which included any wayward encounters, professional or otherwise. Dominic Cross's mirror-man had been over the Wall himself, so knew how the big world turned. That should have given them common ground, but sometimes common ground becomes no-man's-land, and the pair had never clicked. Which might have been why Cross didn't mention that first pass, which was breaking the law in about five different ways. You always mentioned a pass, even if it didn't look like one at the time. You mentioned it when it was a woman, and you mentioned it when it was a man, and if it ever happened that it was a polar bear or a skunk you mentioned that too, because there was no end to the ways in which an approach might be made, and Berlin Rules were clear on the issue. You always mentioned a pass.

But Marta hadn't been making a pass. She was just a woman

who thought she'd lost her purse, until she discovered she hadn't. If it had been a pass, she'd have let him do the talking, which was how these things went: first you opened your trap, then you walked into it. It was a ceaseless wonder how eager joes were to start talking. So she'd have let him buy a second drink, and then sat and let him talk, ears and eyes wide open. She wouldn't have left so soon, not on a rainy night. Not without taking a number or making a date. Not leaving them both with their virginities intact.

So plant or not, Dominic Cross kept her a secret. Didn't mention her to The Shit, which was his private name for his mirror-man, nor drop her name anywhere else. Instead, he told himself he'd forgotten all about her. It had been just another rainy night in a workers' bar, and anyway, he never saw her again.

Until, of course, he did.

It was the following year, about four months later. Far too long an interval for it to be anything other than accident—you didn't keep a man dangling that long. Not in Berlin, where four months might as well be a decade.

And this time it was in broad daylight, on a busy street. She was carrying a shopping bag over one arm, which gave her a domestic look, and they met in the middle of the road, crossing in different directions. Traffic waited, poised to pounce.

"It's you! Hello again."

There are better times, better places, to become reacquainted than the middle of a road, with traffic lights about to change.

"Hello again," he said, and then they were on opposite sides of the street, with traffic flowing between them; a metal river keeping them apart.

If it were a pass, it would have happened sooner. And wouldn't have happened here, with no chance of further conversation; unless one or other of them—unless both—waited until the lights changed again, and allowed passage across the road.

He rejoined her on the far pavement.

"Are you busy?"

He was. He wasn't. It didn't matter.

"We could have coffee."

They could. Anyway, he owed her a drink. And a good spy always pays his debts.

As they made their way to a café, Dominic found himself assessing how she looked in daylight: the eyes sadder than he remembered; the face more lined. The hair not naturally blonde. But a smile that showed she remembered him, and one which he now realised he had been carrying with him ever since that night. Any contact made is a memory filed. Even if that filing is a purely private matter.

And now might be a good time to remind you that we're in a church, and smoking is strictly forbidden.

Because Lamb was holding a cigarette, though Molly hadn't seen him reaching into a packet, or even a pocket. He hadn't lit it, but was making it dance between his fingers, as if hoping to mesmerise her, or possibly himself. The latter seemed likely at that moment, as his eyes were unlit too, reflecting whatever dark spaces filled him.

She sensed his objection without his having to voice it.

"We're all entitled to weave our own tapestries, Jackson. Don't you like a good backstory?"

"Depends whose it is." He looked down at his cigarette, then tucked it up his sleeve, or did something with it anyway: to all intents and purposes, it vanished. "Someone asked not long ago what happened to your legs. Should I have told him?"

Molly Doran wouldn't answer that. "Shall I continue?"

"Do we get a piss break?"

"It depends what you mean by 'we.' They don't have a disabled toilet."

"Well, I've disabled a few in my time," said Lamb. "I'll sort one out for you."

She wheeled back to allow him to exit the bench, and he got to his feet with none of the wheezing histrionics he'd occupied it with. The look he gave her as he passed would have caused a weaker soul to flinch, but even so it was mild, compared to what he was capable of. She watched as, instead of disappearing into the vestry to find a toilet, he went through the side door into the graveyard. To smoke, though he'd probably piss up against a tree while he was at it. The Lamb who'd been a spook in Berlin would have taken the opportunity to fade away: it wasn't dark yet, but Lamb had never needed much shadow to disappear in. But she knew he wouldn't, not now. Not because he'd want to know the end of the story—he knew how it ended—but because he'd want to match her ending against his own.

Though in the end it would all come down to peacock shit: different colours sprayed on the same grey facts.

Their affair began with that second meeting: the café might as well have been a hot-sheet motel, with the waiter bringing condoms along with coffee cups. And though it was weeks before they actually took each other to bed, at that same meeting they began to establish tradecraft, for affairs demand codebooks and secret practices. Dominic was that particular kind of bachelor, the kind you can't imagine being anything else, but Marta was married, even if her husband was such old news she might as well not have been. And this was Berlin, where it was axiomatic that, if you slept with someone, you were sleeping with the enemy; or, at the very least, with someone who had themselves slept with the enemy. So yes, tradecraft. They never met in the same place twice. Should they encounter someone familiar, Marta was from Dominic's old neighbourhood, bumped into by chance. Or Dominic was hoping for an apartment in Marta's building, and she was giving him the lowdown. Threadbare stuff, because it always is, and there's no amateur like a professional with his guard down. Dominic might as well have been walking round town bare-headed, which, for a spook, is as careless as it gets—a hat, in spook talk, is a whole identity. If Dominic Cross was wearing any hat that spring, it was one that identified him as a man in love.

He sublet a small apartment fifteen minutes from the office. There and back inside a lunch hour was doable. He plotted thirteen different routes between the two. He was more likely to be spotted as a spy when not being a spy than at any other time in his career, but what could he do? Her eyes were sadder than he remembered, the face more lined, the hair not naturally blonde. And the way she spoke, the way she called him *my Dominic*, all of it sunk a hook in his heart. He was haemorrhaging his savings, renting their lunchtime safe-house, but if they used his own apartment, it would all become official.

All encounters with civilians are to be logged and appended to the relevant personnel file.

They'd tear her life apart, looking for reasons why she was untouchable.

She had a child, of course. A five-year-old: Erich. This she told him on their third meeting, as if it had slipped her mind until that moment. He pictured a waddling cherub: Eros in lederhosen. Children did not come naturally to him. It was doomed from the start, obviously—he didn't have to be a spy to know that much— but still, he found himself imagining it wasn't.

Repeat encounters require follow-up.

The Shit asked him, "What's put a smile in your trousers?"

"Berlin in the spring," he said. "Always a joy."

"If you say so." Then, with a nod at the teleprinter, "They want you to resend the latest figures from Atticus. Seems they're not convinced."

They, in this instance, meant the Park—sometimes *they* were them, and sometimes *they* were us. And Atticus was an asset, an accounts officer at the second-largest machine-parts factory in the GDR, the output of which cast interesting light on agricultural requirements in the Eastern bloc. Or might do. One of the problems with information is that the useful and the useless can be snowflake-similar, and the ability to know the one from the other comes with hindsight, if at all. The intel Atticus provided, at risk to life and liberty, might be background chatter in the long run. But it all had to be processed, because it all had to be processed. That was written somewhere; maybe on the Wall, in pinks and blues.

Dominic had leave coming, after his quarterly debrief at Regent's Park, and it was an unwritten rule that it be spent well away from Berlin. He usually stopped in London; drinking too much, smoking too much, testing the patience of friends, and the wives of friends. "Something in the Foreign Office." It was a code that had brought him latitude in the past, but everything had its limit. Being thrown out of bars at two in the morning wasn't a good look after a certain age. More than that, he worried about Marta. Couldn't bear the thought of leaving her here, with all the temptations an unhappy homelife had to offer.

The husband was old news, but they still shared an apartment. And she had a five-year-old, Erich . . .

She could easily fall back onto the straight and narrow, Dominic thought. He had lived all his adult life among people for whom lying was the simplest form of communication, and though she had told him she loved him, still, it was Berlin, and people told you what you wanted to hear. Usually in the full knowledge that all parties knew it was a temporary truth; built for the circumstances, and unlikely to survive the first wolf that came huffing and puffing. Was that what was happening here? He didn't want to think so.

Marta had told him—

"No," said Lamb.

"Touching a nerve?"

"Yeah, my piles act up when a torrent of shit's on the way."

"That's so disappointing."

Lamb grunted. Or, if it was a word, it was buried under so much breath, he might have been huffing and puffing himself.

"Let's leave her be, then," said Molly. "But I picture him wondering what kind of life would have been awaiting him after Berlin. Whether he'd have ended up with an office job, maybe

running one of the smaller desks. But he was a joe, not management material. He'd have been a disaster. Made everyone's life a
misery. What do you think?"

"I think you're pushing your luck."

She laughed, a startlingly tinkly sound, something like angelic
merriment.

So Dominic went to London, and had his debrief with David
Cartwright at the Park. It was the usual slow-burn affair: two
days in a windowless office, with the same questions delivered in
the same friendly but unyielding tone; the constant probing for
information he might have but was unaware of; for weaknesses
he was aware of, but didn't want to share. For signs that he was
going native.

"You must be about ready to come home."

"I am home."

"For good, I mean."

For once an error had sailed past David Cartwright. He'd
meant he was at home in Berlin.

"I've a year or two in me yet."

Cartwright had delivered one of those piercing gazes of which
he seemed so proud: *I can read your small print*, it seemed to say.
Dominic wondered how often it had resulted in impromptu
confessions; in ghosts being given up before the haunting was
confirmed. "If you say so," he said, contriving to make the phrase
sound like its exact opposite. Then glanced at the papers in front
of him. "I'd like to talk about Atticus. How do you think he is?"

"Well enough. In the circumstances."

These being that he was betraying his own country to a foreign power, and would face imprisonment, probably death, if this came to light. Balanced against which, he had been promised life everlasting, eventually: a new home, a new job, a lump sum, a different horizon. Though, as was ever the way with such new starts, this always seemed to be receding into the distance. Atticus had been asking for an escape route for more than a year. Dominic had been explaining the difficulties involved, their imminent solution, for precisely as long.

"Are you confident his product is still sound?"

"It's facts and figures, David. I can't answer for their usefulness. I'm not an analyst."

"The last two reports, they've been wildly out of kilter with the previous few months."

"So things are changing. Isn't that what we're supposed to be on the alert for?"

"Some of our chaps, they're wondering whether we're being fed inaccurate data."

"You think he's been compromised?"

"I don't know, Dominic. What do you think?"

"I think he's been risking his life for little reward. I think he deserves our trust."

"It's important that we remain clear-eyed. Obviously, we want to do our best by Atticus. But if he's been blown, he's already beyond our help. And attempting to assist him further would be to put ourselves—to put you—at considerable risk."

David Cartwright had leaned across the table, as if to demonstrate their togetherness on this issue.

"And it's not as if he's high-value. I mean, all intel matters, I don't mean to suggest otherwise. But he's one small segment of a big jigsaw. We can work out what the landscape looks like with his part missing."

Dominic said, "Are you telling me to cut him adrift?"

"Of course not. But let's treat his product with caution. If they're using him to feed us sawdust, let's not put it in our loaves." He sat back. "Trust is our currency. Of course it is. But we have to know when to cash in."

There were other assets, other issues. Two days was a long time.

Dominic spent the tea breaks thinking about Marta, and counting minutes.

Somewhere out in Hampstead's wilds, a bell was ringing. Perhaps a local school, releasing its charges for the day. There were always bells somewhere. This was London.

Lamb, well-practised at sleeping through alarms, paid it no attention. His eyes were closed; his mouth slightly not. But he wasn't still, or not as still as he was capable of. Every so often something rippled through his frame: a digestive rumble perhaps, though if so, an uncharacteristically silent one. It was as if his whole body were frowning.

"I'm not sending you to sleep, am I?" Molly asked.

"No," he replied at length. "You're keeping me awake."

"It's your fidgeting doing that. I never had you down for the fidgety type. Memories stirring?"

Lamb opened his eyes, and yawned. "Might be crabs. Christ knows who sat here before me." He stood, suddenly, and his head broached the shaft of light falling from a window. Jackson Lamb, enhaloed. An unexpected sight. "Am I supposed to believe you've read transcripts?"

"The debriefing's on record. And I'm an archivist, remember?"

"'He spent the tea breaks thinking about Marta, and counting minutes,'" Lamb quoted. "Funny fucking records someone's keeping."

"I fill in gaps. It's what I do."

"These aren't gaps. They're canyons."

"What are you worried about? That I'll get things wrong? Or get them right?"

"It was all years ago," said Lamb.

"That's not an answer."

It was the best she was getting. After turning for a moment to face the light, Lamb sunk onto the bench again. His gaze was fixed on the altar, but Molly was pretty sure he wasn't seeing it.

"I think," she said, "that it was immediately after he returned to Berlin that Dominic was approached by an agent of state security."

GDR state security, that is.

Marta was rarely available in the evenings, and Dominic, on those nights when he wasn't working, often found himself drifting through the city, joining its dots. Most of these were clubs and bars, but the streets held fascination too. Amidst the larger sectors carved out by politics and history, Dominic had his own areas determined by appetite and inclination. He was far from alone in this. Students, young people, often huddled near the Wall, sitting round fires, smoking, drinking, making music, while being studied overhead by watchful soldiers, their rifles unslung from their shoulders, as if the youth might be planning an assault. There were few things most students looked less capable of. On the other hand, Dominic thought, if anything were to shift that barrier, it would be the will and cooperation of the young, not the machinations of their elders. If politics was the art of banging your head against a wall, in Berlin it had found its apotheosis. As such, it seemed unlikely to provide solutions.

But that was no surprise. After years in a divided city, he had long ceased to expect it would ever be anything but. Even if the Wall were to disappear overnight, its stones picked apart by the youngsters who'd grown up in its shadow, where would that leave everyone? Berlin was a city twinned with itself: it had two zoos, two operas, two everything. Even if it healed, its divisions would remain; it would be a pair of mirrored images, neither side trusting the other. No wonder it was a habitat for spooks. Thoughts like this propelled him on his wanderings, and he found himself drawn, as so often before, to the watertower, a halfway point between two of his usual bars, and a place to sit for a smoke, or have a piss in the bushes, which is what he was doing when he found he wasn't alone.

"I hear you've been keeping company with my dear friend Marta."

Dominic braced himself for a punch in the kidneys, which didn't come, so he finished what he was doing, zipped himself away, then turned.

"I think you must have me mistaken for someone else."

"In that case, I apologise. It must be a different Dominic Cross I took you for."

That the stranger was a thug was no surprise; that he was a civilised thug was less expected. He wore a soft brown raincoat to match his soft brown shoes, and Dominic knew he could peel layer after layer from this man, and everything he found would be soft and brown, right to the steel black core. For one brief moment he considered throwing a punch, just to short-circuit whatever was about to happen, but it wouldn't help in the long run. Not that violence couldn't be a solution, but it was best to have the problem laid out in full beforehand, in case he was asked to show his working.

"What do you want?"

"I think a beer would suit the purpose. Over there, perhaps?"

A lit corner of the nearby square.

"They serve a reasonable Guinness. That's your drink, am I right? In this part of town?"

There might have been a soft brown space in the air behind him as he walked away.

Dominic followed. He didn't see what else he could do. There were tables outside the bar, though the night was cool and curtained with damp, and it was here that his new friend chose to sit. He was lighting a cigarette when Dominic caught up, and a waiter was already asking if the gentlemen wouldn't prefer to be inside, and quickly understanding that the gentlemen wished only to be served their drinks, and then left well alone. Two beers arrived shortly afterwards. By then both men were smoking, and from a distance might have been taken for old acquaintances, comfortable in each other's company, and finding no need to talk.

An old woman walked past tugging a dog on a string, as if it were a reluctant kite.

The man spoke at last, continuing an interrupted conversation. "She is a citizen of the Democratic Republic."

Choosing to misunderstand would have been a waste of time and breath.

"She's a West German," Dominic said.

"Oh, is that what she told you?"

He sounded genuinely curious.

Dominic didn't reply. He had never asked, it occurred to him. Marta was here, in the West; of course she belonged. For her to be otherwise would have cast their reality in doubt.

The stranger was watching him through their joint veil of cigarette smoke. Like his overcoat, like his shoes, his eyes were soft and brown. The colour was probably his by birth, but the softness was a disguise he'd donned since. He said, "She was granted exit papers nearly twenty years ago, to visit an elderly grandmother who had the misfortune to be stranded on your side of the anti-fascist barrier. And she never returned after the grandmother's death."

He might have been remarking on the dampness in the air; how, for all its lack of bite, you could still catch your death if you lingered too long.

Dominic said, "She's lived here for years. Her papers are perfectly in order."

"I'm sure that's true."

"And it's not like they'll send her back."

His new friend was nodding: this also was true. They could hardly be more in agreement. "And yet, if she were to stray across the border by accident . . ."

"Nobody crosses the border by accident."

"But you know what they say. There is a first time for everything."

The old woman and her dog were long gone.

"What do you want?"

"I want you to know that we have your best interests at heart, Dominic. That there are many of us who wish to see a happy ending for you, and for your Marta. And we would be so unhappy were anything to come between you."

He flicked his cigarette in the direction of the Wall, and left Dominic with an unfinished beer.

This time, there was no doubt. It was a pass. But the moment for confession had gone: if Dominic bared his soul now, there was only one possible outcome. He'd be on the next flight home. What happened to Marta afterwards, he might never know. Perhaps nothing. If he was out of the picture, Soft Brown Raincoat might heave a soft brown sigh and move on, leave Marta untouched. But Dominic didn't think so. The morning after their encounter, he'd gone through their files on Stasi agents: Soft Brown Raincoat was one Helmut Stagge, whose paperwork was marked with a satanic squiggle, a line drawing of a horned devil whose meaning didn't require a footnote.

That lunchtime, Marta didn't turn up. He spent an hour pacing the bare floorboards of the flat, pulsing at every squeak; called her eventually, from a café four streets away.

"Erich isn't well. What could I do? I couldn't phone you. Not at work."

An unshakable rule, except in absolute emergency. Which this was, though she didn't know that.

"There's a man I met last night, he says he knows you."

"What's his name?"

"I can't remember. He has brown eyes? A brown coat?"

She laughed. "These are not distinguished features."

"Distinguishing."

She had to end the call; Erich, she said, was wailing again.

Blackmail was a favourite weapon—he'd used it himself, many times. You didn't always recruit an asset by showering them with kindness, or appealing to principle or greed. So by the time Stagge showed up again, two days later, Dominic had grown weary of expecting him. He knew that sometimes a joe was happy to be caught, or if not happy, at least aware that a weight had been lifted. Part of that was guilt, but mostly it was the relief of not having to wait any longer; of knowing that, whatever it was you feared, it had arrived, and now you would discover how well you might face it.

"It's simple enough," Stagge told him. They were on adjacent tables outside a café, and the recent glum weather had subsided at last: spring was here, and graffiti had bloomed fresh and new in the sunshine. Stagge had appeared as suddenly as birdsong a few minutes after Dominic had chosen this spot to nurse his hangover. Across the square a group of mime artists had set up shop, and were acting out agony or unspeakable happiness. It was hard to tell. As far as mimes went, Stagge was the better. He was enjoying a pastry with his coffee, and to the casual observer was ignoring Dominic and reading a newspaper.

"Whatever it is, I'm not doing it."

"Then I hope you've made your goodbyes. We'll be glad to see the prodigal return." The newspaper rustled in his hands. "Her son, though, his place is with his father. He'll be staying here."

This was delivered as fact, like a builder with an estimate. *This will be made to happen. I have all the tools at my disposal.*

Dominic's hand shook as he raised his cup to his lips. Experience with hangovers accustomed you to them, but didn't lessen their effect. He knew that Stagge could fulfil his threat. The very fact that he wandered at will through West Berlin would have indicated his status, even if Dominic hadn't been through his file. That satanic squiggle some Stasi-watcher had doodled: it might have been a comic flourish, but it wasn't a joke. So yes, Stagge could do as he threatened, and in the end it would just be another Berlin story: one that got away turned out not to have done so after all. Nobody strayed across the border by accident. But it was possible to end up in the boot of the wrong car, and wake up in your own past.

He wasn't aware of having spoken the words. Maybe he had picked up a trick from the mime group, and whatever expression was plastered across his face had done the work for him.

"A token of goodwill, that's all. You give me one of yours. I let you keep one of mine."

"She isn't yours."

"But she can be. You're not in a position to protect her, are you? A secret flat? Really?" Stagge bit into his pastry with care. A few, not many, crumbs fell free. "If your Service knew you were having an affair with a local, you wouldn't be going to such lengths. But then, that's the trouble with spying, isn't it?" His tone sounded almost kind. "It becomes an addiction. All this secrecy."

"I have nothing to offer you."

"I'm not looking for the crown jewels. A name. There must be many to choose from. One name, that's all. Anyone you like. You give me something I can take home to my masters, and your mistress can stay here with you." He smiled at his newsprint, proud of his wordplay.

"I see you again, I'll bring you in," Dominic said. The threat was for his own sake, they both knew that. Berlin Desk would have a stroke if he did any such thing, and besides, Stagge could cut him off at the knees without dropping what was left of his pastry.

"That watertower you're fond of," Stagge remarked to his paper. "There's a loose section of brick round the back."

"I'm not interested."

"One name," he said. "Is it really so much to ask? One name. Twenty-four hours."

Dominic watched as he strode off across the square, pausing only to drop a coin or two into the mimes' hat as he passed.

The bells had ceased, and nothing now disturbed the sanctified air, unless it was the aroma of stale cigarettes unleashed by Lamb's restless movements, or the whisky-tinted breath he expelled in a soft belch as it became apparent that Molly had come to an end, of sorts.

At last he said, "Mimes?"

"I told you. I fill in gaps."

"And that's what you brought me here for? To let me know you'd uncovered this little episode from the past?"

"Your past."

Molly reversed her wheelchair, and came to rest by the same stretch of wall she'd been looking at when he joined her. Lamb, for his part, stood again, and stretched loudly. A cigarette had appeared behind his ear. It was possible, she thought, that they grew there, like fungi. She was surprised, truth to tell, that he'd suffered in more or less silence this long: it would have been in character for him to leave as soon as her subject became clear. But he owed her, as he'd said. And spooks pay their debts, or the best of them do.

They both knew the ending of her story, of course, but she suspected the endings they knew were different.

She said, "So tell me what happened next."

"You know what happened next."

He sounded bored.

"I know what happened officially."

"Ought to be enough. That's your job, isn't it? Keeping the truth and the bullshit separate." He collected the cigarette from his ear and inserted it in his mouth. "But you seem to be treading a lot of bullshit around today."

"Atticus was for the chop," Molly said. "David Cartwright had made that clear. And maybe he'd already been compromised, but even so, he was still in play, and offering him to Stagge would have been a show of good faith. Enough to buy a little time."

Lamb said, "Stagge wouldn't have accepted a name he already had. And either way, he'd have wanted another one two days later. When a shark tastes your toe, he comes back for the rest." He moved the cigarette back to his ear. "But here's me, preaching to the legless."

"So he did nothing. He called Stagge's bluff. Remind me, how did that turn out?"

Lamb shrugged. "About how you'd expect."

"Marta disappeared."

He said nothing.

"Well, I say disappeared, but we both know where she went. They took her over the Wall. That must have been . . . difficult."

Lamb said, "No, they were pretty good at that. Ambulances were popular." He made a gentle swipe at the air, demonstrating a swift passage through all obstacles. "Unconscious patients don't fuss much at the border."

"Not what I meant. Do you think she was a plant?"

"I don't much care. It was a long time ago."

"There's a lot of stuff you don't care about, but the difference between a joe and a civilian was never one of them."

Lamb didn't answer for a while. At length he said, "I thought she might have been at the time. But it turned out there really was a kid, and he stayed behind when she left. So no, I don't think she was a plant. I think she was who she said she was. Just a woman called Marta."

"What about Atticus?"

"He was compromised, like Cartwright said. They fed us fake figures a little longer, but their heart wasn't in it. They knew we knew they had him. He went off air a month later. There was a report of a firing squad. We assumed that was him."

Molly patted the armrest of her chair. "So nobody got to live happily ever after."

"Imagine my surprise."

"Maybe a swap would have been a better outcome. Atticus for Marta."

Lamb said, "Sharks, toes. Remember?"

"So, then. No regrets?"

"What do you expect me to say? That I'd have done it differently now?"

She said, "That's what I thought."

He paused, then said, "Oh, Christ. That was a schooltwat's error, wasn't it?"

"I was already sure it was you," she said. "Not Dominic."

"No," he said. "It wasn't Dominic. Dominic gave up Atticus. I was the one took him back."

"No wonder he called you The Shit," Molly said.

"I saved him," Lamb said at last. "Even if he wouldn't have seen it that way."

"From what, exactly?"

"From leaving a name in a dead letter drop behind a loose brick in a watertower." He lit his cigarette in a brief, almost invisible gesture. Smoke pretended to be incense for a while, weaving in and out of coloured light. "From sacrificing an asset."

"So you waited till he used the drop, then removed the letter before it was collected. How long had you been following him?"

"Months, on and off. He was clearly hiding something. And I was his mirror-man, so I was the one he was hiding it from. That never lasts." He sat down. "So I knew about the apartment, I knew about Marta. I knew it was only a matter of time before someone put the screws to him. It didn't matter whether Marta was a plant or not. Bait doesn't have to know it's bait."

"But you didn't throw him to the wolves. *Our* wolves."

"He didn't like me. I didn't like him. But he was a joe. He'd earned the benefit. And Atticus was one of ours."

"Atticus was already lost."

"Doesn't matter. You never pull the plug. How did you know about Stagge, anyway?"

"His report turned up in a Stasi file we bagged in the nineties.

He had it down as a failed attempt to turn a British agent." She smiled a sour sort of smile. "He thought Dominic had chosen duty over love."

"Like I said," said Lamb. "Barbara fucking Cartland."

Molly said, "Did Dominic discover what you'd done?"

Lamb shrugged.

"When Marta disappeared, he gave up, didn't he?" Molly said. "Came back to Blighty and drank himself to death inside a year."

"In a manner of speaking," Lamb said. "Hanging himself helped, mind."

"He was drunk at the time," said Molly. "And at least he got a plaque." She nodded towards the name at her eye level: Digby Palmer, which was who Dominic Cross was once he ran out of names. A pair of dates was his only epitaph. "I'm glad it wasn't him who sold Marta out."

"No. He sold Atticus instead."

"He wasn't in love with Atticus."

"What the fuck's that got to do with it?"

Molly silently allowed that this had no answer that Jackson Lamb might accept.

While he rammed his hands into his raincoat pockets and stood, all in the same huge motion, putting her in mind of a bin lorry performing one of those complicated hoisting operations which always threaten to leave spillage everywhere, she reached out and traced Digby Palmer's engraved name with her right index finger, feeling the shape of each letter unfold under her touch. She meant what she had said: she was glad that he had intended to sacrifice one of his agents for the woman he'd loved; but equally and inconsistently glad that this intention had been thwarted by Lamb. Mostly glad, though, that she could stop wondering where the truth lay. And it occurred to her to ask whether Lamb had ever met Marta, and if so whether he understood his poor mirror-man's fascination with her, but by the time her finger finished tracing the last dead letter of Digby Palmer's name, Lamb had gone.

STANDING BY THE WALL

. . .

"Ho."

The name wasn't so much dropped as thrown from the top of Slough House, and like a snowball finding its target struck Roddy Ho, two floors down, on the back of his neck. He looked up from his screen, senses quivering. He was needed.

"Ho!"

This iteration carried more force; less a snowball, more a local-ised collapse, as when poor insulation causes a roof to loosen its grip, and its burden of snow hits the pavement with a *whump*. Roddy was already out of his chair, the sleek dynamism of a panther fuelling his every move as he sashayed round his desk, hop-skip-jumped a broken printer, pirouetted past a waist-high stack of pizza boxes, and faceplanted on the landing. Damn car-pet! He was hearing bells as he picked himself up, and was almost swept away when the third call came: this one a snow tiger cas-cading down a mountainside, uprooting everything in its path.

"HO!"

Like being summoned by an angry Santa.

On the threshold of Lamb's office he paused, adjusting his expression. Decided to go for quizzical: Spock responding to

Kirk's urgent directive with his customary calm, secure in the knowledge that, beneath the necessary camouflage a command structure imposed, they were friends and equals. The captain, subject to the pressures of office, might skirt the boundaries of decorum, but to the practised ear respect was the bedrock of their every exchange. With eyebrow at optimum angle, Ho pushed the door and entered Lamb's den.

"What took you so long, goat-breath? Stop for a dump on the stairs?"

Bantz.

Lamb, Ho noted, was in festive mode, his shoeless feet, currently on his desktop, rejoicing in a pair of Rudolph socks: a browny-grey reindeer colour, graced at each tip with a bulbous red nose. And on the desk in front of him were scraps of gift-wrap that looked like a cross dog had ripped its way free from, the paper's recurring motif—angels and bells, bells and angels—only discernible if you had the kind of mind to reassemble patterns. Roddy was lining up a seraphic chorus, mentally repairing torn wings and cracked casings, before he clocked what been in the wrapping: a shiny white sheet Lamb was holding, twelve inches by ten, give or take. Any illustration or writing it bore was on the side cradled to Lamb's stomach.

A star-shaped gift tag had fluttered to the floor, attached to a length of green ribbon, on which an actual small bell hung. A message Ho couldn't read was scrawled across the tag, unless a drunk beetle had used it as a short cut on its way home from an inkwell.

Lamb said, "Hello? It's like talking to a crash-test dummy."

"I'm here," said Ho, briefly contemplating, and as swiftly

rejecting, denying the whole dump-on-the-stairs thing, because if Lamb had a fault, it was his occasional inability to put a joke aside before he'd squeezed every last drop out of it. Then again, Roddy reminded himself reasonably, it wasn't everyone had natural comic timing. You had your Roddy types, whose verbal dexterity just naturally brought the sunshine, and then you had your straight men, who milked the laughs by falling flat on their faces. He rubbed his cheek, studded with carpet grit. "What do you need?"

For a moment, his boss stared off into a middle distance Slough House's walls couldn't contain. "Christ," he said. "The idea that I might need stuff you might supply. Makes me wonder if I took a wrong turn." Then he pulled his gaze back, and took in the peeling wallpaper, the overflowing desk, the broken slat on the blind covering the dirty window. "Nah. Living the dream."

He flipped the sheet he was holding, and held it in the grubby yellow light cast by his lamp.

Which added a sepia tint to the photograph it turned out to be, not that this was a term Roddy reached for. Instead, Roddy just thought: *Old* . . . It was black and white; one of those snapshots of the long-ago that caught, in its subjects' faces, a hint of the melancholy they must feel for a future they'd be too crumbly to enjoy: one in which they wouldn't have to wear baggy suits and hugely-lapelled raincoats, or—in the case of the woman—a drab mid-thigh length dress, with buttons the size of saucers. The three stood in front of a wall, facing the camera: the man in the middle beaming broadly; the woman, on his left, wearing a shyer smile, as if she weren't sure this assignation should be made public. The remaining figure was strangely expressionless, as if caught between two moods, something about him reminding Roddy of someone, he couldn't think who. The woman, meanwhile, was a solid six, maybe seven if she made an effort, but on this showing was all washed out: word to the wise, babe; a touch of the old slap wouldn't go amiss. Anything that gave the sisterhood a leg up got Roddy's vote, and he'd seen enough movies to know that a quick makeover, en route to the lingerie department, could push a six to an eight and a half if you had feminist leanings, and weren't too fussy. But that wasn't happening here, though you could never know for certain about lingerie. As for the man in the middle, he wore a wide-brimmed gangster hat pushed back on his head, as if decked out as an extra for a roaring twenties' revival. Both men's shoes were oddly shapeless. Roddy glanced down at his trainers while making this observation: Tommy Hilfiger, dude. Count 'em and weep.

This photo, though. Lamb had been sent it as a Christmas present? Someone didn't like him much. On the other hand, Roddy didn't want to be stepping on anyone's toes whatever their footwear. So he pursed his lips and nodded thoughtfully; eased back a little to adjust his focus, forward to zoom in on the detail. His nodding grew more assured. He stroked his chin and delivered his verdict.

"That's, em, yeah. Art, right? It's, like, yeah. Cool."

Covered the bases.

Lamb blinked twice, then said, "It's like Ruskin's in the room."

"Who's—"

"Shut up. Now, ordinarily the reason I make you run up those stairs is I don't like you and I want you to die. But today, as it happens, I've a job for you." Still holding the photo so it was facing Roddy, he slapped a meaty hand over the face of the man in the middle, blotting his wide grin. "I want you to get rid of this guy. Think you can handle that?"

Get rid of this guy . . .

I mean, dude, why not? This was the security service, and if a wet job was on the cards, Roddy was precisely the high-precision tool required. Not that he'd done it before. Had come close a time or two—he could think of a couple of encounters in clubs that would have ended *very* differently if he weren't so self-disciplined—but this, no, this was next level. This was the HoMeister being let off the leash. He could feel his features hardening as he ran down a mental check-list of methods: apparent accident, evident suicide, inappropriate touching. That last wasn't technically an assassination method, but according to Louisa and Ashley, who'd been discussing it in the kitchen last week, it could definitely end in death.

But Lamb was shaking his head. "Hold your horses, double-oh dickless. If I wanted someone dead, you'd not be the person I'd ask to make it happen. You'd be the person I'd want it to happen to." He laid the photo on the desk, and reached for a steel ruler Ho dimly remembered as having once been his own. "Don't worry. Being a desk-bound twat might not put you on movie posters, but it suits my purposes, which is a lot more important."

Roddy allowed a twinkle to show in his eye, to let Lamb know he knew he was kidding. "So get rid of him how?"

"Like he was never in the photograph. That's the kind of deepfake mindgame you cellar-dwellers specialise in, right?" Reaching out with the ruler, he scratched one of his Rudolph noses, which, Roddy now noticed, were peculiarly toe-shaped. In fact, *precisely* toe-shaped. "Only this time you're on the side of the angels."

"Yeah, so how—"

"Do I look like I'm interested in hows? I only care about whens. So let's say end of the day, shall we? Gives me something to look forward to, and keeps you out of mischief. Win win."

"But it's already gone four!"

"What's your point?"

"It's Christmas Eve!"

"Why, did you have plans? No, let me rephrase. Did you have plans that matter? Good." Lamb pointed with the ruler at the photo, and then, when Roddy had reluctantly picked it up, waved at the door with the same implement. "Don't make me have to tell you to fuck off." He beamed, kindly. "Not on Christmas Eve."

With grudging tread, Roddy left the room.

Back in his office he scowled. Plans? Of course he had plans. It was Christmas Eve! *Die Hard, Die Hard 2* and *Elf.* Unless the others were planning an evening in the pub, which he thought might have happened on previous Christmas Eves, and which he'd allow himself to fall in with if it happened tonight. Spread a little Roddiness. And with every other office worker in the capital heading out for a spot of seasonal insobriety, there was a distinct possibility of the mistletoe effect going viral: Christmas crackers, eager to be pulled! Instead of which here he was, in his office; the streets outside already dark; the dim murmur of conversation in the room above his—who *was* that speaking; they sounded weirdly familiar?—and a way-past boring technical task facing him when he'd been planning on killing the last working hour browsing stocking-filler sites. Sometimes, being Slough House's go-to guy was a pain in Ro-Ho's arse.

He paused, checked his scowl, took a selfie. Not bad, actually. But time was ticking on, and he had a job to do.

The photo was smaller than he'd thought; ten inches by eight, with a white border. Laying it flat on his desk, he photographed it, downloaded the result onto his desktop, imported it into a manipulation program the Service carried on its intranet, accessible only by a handful of registered users—yeah, right; big smile, boys, you've been Roddied—and opened it on his main screen. So far, piece of piss.

The next part of the job—making the man disappear—wouldn't stretch him either. Currently, this guy took up the foreground, one arm around the waist of the woman to his left; the other hanging free by his side, with a small but perceptible space between him and the second man, as if one or both were keen to avoid intimacy. The second man's hands were jammed inside his pockets. The look on his face hadn't altered since Roddy first clocked it, that caught-between-two-moods expression, as if he were about to turn one thing or another: nice or nasty. But the first man looked more confident now Roddy had cranked him up, that thirty percent magnification adding ballast. Not that he needed it. He wasn't beefy exactly, but was well enough built; not the type to impress Roddy, whose wiry frame was the perfect container for the relaxed energy he embodied, but the sort who would make a decent sidekick: not too weighed down by the old brainpower, but able to take a beating. Fancied himself a bit, though. You could tell there was self-satisfaction there, because— dead giveaway—out of his breast pocket poked a jaunty little tongue of handkerchief. Roddy gave an amused shake of the head. Vanity. The vice of mediocrities everywhere.

But no, excising this chump would be the work of minutes. What would take time was joining up the background, leaving no jarring misalignments visible. The background was a brick wall. A grid pattern wasn't the hardest thing to work with, but it meant a lot of straight lines had to meet each other cleanly, and the bricks had to remain of uniform size. The sort of task, in a perfect world, Roddy would hand to an assistant; ideally a blonde with thick-framed glasses she'd remove in pensive moments, tucking the end of one arm behind her lower lip while her eyes went softly out of focus . . . He made a mental note to Google himself some of that, then unglazed his own eyes and activated an outlining tool from a dropdown menu. Using a pencil on his mousepad he traced a thin white line round the target, highlighting him, making him momentarily brighter, more dazzling, than his companions. Roddy left him hanging like that for a moment, a man from the past in a spotlight cast by the future. Then he pressed a key and *pow*, the figure vanished, leaving behind only a blank space; the nothingness of a background that had disappeared along with him. Making a gun of his fingers, Roddy raised its barrel to his lips, and blew away imaginary smoke.

It was too sudden to be truly awesome, though. The cool way would be a slow melt; the character shimmying away in a *Back to the Future* style fadeout, taking all his potential, all his impact, with him. Yeah, what would be really aces would be if this guy hadn't just vanished but had ceased to ever be. And what would the ripple effect be like, Roddy wondered? This guy, blinking out of existence: it could cause havoc with the space-time continuum,

it didn't take Stephen King to work that out. *Haw*king. Whatever. One moment he's securely rooted in the history of those
around him; the next, there's not a pixel of him left. So how
would this other pair find it if he just vanished from their lives,
and all the things he'd done had never happened? Perhaps they
wouldn't have met—perhaps this vanished dude introduced
them. Perhaps, without him, they'd have floated away down
different paths, leading different lives . . . Roddy shook his
head at the philosophy of it all. For an even bigger thought
had just landed, one with breathtaking implications—what if
Roddy Ho were to just vanish; his entire identity, all his adven-
tures, put back in the box like an unstruck match? Talk about
the ripple effect. You'd be looking at a tsunami. As he sat there,
gazing at his screen with its blown-up image of a trio reduced
to a couple, his thoughts shimmied away into a parallel world,
one from which the Rodster and all his works had been
plucked; a duller, greyer, tone-deaf place, lacking in joy and
spectacle. It was hard not to get a little misty-eyed at the
prospect, and more on others' behalves than his own. Imagine
the heartbreak, he thought. And he allowed himself to do just
that; to sit back and picture the world—Slough House—bereft
of his presence; touring the ruins as if in the company of a
passing angel, who had taken him by the hand to show him
how grievously he'd be missed.

"So. Miss me?"

"You've been away? We didn't notice."

"Except," said Lech Wicinski, "there was maybe a tiny uplift
in the average IQ?"

He held his finger and thumb a few inches apart, to demonstrate just how tiny.

"And less dicking about," Shirley said. "Fewer slammed doors
and not so much moody stomping around."

"Well, coming from you—"

"And a calmer atmosphere," Louisa agreed. "Less sexual depri-
vation in the air."

"Yeah, that's no longer a—"

"We don't want to hear about it," said Lech.

"And everyone felt better dressed," Shirley said.

"So on the whole," Louisa concluded, "no, I have to say, it's
surprising how well we coped."

Yeah, thought River. They'd missed him.

Slough House hadn't altered in his absence, or not so he could
tell. There was a new occupant, but that was a change often felt
least of all: some slow horses had a way of merging with the wallpaper, adopting its rancid pattern, during their first months of
tenure; as good a way as any, he supposed, of demonstrating that they
belonged here. But once the soul-deadening realisation that this
wasn't just a career glitch—that this was their future made solid
and served up in one indigestible lump—once that was out of
the way, some started to reassert themselves, unless they'd given
up by then. Half a year spent fiddling about on the margins of
the nation's security—passing your days, say, checking passen-
ger locator forms against NHS records, on the vanishingly
small chance that any discrepancy was down to a bad actor's
inadequate cover rather than human error, form-fatigue or sheer
bloody-mindedness—and you'd know whether you were prepared
to dig your heels in long-term, or accept that your mental

well-being and sense of self-worth depended on finding alternative means of employment, despite the hole in your CV you'd be carrying forever. As far as the Service was concerned, if you bailed on them—even, or especially, if they wanted you to—you ceased to exist.

Of course, remaining on the Service's books when the volume in question was Slough House wasn't that much better a prospect. There were those who'd prefer the clean start, even if that left you way down the ladder, admiring the arses of those who'd made more considered career choices, like accountants or window cleaners or jugglers.

Ashley Khan, the trigger for this line of thought, was leaning against the wall.

"So you're Ash."

"Uh-huh."

"How's it going?"

"What is this, a royal visitation? Ask me how far I've come, why don't you?"

"I know exactly how far you've come," River said. "We all used to work at the Park."

"And some of us got screwed over," she said. "While the rest of you fucked up."

"Right. Looking forward to sharing an office with you."

"Yeah, I've taken your desk, by the way."

"That's fine," River said. "I don't start for a month. Plenty of time to vacate it."

"That's gonna happen."

"Then we're both happy."

Ash stood. "We'll have lots of time to get to know each other. Don't see any point in wasting this afternoon too."

She left.

River looked at Louisa, who shrugged. "You were hardly a bundle of joy either. Back in the day."

"She's kind of . . ."

"Uptight?"

"I was going to say arsey."

"I like her," said Shirley.

"You would."

"She's over-sensitive," said Lech. "Like many millennials. Some of them find punctuation aggressive."

"Yeah? How'd they feel about a punch in the mouth?"

"Hello, River."

Catherine Standish had chosen that moment to appear.

Speaking of not changing, here was the touchstone. For as long as he'd known her, Catherine had dressed the same way, moved on the same rails, transmitted on the same frequency: one of measured calm despite the daily aggravations. If Slough House was where you found out what you were made of, River thought, Catherine must have discovered pure titanium below her apparently delicate surface. The clothes she wore might have graced a Victorian doll; her hair, from a distance a grey dull cap, was a wispy fair web where it escaped the slides keeping it tamed. He might have seen her yesterday. He was glad to see her now.

For a moment, he thought she was going to embrace him. That moment—if it actually was one, and not his imagination—passed. But there was warmth in her smile when she asked, "How are you?"

"Fine. You?"

"No, I meant really."

"I passed the medical, Catherine. I'm fine."

And he was, or he was if anybody asked. Anyone bar Sid, that is—she was privy to his nightmares, which were not so much a summoning of the demons his brush with Novichok had tarred him with as a tour of other, earlier griefs. These dreams took him by the hand and led him through his grandfather's house: the rooms, bar one, emptied of possessions; only the study still furnished. In this version, though, it had been ransacked by some furious intruder, its hundreds of books spilled into a heap that might have boiled up from some underground chamber, and he—River—was tasked with putting each back in its rightful place, according to a system ordained by his grandfather, and never revealed to anyone else. Unspecified punishments awaited should he shelve a title wrongly. These dreams, or this single recurring dream, his waking mind interpreted as a mission to restore order where he found chaos, a diagnosis which caused Sid no small amusement. That didn't sound like the River Cartwright she knew. No; his nightmares were random assaults made by his subconscious, just like everyone else's. Deal with it.

The pair of them, though. Sid, River had once bent over on a pavement wet with blood, a bullet in her brain; River, Sid had found on his grandfather's kitchen floor, laid low by a Russian nerve agent. If not made in heaven, their relationship was at least ratified by intensive care.

"When do you start back?"

"Not for a few weeks. Just thought I'd drop in, say hello."

"That's kind."

"Wish you all a Merry Christmas."

Louisa said, "Who are you, and what have you done with River?"

Catherine tilted her head to one side. "All of us?"

"Haven't decided yet."

Because sticking your head round Lamb's door to say hello wasn't established practice. He had a way of making you feel unwelcome even when he'd specifically demanded your presence.

"How is he, anyway?" he said.

"Same as ever."

"That bad?"

Lech said, "He had an email from HR yesterday, about something called an equality impact assessment."

"Bet that went down well."

"He emailed back asking how high a window he could use."

Shirley said, "If they start checking in with him about our preferred pronouns, he might have a stroke." The idea obviously pleased her. She looked around. "So, we going to the . . ." She glanced at Catherine, then away. "You know."

Catherine rolled her eyes. "I'm not about to have a fit of the maidenly vapours just because someone mentions the pub."

"Yeah, it's just, you're not invited."

"Of course you are," Louisa said. "Shirley's kidding. Aren't you, Shirley?"

"Only if it's understood that, just because she doesn't drink doesn't mean she gets out of buying her round."

Lech shook his head in what, in a better place, might have been disbelief, but in Slough House was more likely recognition.

"Thanks for the gracious offer, I'm sure," Catherine said. "But the pubs will be crowded and I'd rather get home."

"That was nice," Louisa said, once Catherine had left the room.

"Why's everyone looking at me?" said Shirley.

River closed his eyes briefly, allowing the familiar discomforts of a broken-backed chair and fractious colleagues to welcome him back to Slough House. But amid the call and response of office life—the jibes and barbs, the occasional harmonies, the inevitable grating discords—a stray thought kept sneaking up on him: *it feels like there's someone missing.*

For the life of him, River couldn't think who.

There were too many moments to recall, to many examples to list, but when you looked back over the last few years—which somehow felt like a decade or more, though obviously wasn't, or they'd all be older—when you did that, no question, it was Roddy Ho holding Slough House together; Roddy whose technical wizardry stopped things going tits up on a regular basis, and kept them tits down the rest of the time. Accessing databases, check. Hacking Service files, check. Verifying the locations of colleagues or minor characters armed with nothing more than their phone numbers, check. Some of this shit bordered on science fiction, and might as well be for all the attention the slow horses paid, as they sat slack-jawed, watching the Rodmeister's hands blur across his keyboard: bish bash bosh—job done. They didn't see the magic. Maybe they had their uses when you needed a blunt object, but for subtlety and grace there was only one Roderick Ho, plus, come to think of it, only one Roderick Ho's car: a Ford Kia, not *exactly* a common sight on the streets. How often had the HoMobile been called into action when a reliable and stylish mode of transport was required? From Wimbledon Common to the woolly wilds of Wales, how many tight squeezes had HotRod's hotrod rescued hapless spooks from? They were utterly clueless, the whole pack. So no, a world from which the Rodster had been erased was a world devoid of happy outcomes for Slough House, and Roddy didn't need a guardian angel to tell him *that*.

Didn't need one to tell him what to do next, either, which was move the two remaining characters in Lamb's photo closer together. And that was Roddy in a nutsack: always bringing the extra noise. Because clearly, with the central figure no longer there, this pair were going to have to shuffle up a bit, otherwise you'd have this weird disconnect going on; an obvious absence keeping them apart. And then, of course, there was the background to be filled in, the wall which was neither obviously new nor evidently old but had to be got right, brick by brick, so that as each pixelated unit slotted into place, you'd have the sense of a world healing itself, coming to terms with the loss of whoever had just vanished . . . Who'd been no one special, Roddy had decided, if all it took to fill the gap he'd left was some CGI brickwork. Compare and contrast with the Roddyless scenario. What kind of grief would be coming Slough House's way, if the world blinked once and Roderick Ho ceased to be? Even leaving aside all the hairsbreadth escapes he'd been responsible for—the countless times he'd waved the Roddy wand and pulled a Roddy rabbit from his hat, without which most of the slow horses would be smears across the landscape by now—there'd be the devastating emotional consequences to contend with. Louisa would suffer worst, without even knowing what caused her sense of loss; deep inside her there'd be a Roddy-shaped hole, and she wouldn't even know it. As for the others, well. For Shirley, the Rodster had

always been off-limits, of course; be like a donkey expecting to
get it on with a thoroughbred, but people couldn't always tell
what league they belonged in, and Shirley too would be bur-
dened with a vague awareness of lost possibilities, of never-weres.
Ash's chances of a close encounter of the Roddy kind had been
higher, making her outlook that much more blighted, but she
was young and might get over it. Catherine, though—who
looked on Roddy as the son she'd never had—there was no
happy outcome there. The best you could hope for was that
someone would toss a bunch of flowers into whatever lonely
well she ended up in. And Lech Wicinski—well, Lech could
fuck off. Even the Rodster's famous compassion had its limits.
But for Lamb, for Lamb it would be a case of missing limb
syndrome. Every time he had an emergency, every time he had
a crucial task, it would be like he was reaching for something
that wasn't there, with an arm he no longer had. Imagine the
frustration—

"Ho."

—imagine the grief—

"Ho!"

—imagine the anger—

"HO!"

Roddy hit the printer button and scampered upstairs with
his doctored photograph like a man chased by an angel.

Ho, Ho, HO! . . .

Roddy, thought River. How could he have forgotten Roddy?

More to the point, if it was that easy, how come he hadn't
managed it years ago?

Must have been the medication he'd been on these past six months. Side effects include: nausea, vomiting, sleeplessness and an eradication of arsewipe colleagues.

The others were deep into discussion about which pub they should head for after work—a formula which rather skated over the notion of how much work was going on—Shirley holding out for a dive on Whitecross Street she claimed did a nice line in craft beers, but whose attractions, the assembled company knew, were more to do with the illicit substance dealing it also specialised in, and Lech and Louisa hoping for somewhere you could be guaranteed a seat, and maybe food. River, meanwhile, was gauging his levels of strength. *I'm fine*, he told everyone, all the time; *I'm fine*, he'd told Sid earlier, when she'd queried the wisdom of this visitation. He wasn't fine. He put on a good show, mostly, but right this moment, for example, he wasn't sure he could stand up without keeling over.

Lech and Shirley were getting loud about what made a good pub good.

"Comfortable seating and no rap on the jukebox," said Lech.

"Wide range of lagers and flavoured gin," said Shirley. "Give the punters a party in their pants."

"Leaving aside the lager abomination," Lech said, "'a party in their pants'?"

"What's wrong with that?" Shirley, aggrieved, sounded a lot like a twelve-year-old. "It's an everyday expression. Like 'look before you leap.' Or 'Prince Andrew denies the allegations.'"

While they argued, Louisa rolled her eyes and tapped River on the shoulder. "You okay?"

"I'm fine."

She nodded, but not in a way that suggested belief.

To distract her, or maybe just to indicate his grasp on how many slow horses there were, he said, "Roddy part of this plan?"

"Probably not," she said, glancing in Lech's direction.

"Hard feelings?"

"Long story," she said, "but Roddy ran him over."

"With a car?"

"With a car."

"... Okay."

"So things are a bit ... tetchy."

River could see how that might be the case.

He heard Ho leaving Lamb's office and briefly saw him through the open doorway as he clumped downstairs. Catherine, he assumed, was in her own office, doing whatever it was she did when she was alone, which probably involved more dedication to tasks in hand than the rest of them managed. Ash was now coming out of her room—River's room, that is, but she'd learn—just across the landing from Louisa's, where Lech and Shirley had reached some at least temporary resolution as to which pub they'd grace with their favours. River had been on office outings before, and knew from experience that any such expedition involving more than two slow horses could end abruptly, with harsh language and the occasional slap. It being Christmas might make a difference, of course—everyone he knew and had ever known, however ill-tempered and misanthropic they might seem the rest of the year, proved themselves to be, deep down, at least twice as bad as that at Christmas.

Louisa was putting her coat on. "Ready?"

"You go ahead," he said. "I'll just say hi to," and he tilted his head to indicate the man upstairs.

"Seriously?"

"I've been pumped way full of drugs this year," River said. "I'll probably survive a few minutes in his room."

Though in truth, he wanted to remain static a little longer, rather than have anyone witness his attempt to stand.

Louisa said, "You'd have to be on something to even want to make the effort." She glanced towards the window, as if gauging the weather. It was dark, cold and damp. She named the pub the others had nominated: a big place on the corner at Smithfield Market. "You'll catch us up?"

"Sure. Probably. I may have to get home."

"But you're fine."

"But I'm fine."

She nodded, and steered the others out, Ash joining them on the landing. River heard them negotiating the stairs; heard the usual tussle with the back door, which stuck in all seasons; heard the final scraping crunch as someone shouldered it into place. Then Slough House was quiet, which meant there was merely the wheezing of the pipes, the groaning of the floorboards, the humming of the lightbulbs; and also, as long as he was paying attention, the whirring of computer tomfoolery from Roddy's room below, and the gentle tap of Catherine's feet above, as she crossed the small landing with her customary unhurried pace, and entered Lamb's lair.

Lamb's office, Catherine thought—not for the first time—was a synaesthete's daydream: tobacco, sweat and alcohol, along with the fug of unshared secrets, which had discoloured over the years, adding a rank shade to the spectrum. And under that rainbow Lamb sat, twisting something in his hands, and wearing what the others called his resting bastard face: an expression of wistful viciousness, as if he were remembering a bad turn he'd done someone, and wishing it had been worse. Whatever he was fidgeting with made a small tinkling sound as it dropped to the desk. It was a strip of ribbon, used as gift wrap, to which a small bell was attached.

"You realise that every time a bell rings," Catherine told him, "an angel gets its wings?"

Lamb said, "Yeah, but every time I break wind Tinkerbell punctures a lung. So I figure I'll come out ahead." He shifted in his seat, and for a moment she feared he was about to demonstrate his organ-deflating abilities. Instead, he reached for a plastic lighter, and dry-clicked it several times. "What's all the noise downstairs? As if I didn't know."

"He'll be up soon, I'm sure. To pay his respects."

"I'd sooner he paid my bar tab. Anyway, his sick leave's still running, isn't it? Shouldn't he be playing shitty sticks in some country retreat, with the other casualty?"

"It's called Poohsticks," Catherine said.

"Yeah, well, tell him to fuck off. If he's on sick leave, he shouldn't be on Service property. In fact, why not just set the Dogs on him?"

"Because it's Christmas?" She collected the empty mugs from his desk, each half full and rejoicing in at least two drowned cigarette ends. "Speaking of which, I see Molly sent you a gift."

"Molly's yanking my chain. It's not the same thing."

He slumped back in his chair, and into a state familiar to Catherine: one he adopted when pursuing a marathon brood. As a drinker—even if the last glass of alcohol she'd raised to her mouth had been years ago—she recognised the condition: one in which the brooder stared into an oblivion of his or her own making, an oblivion which stared right back, if you let it. Or you could open another bottle, pour another glass. There was a bottle on Lamb's desk now, a detail which barely needed mentioning. A glass too, its surface sticky, a stray hair clinging to its rim.

If she ever needed reminding why she no longer drank, all she needed to do was walk into this room, imagine it her own.

She had known that Molly Doran—Regent's Park's keeper of the files, who guarded her wheelchaired domain like a single-minded Cerberus—was the gift-giver because she had recognised the handwriting on that morning's envelope, sent through the mail rather than the internal courier system, which might indicate a scrupulous awareness of what did and did not count as official Service business, or perhaps just meant that Molly had wanted a 50 percent chance of it arriving within the fortnight, which was about how often the internal courier made it to Aldersgate Street. That the envelope contained a photograph, Catherine had deduced from the 'Do not bend—contains photograph' sticker, and that Lamb had not been expecting it from the distracted mood he'd been in since. He generally marked the festive season with an increase in hostilities. Today he'd barely ventured from his room other than to bellow for quiet or tea four or five times, and, Roddy apart, had invited nobody to suffer his company, preferring to stew in solitude and—one massive coughing fit aside—relative silence.

And the silence of the Lamb, more often than not, was an indication of disquiet.

As for the photograph, Catherine hadn't seen it earlier, but it now lay on the desk in front of him, and he was making no attempt to shield it from her gaze. So gaze she did: a couple, in black and white, standing in front of a wall somewhere, years ago. She didn't recognise the woman, though had the vaguest sense that she ought to, but the man was Jackson Lamb.

Who, as if hearing her think his name, stirred and curled his lip.

"Do you want more tea?" she asked, to forestall his asking why she was still there. But he didn't answer.

The photograph was at an angle to her, not far from upside down, but like many a long-time Personal Friday, Catherine could read, absorb and digest printed material from most perspectives, and had little difficulty assessing the image offered. Her initial response was that Jackson cut a surprising figure back when this picture was taken. Not attractive or youthful or fit or healthy, mind; it was, simply, surprising to note that he'd not always been a shambolic mess, but had once been someone you might not bat an eyelid at if they, say, ran up a flight of stairs, or didn't light a cigarette. So this picture was from his war years; not the actual war, obviously; not even the actual Cold War, since that had been over thirty years ago, and the figure in the photo didn't look young enough, but from that period, anyway, when Jackson Lamb had been a warrior, and the enemies he faced flesh and blood, rather than the dim and distant ghosts that bothered him now.

The woman, though . . . She didn't have the look Catherine might have expected from one consorting with the likes of Lamb.

Did not, to put it bluntly, look like a professional, by which Catherine didn't mean on the game—or not necessarily on the game—but, rather, in the picture; someone who knew the world Lamb lived in, and had been trained to walk within it too. Instead, she had the appearance of one about to choose a gateway in a riddle. The first would lead to love and fortune, the other to disgrace and loneliness. Catherine preferred images of such women before they'd made that choice, their excitement not yet drowned by apprehension. The dress she wore was eye-catching; its buttons indicating a style classic, though Catherine couldn't put a name to the designer. She wondered if this woman were one of Lamb's dim distant ghosts . . . There was something ghostly about the picture, come to think of it. As if there hovered above the captured pair an unseen spectre, one that had faded into the brickwork, but whose memory remained. Not much given to fey speculation, Catherine dismissed the thought before it could take root, and leave her wondering whether the ghost was friend or foe.

"Are you still here?"

She said, "I was asking if you wanted more tea."

"Well don't talk to me when I'm not listening. It's a waste of everyone's time." As he was speaking, Lamb seemed to notice that his photo was exposed to Catherine's view, and he reached for it and flipped it over. It was on paper, not card, Catherine noticed, and she wondered why the instruction on the envelope had cautioned against bending.

Not caring that he'd know she'd been studying the image, she said, "Taking a peek into the past?"

"Why would I want to do that?"

"It's the time of year for memories."

"I don't do memories."

But they do you, she almost said. Lamb, she felt, would be steamrollered by memories if he let his guard down. Though she no longer speculated, or not often, about what had happened to make him this way, she'd long assumed that when the lists were drawn up of who did what to whom, and at what cost, he'd turn out to be at least as much sinning as sinned against. And that, she knew, could make for sleepless nights.

"Are you still here?" he asked again, and she shook her head. Tea mugs in hand, she closed his door behind her, and paused on the landing, hearing River coming up the stairs. If that photo came from Molly, she thought, Molly must have found it in her archive. Which meant that the image it held wasn't just from Lamb's past, it was from his job. The wall it showed him standing in front of might not be the actual Berlin Wall, but it could easily be a wall in Berlin. He might look like a younger version of himself, but he was pretending to be someone else entirely. And who the woman was was anybody's guess.

I don't do memories.

For a good liar, Lamb came across like a shocking amateur on occasion.

Some minutes after the others had left River stood, and was relieved to find that his legs supported him. There'd been times, as recently as the previous week, when standing upright had proved a bridge too far.

He had reacted to such setbacks with his usual poise.

"There's no point rushing recovery," his physiotherapist had said.

"There's every fucking point," River had assured him.

Because becoming whole again, learning to trust his own body, wasn't something he could approach gradually. He had to know that he was back on track, and had to know it soon. Had to know that, by the time he reached his peak again, he wouldn't be over the hill.

"The physio knows what he's talking about," Sid had said. Repeatedly.

"Yeah, but he's not the one this is happening to."

"Very adult."

"It's these sudden . . . weaknesses I can't stand. One moment I'm normal, the next it's like someone's cut my strings. It's as if my body's housing a traitor."

Sid laughed. "This is news to you?"

"It's not to you?"

"Well, you've already got a mole on your upper lip."

". . . Very funny."

"River," she said. "I get it that you're hoping for a full and fast recovery. You know why I get it? Because I was shot in the head."

He shook his own head now, remembering that conversation. He and Sid had a good thing happening, he reminded himself. It would be a shame to mess that up by being a dick.

Before he reached the top landing Catherine came into view, cautioning him away with a mug-handed gesture towards Lamb's door and a shake of the head. "I wouldn't."

If it was anyone else but Catherine, talking about anyone else but Lamb, River would have pressed on anyway, but that wasn't going to happen here. He stopped on the stairs and gave her a half-wave—"Bah, humbug, Catherine." "Happy Christmas,

River."—then turned and headed back down. He could join the other slow horses in the pub, get used to being in their company once more, or head on home and be with Sid. He decided to head on home and be with Sid. Nothing to do, of course, with not feeling up to a crowded pub. Tip-top form, that was River Cartwright.

He passed Roddy's office, its door half-open, and glimpsed Ho at his desk, steering his software towards some distant destination. He was almost at ground level, gearing himself up to tackle the door that never worked, when he stopped, chewed his lip for the best part of thirty seconds, then turned and walked back up. On the first landing he stood for another moment before putting a finger to Roddy's door and pushing gently. It swung open.

When Roddy saw who was invading his space, he scowled. "Thought you weren't back till next month."

"I'm fine. Thank you." He thought about moving further into the room, then decided leaning against the door jamb was a better bet.

A glance around confirmed that Roddy's office hadn't altered much in his absence, beyond having had a window pane replaced with a grease-stained cardboard mosaic. There was probably a story there, but Roddy was unlikely to reveal it. Roddy wasn't revealing much, in fact, except for an obvious distaste for River's presence, which was a good enough reason, where River was concerned, for prolonging it a while. If his initial motive in returning—a quantum of sorrow that Roddy had been frozen out of the pub trip—had instantaneously morphed into a desire to wind him up, that wasn't a headline-grabbing development. Few benign feelings survived more than a moment or two of Roddy's company. Most would crumble into dust faced with the look he was giving River now.

"What's up with you?" River asked. "Did they stop making pizza?"

"No, and anyway, what's up with *you*? Did they stop . . ."

River waited.

". . . putting Novichok on doorknobs?"

"Not soon enough to suit me," said River. "What you up to?"

"None of your business."

"Well of course it's none of my business. I wouldn't be asking otherwise, would I? Haven't you worked out what spies do yet?"

Roddy tilted his monitor, in case River had developed the ability to review a screen's contents from its reverse side. "Special job."

"A phrase I often associate with you."

"For Lamb."

"What would he do without you? In fact, what would any of us?"

Roddy gave a bored look, as if he'd long plumbed the depths of that particular question.

"You joining the others for a Christmas drink?" River asked.

Roddy looked shifty. "Why?"

"Because they're going down Smithfield Market. That big place on the corner?"

"Yeah, right."

"Instead of the one on Whitecross Street."

"Yeah. Right."

"I'd hate you to end up in the wrong place."

Roddy stared, a mixture of doubt and aggression stirring just below his surface.

"Absolute opposite direction," River said.

"Yeah," said Roddy. "Right."

"Have a good Christmas."

Roddy grunted.

"I hope you get everything you deserve."

"And I hope you get a Novichocolate Santa in your stocking."

That was actually pretty good, thought River.

"And some Novichocolate reindeer."

But now he was just milking it.

"Don't forget," he said, turning to go. "Whitecross Street."

"You said Smithfield!"

"That's what I meant."

Down the stairs again, and this time River made it all the way out through the back door, which he was glad no one was around to see him making a meal of. In the yard, its mildewed walls pungent in the cold, he paused while pulling his gloves on and looked back at the building, its only sign of life on this side a dim light on the top floor, leaking through Lamb's blind. He wasn't sure what he'd been expecting from the afternoon—though he'd been glad to see Louisa and Catherine, and even Lech and Shirley, and even, *even*, didn't feel entirely soiled by having seen Roddy too—but had imagined it would involve encountering Lamb, and felt slightly cheated that it hadn't. But not as bruised, he admitted to himself, as he'd probably have felt if it had. As it was, Roddy's blunt barbs aside, the worst he'd been offered was the new recruit's comment about a royal visitation—ha! The return of the prince . . . Did she imagine he thought he was special? In truth, he had once, probably, but his time as a slow horse had mostly cured him of that. And royalty, no, seriously; this was Slough House, not

Clarence House. Which rang a bell, but what did 'Clarence' have to do with anything? And then he remembered Springsteen's saxophonist, and 'Santa Claus Is Coming to Town.' That was it.

It would have been nice if a few flakes of snow started drifting earthwards as he made for the Tube, but they didn't. In ordinary weather for the time of year, River Cartwright joined the crowd heading into the underground, and went back home to Sid.

Meanwhile, back in his office, Roddy Ho put the final touches to the photograph, incorporating the further change Lamb had demanded; one which made little sense to him, but who was he to argue? When the boss was ready to share, it'd be Roddy he'd turn to. And he remembered Cartwright's question, *What would Lamb do without you?*, and supplied the answer he'd come up with earlier: he'd suffer missing-limb syndrome. Which just went to show: when Roddy was right, he was right.

He printed it off, admired it, then took it upstairs, where Lamb had stirred himself enough to pour whisky from the bottle into the glass, and from the glass into his mouth, at least four times since their previous exchange. This one lasted little longer. Roddy put the printout on Lamb's desk and Lamb glanced at it, nothing in his expression changing while he took in the further alteration Roddy had made. Then he picked up his glass, drained it, and set it down again. Something tinkled on his desk when he did so: a plasticky little noise that barely lasted a moment.

"Okay," he said at last. "Bah humbugger off, then."

"Hamburger . . . ?"

"Go," said Lamb, "away."

"Oh. Right." But he paused at the door. "Merry Christmas."

"Huh."

"Doing anything special?"

"I hate to sound like I'm part of the whole snowflake cancel-culture scene," said Lamb, rearranging his feet on the desk. "But I'm going to spend most of it pretending none of you exist."

Roddy went on his way, chuckling.

As he left the building ten minutes later, negotiating the stairs with his usual lithe grace, he ran through the day's events in his mind, satisfying himself that he'd been indispensable once again. Not just the tech wizardry—when had he ever let anyone down in that department?—but the general rolling with the punches, staying ahead of the game, knocking things out of the park, and besting River Cartwright in a verbal duel. Yes, it was beginning to feel a lot like Christmas.

Roddy Roddy Roddy!

Ho ho ho!

It's an awesome life, he thought. Or mine is. And after the briefest of moments in which he allowed himself to pity all those lacking his very special sets of skills, he crossed the road and headed off to Whitecross Street.

Leaving Lamb in his top-floor office, its soft light softened further by a veil of cigarette smoke, so that any observer of a sentimental nature might imagine him a grubby Santa, putting the grot into grotto. But there were no observers, sentimental or otherwise— Catherine having departed, to pursue her own vision of Christmas in her calm and quiet, not unhappy way—so there was no one to flinch when, with surprising suddenness, Lamb swung his shoeless feet to the floor and went barrelling out of

the room, entering Catherine's office like a Viking on manoeu-
vres. Flakes of plaster fell from the ceiling when the door
slammed against the wall; more drifted free as he pillaged desk
drawers with the kind of controlled fury that this room alone,
of all Slough House, generally provided sanctuary from. Most
of what he found he dropped to the floor—reels of sticky labels,
cellophane folders, account books, boxes of Biros, treasury tags;
all this junk from another era, as if he were trashing a museum
installation—littering the carpet with a mess of ancient stationery. But at last he found what he was after, a packet of A4
envelopes, and with this under his arm he stalked back to his
domain, leaving the bruised, assaulted room to adjust itself to its
new arrangements.

The doctored photograph lay on his desk. Tossing the envelopes aside Lamb crashed into his chair, simultaneously groping
for a cigarette and snatching the picture up so he could glare at
it from a distance of six inches. For a long while he became still,
and whether he was examining the picture for the new truth
Roddy's tampering had imbued it with, or looking beyond that to
whatever ancient lie it had originally captured, was impossible
to say. At last he fumbled in a pocket, produced a plastic lighter,
and struck flame on the third or fourth attempt. He held it to his
cigarette, and in the following moment seemed ready to apply it
to the photograph too, putting a fiery end to whatever speculative
journey he was on. But the flame choked of its own accord, and
gasped a little, and went out. After maintaining the pose for a
few seconds, Lamb gave a flick of the wrist that sent the lighter
spinning into the darkness behind him. He laid the photo on the
desk again, and sprawled back in his chair, smoking.

It was much later that he left Slough House, and in the meantime, evidently, he'd found a stamp; had evidently found a pen. But tradecraft, perhaps, prevented him from dropping the sealed envelope he now carried into the first post box he passed, or even the second, and it was still securely under his arm when he arrived on Old Street, which was not his route home. He turned right, his gait steadier than was reasonable given the quantity of Scotch he'd put away, and directed himself towards the far roundabout, its huge video screens releasing visions of Yuletide splendour into the night air, as if the steady beating of mercantile drums might be mistaken for the sound of distant reindeer. Around him the street pulsed with out-of-office life, much of it wearing party hats; there was a constant weaving in and out of the various establishments along the road—eateries, bars and pubs—but Lamb's pace didn't waver as he made his way through the crowds, though at no point did he make as much as elbow-contact with those around him. And at some point he dispatched the envelope he was carrying, or at any rate, it was no longer in his possession when he arrived at the roundabout's video windmills and turned and stared back the way he'd come, as if trying to discern the ripples his passage had caused along that crowded thoroughfare, the thousands of tiny accommodations others had made for his passing bulk. But whatever perforations his journey had caused, no trace of them could be seen now. Whether this satisfied him or otherwise couldn't be said, but he stood unmoving for a while, a silent stony figure among a carnival of noisy excess, until at last he jammed his hands in his pockets, and made his way round the huge roundabout, and disappeared somewhere on the other side.

• • •

As for the envelope, it re-emerged into the world in the new year, arriving at Regent's Park to be X-rayed, prodded, and decreed harmless before being sealed in a suitcase-like plastic shell along with the rest of the day's post and sent down to Molly Doran's floor, where the light was blue and the air chilled to a little below body temperature, which many thought less about the requirements of ageing documents and more about Molly Doran's antipathy to visitors. When she saw it she studied it briefly, then set it aside before attending to the rest of the day's deliveries, and if the envelope weighed on her mind through the hours that followed no sign of this played on her face, which was the usual powdered mask of too much white and too much red, and somehow not enough colour.

But later, once office hours were done, and the lighting on the floor had powered-down to a darker blue, she completed one last circuit of her domain, then made her way to her favourite nook in the centre of the labyrinth, one into which her wheelchair slotted as neatly as if it had been designed for the purpose. Removing the envelope from her chair's pocket, she laid it flat on the small table. Christmas was over, and the stamp that Lamb had found, on which an angel blew lustily into a horn, seemed crudely out of place, as if it were summoning revellers to a party long disbanded. That Lamb had affixed it there, she was certain, though his handwriting was never readily identifiable, and this example—she thought—had been written left-handed. But that he would make some riposte to her admittedly provocative gift, she'd more than expected. He was not a man to ignore a challenge. Those who thought him lazy knew only half the story: he put an enormous amount of effort into avoiding activity, true, but he couldn't resist poking at the grit and clinker left by the fires he'd started along the way. Which was what the photograph had been, of course. Grit and clinker. The record of a moment Lamb had gone on to torch.

Molly had found the original down here, among her treasures. She had known it existed, though the file it was from had been stamped [CLOSED] long before her own tenure at Regent's Park had begun. But she also knew that closed files had a way of opening again. The word *Monochrome* was in the air, an inquiry everyone knew would prove fruitless, but which nevertheless had to justify its existence. So wheels were in motion, and Molly knew first-hand that without an effective brake, wheels in motion tended to stay that way. Sending Lamb the photograph hadn't been a warning, exactly. More of a notification.

And now she opened the envelope, to see what response this notification had generated.

If Lamb had intended to cause Molly pain with his tinkering, he would have been disappointed, for when she examined the doctored photograph her face betrayed no emotion; remained a study in professional detachment. The nature of that profession, true, might be open to question, given the over-generous application of powder and paint, but its commitment could not be doubted. For a while all remained still, the only noise the lift passing the floor on its way to the hub. Molly's eyes were clear, alert. And when she at last reacted it was to nod once, as if in appreciation of an opponent's well-considered move, and then to speak aloud with a certain self-conscious playfulness.

"Ho, ho ho," she said.

Roddy Ho, in fact. Lamb had set his computer munchkin on

the job, and the photo he'd returned was both commentary on, and updating of, the original image.

Otis was gone. This was the most obvious emendation; Otis was gone, as if Lamb thought that by obliterating his image, all that he'd wrought in the long-ago could be undone. Except, of course, Lamb knew nothing of the sort was possible—that was clear from the other change he'd had Roderick Ho introduce; one that underlined all the damage that Otis, wilfully or not, had caused. It was a change many would have thought cruel, but as far as Molly was concerned, there'd have been more malice in leaving the image intact. When the original photo had been in her hands, she'd spent an age looking at the third figure, the young woman who both was and was not entirely familiar. It had been like peering down a well, trying to make out a reflection; or staring at someone she'd started a journey with, only to part company when the going got rough. It was impossible to know where the woman in the picture might have ended up, but difficult to imagine it would have been anywhere like Molly's own destination: this wheelchair, this archive, this solitary late middle age. No, in having Roddy digitally erase the figure's legs, Lamb had not intended cruelty; he had, rather, been asserting the inevitability of the here and now. All paths lead to the present. His own story proved that much: all the different histories he'd had, and all had converged on the same ending, as if it were the one he'd chosen for himself. But however deep he'd buried it, sooner or later Lamb would have to face his past. Molly rather thought that time might be coming.

She took one last look at her younger self, her body floating above the ground, and allowed herself to smile. There had been no floating—the pain had been as powerful as gravity—but it had been a long time ago. The woman in the photograph existed no more. Even so, she'd keep this bastardised record of her one-time self. It was of no probative value, of course, but she would preserve it, because an archive was not intended simply to capture the past, it was there to seed future reckonings. In the cabinets all around her consorted ghosts from the past, ghosts from the present, and ghosts from futures yet to come, and the potential consequences of an uncontrolled assembly of any of these made this the most dangerous room in Regent's Park. She'd long been aware of this. It was possible she was the only one who was. But others would find out. You can't seal ghosts up forever.

For the moment, though, she sealed this one back in its envelope. There were several rubber stamps on the desk in front of her, and she collected three of them in her grasp, examining the handles, neatly colour-coded—the red, the green, the black. But there was no real choice to be made. Dropping the other two, Molly held onto the green, and stamped the envelope [PENDING]. Then laid it flat on the desk before reversing her wheelchair out of her favourite nook, and rolling once more through the dangerous labyrinth of the past, towards the lift.

Continue reading for a sample of Mick Herron's

NOBODY WALKS

1.1

The news had come hundreds of miles to sit waiting for days in a mislaid phone. And there it lingered like a moth in a box, weightless, and aching for the light.

The street cleaners' lorry woke Bettany. It was 4:25 A.M. He washed at the sink, dressed, turned the bed's thin mattress, and rolled his sleeping bag into a tight package he leaned upright in a corner. 4:32.

Locking the door was an act of faith or satire—the lock would barely withstand a rattle—but the room wouldn't be empty long, because someone else used it during the day. Bettany hadn't met him, but they'd reached an accommodation. The daytime occupant respected Bettany's possessions—his toothbrush, his sleeping bag, the dog-eared copy of *Dubliners* he'd found on a bus—and in return Bettany left untouched the clothing that hung from a hook on the door, three shirts and a pair of khakis.

His own spare clothing he kept in a duffel bag in a locker at the sheds. Passport and wallet he carried in a security belt with his mobile, until that got lost or stolen.

Outside was February cold, quiet enough that he could hear

water rinsing the sewers. A bus grumbled past, windows fogged. Bettany nodded to the whore on the corner, whose territory was bounded by two streetlights. She was Senegalese, pre-op, currently a redhead, and he'd bought her a drink one night, God knew why. They had exile in common, but little else. Bettany's French remained undistinguished, and the hooker's English didn't lend itself to small talk.

A taste of the sea hung in the air. This would burn off later, and be replaced by urban flavours.

He caught the next bus, a twenty-minute ride to the top of a lane which fell from the main road like an afterthought, and as he trudged downhill a truck passed, horn blaring, its headlights yellowing the sheds ahead, which were barn-sized constructions behind wire-topped fences. A wooden sign hung lopsided from the gates, one of its tethering chains longer than the other. The words were faded by weather. Bettany had never been able to make them out.

Audible now, the sound of cattle in distress.

He was waved through and fetched his apron from the locker room. A group of men were smoking by the door, and one grunted his name.

"Tonton."

What they called him, for reasons lost in the mist of months.

He knotted his apron, which was stained so thick with blood and grease it felt plastic, and fumbled his gloves on.

Out in the yard the truck was impatient, its exhaust fumes spoiling out in thick black ropes. The noise from the nearest shed was mechanical, mostly, and its smells metallic and full of fear. Behind Bettany men stamped their cigarettes out and hawked noisily. Refrigerated air whispered from the truck's dropped tailgate.

Bettany's role wasn't complicated. Lorries arrived bearing cattle and the cattle were fed into the sheds. What came out was meat, which was then ferried away in different lorries. Bettany's job, and that of his companions, was to carry the meat to the lorries. This not only required no thought, it demanded thought's absence.

At day's end he'd hose down the yard, a task he performed with grim diligence, meticulously blasting every scrap of matter down the drains.

He switched off, and the working day took over. This was measured in a familiar series of aches and smells and sounds, the same actions repeated with minor variations, while blurred memories nagged him uninvited, moments which had seemed unexceptional at the time, but had persisted. A woman in a café, regarding him with what might have been interest, might have been contempt. An evening at the track with Majeed, who was the nearest he'd made to a friend, though he hadn't made enemies. He didn't think he'd made enemies.

Thoughts became rituals in themselves. You plodded the same course over and over, like any dumb beast or wind-up toy.

At about the time citizens would be leaving their homes in clean shirts Bettany stopped for coffee, pitch black in a polystyrene cup. He ate a hunk of bread wrapped round cheese, leaning against the fence and watching grey weather arrive, heading inland.

From three metres' distance Majeed detached himself from a group similarly occupied.

"Hey, Tonton. You lose your mobile?"

It spun through the air. He caught it one-handed.

"*Ou?*"

"*La Girondelle.*"

The bar at the track. He was surprised to see it again, though the reason why wasn't long in coming.

"*C'est de la merde.* Not worth stealing."

Bettany gave no argument.

The piece of shit, not worth stealing, was barely worth ringing either, though still had a flicker of charge. Four missed calls in nine days. Two were local numbers and hadn't left messages. The others were from England, unfamiliar streams of digits. Odds were they were cold calls, checking out his inclinations vis-à-vis internet banking or double-glazing. He finished his coffee undecided whether to listen or delete, then found his thumb resolving the issue of its own accord, scrolling to his voicemail number, pressing play.

"Yes, this is Detective Sergeant Welles, speaking from Hoxton police station. Er, London. I'm trying to reach a Mr. Thomas Bettany? If you could give me a ring at your earliest convenience. It's a matter of some importance." He recited a number slowly enough that Bettany caught it the first time.

His mouth was dry. The bread, the cheese, grew lumpy in his stomach.

The second voice was less measured.

"Mr. Bettany? Liam's father?" It was a girl, or young woman. "My name's Flea, Felicity Pointer? I'm calling about Liam ... Mr. Bettany, I'm so sorry to have to tell you this."

She sounded sorry.

"There's been an accident. Liam—I'm sorry, Mr. Bettany. Liam died."

Either she paused a long while or the recorded silence dragged itself out in slow motion, eating up his pre-paid minutes.

"I'm sorry."

"Message ends. To hear the message envelope, press one. To save the—"

He killed the robot voice.

Nearby, Majeed was halfway through a story, dropping into English when French wasn't obscene enough. Bettany could hear the creaking of a trolley's metal wheels, a chain scraping over a beam. Another lorry trundled down the lane, its grille broad, an American model. Already details were stacking up. More blurred snapshots he'd flick through in future days, always associated with the news just heard.

He reached for the back of his neck, and untied his apron.

"Tonton?"

He dropped it to the ground.

"*Ou vas-tu?*"

Bettany fetched his duffel from the locker.

1.2

The crematorium was single-storey, stucco-clad, with a high chimney. On one side creeping plants swarmed a cane trellis that bordered an array of small gardens divided by hedges. Japanese stones neighboured ornamental ponds and bonsai trees peered from terracotta pots. Other patches echoed formal English styles, orchards, terraced rosebeds, in any of which you might strew the ashes of the departed, supposing the deceased had expressed a preference.

Bettany imagined Liam saying, *When I'm dead, scatter me on a Japanese garden. Not in actual Japan. Just anywhere handy.*

A mild English winter was turning chill, but all that remained of the morning's frost was a damp smudge on the pavements. The imprints of vanished leaves were stamped there too, like the work of a graffiti artist who'd run out of things to say.

Bettany's once-blond shaggy hair was now streaked grey, like his ragged beard, and while his eyes were strikingly blue, their expression was vague. His hands, large and raw, were jammed in the pockets of a cheap raincoat, and he rocked slightly on feet cased in work boots that had seen better days. Under the coat he wore jeans, a long-sleeved crew-neck tee and a zippered top.

These were the spare clothes from his duffel bag, but three days'
wear had taken their toll. The duffel itself he'd abandoned in a
bin, he couldn't remember which side of the Channel. For all the
hours he'd spent on buses, he'd managed little sleep. His only
conversation had been a brief exchange on the ferry, when a
French trucker lent him the use of a phone charger.

His first stop on reaching London had been Hoxton Police
Station.

Detective Sergeant Welles, once located, had been sympathetic.

"I'm sorry for your loss."

Bettany nodded.

"Nobody seemed to know where you were. But there was an
idea you were out of the country. I'm glad you got back in time."

Which was how he discovered the cremation was taking place
that morning.

He'd sat in the back row. The chapel of remembrance was
quarter-full, most of the congregation Liam's age, none of them
known to him, but an introduction contained a familiar name,
Felicity Pointer. Flea, she'd called herself on the phone. She
approached the lectern looking twenty-five, twenty-six, brunette
and lightly olive-skinned, wearing black of course. Hardly looking at the assembled company, she read a short poem about
chimney sweeps, then returned to her seat.

Watching this, Bettany had barely paid attention to the main
object of interest, but looking at it now he realised that what he'd
been feeling these past three days was not grief but numbness. A
pair of curtains provided the backdrop, and behind them the
coffin would soon pass, and there the remains of his only son
would be reduced to ash and fragments of bone, to the mess of

clinker you'd find in a grate on a winter's morning. Nothing of substance. And all Bettany could make of it was an all-consuming absence of feeling, as if he was indeed the stranger his son had made of him.

He rose and slipped out of the door.

Waiting by the trellis, it struck him that it was seven years since he'd been in London. He supposed he ought to be noticing differences, things being better or worse, but he couldn't see much had changed. The skyline had altered, with new towers jutting heavenwards from the City, and more poised to sprout everywhere you looked. But that had always been the case. London had never been finished, and never would be. Or not by dint of new construction.

Seven years since London, three of them in Lyme. Then Hannah had died, and he'd left England. Now Liam had died, and he was back.

Welles had given him a lift here. There might have been a hidden agenda, pump the father for information, but Bettany had none to offer and the flow had gone the other way. How it had happened, for instance. Up through France, across the choppy Channel, Bettany hadn't known the how. Of the various possibilities some kind of traffic accident had seemed most likely, Liam driving too fast on a fog-bound stretch of motorway, or a bus mounting the pavement, Liam in the wrong place. He could have called and spared himself conjecture, but that would have been to make imagination fact. Now he learned that there had been no cars involved, no buses. Liam had fallen from the window of his flat.

"Were you in close contact with your son, Mr. Bettany?"

"No."

"So you wouldn't know much about his lifestyle?"

"I don't even know where he lived."

"Not far from here."

Which would make it N1. Not somewhere Bettany was familiar with. He gathered it was trendy, if that word was used any more, and if it wasn't, well then. Cool. Hip. Whatever.

Had Liam been hip? he wondered. Had Liam been cool? They hadn't spoken in four years. He couldn't swear to any aspect of his late son's life, down to the most basic details. Had be been gay? Vegetarian? A biker? What did he do at weekends, browse secondhand shops, looking for bargain furniture? Or hang around the clubs, looking to score? Bettany didn't know. And while he could find out, that wouldn't erase the indelible truth of this particular moment, the one he spent outside the chapel where Liam's body was being fed into the flames. Here and now, he knew nothing. And still, somehow, felt less.

Overhead, a stringy scrap of smoke loosed itself from the chimney. Then another. And now here came the rest of it, billowing and scattering, a cloud for only a moment, and then nothing, and nowhere, ever again.

1.3

The chapel had both entrance and exit, and fresh mourners were congregating at the former. Leaving them, Bettany wandered round to the back, where those who'd come for Liam were dispersing. He was the only blood relative here—there were no others. Liam, an only child, had been the son of only children. And his mother was four years dead.

Loitering under a tree, he watched Flea Pointer emerge. She was talking to an older man, himself flanked by another—flanked, as if the second man were a minder or subordinate. The first man was mid-thirties or so, and while dark suits were the order of the day his seemed of a different cut, the cloth darker, the shirt whiter. A matter of money, Bettany supposed. His short hair was fair to the point of translucence, and his wire-framed glasses tinted blue. As Bettany watched Pointer leaned forward and kissed him on the cheek, her arm curling round his back for a moment, and the man tensed. He raised his hand as if to pat her on the back, but thought better of it. Releasing him, she brushed a palm across her eyes, sweeping her hair free or dabbing at tears. They exchanged inaudible words and the men moved off, down the path, through the gate into the street, and disappeared inside a long silver car, which pulled off with barely a noise. Flea Pointer still hadn't moved.

She was the same age as Liam had been, though unlike Liam was petite—Liam had been a tall boy, gangly, with arms and legs too spindly to know where their centre of balance lay. He'd filled as he'd grown, and had maybe kept doing so. He might have barrelled out since then. Bettany didn't know.

As he stood thinking such things, the girl looked round and saw him.

Flea Pointer watched Vincent Driscoll climb into the limo and pull away, Boo Berryman driving. She had felt him flinch when she put her arm round him—Vincent wasn't much for human contact. She had forgotten that in the emotion of the moment, or else had thought that he might forget it in that same emotion. But he hadn't, so he'd flinched, and she was left feeling gauche and adolescent, as if there weren't enough feelings washing around her now. Tears were not far away. The world threatened to blur.

But she blinked, and it shimmied back. When vision cleared, she was looking at a man standing under a tree like a figure in a fable. He was tall, bearded, shaggy-haired, inappropriately dressed, and she wasn't sure which of these details clinched it, but she knew he was Liam's father. With that knowledge slotted in place, she approached him.

"Mr. Bettany?"

He nodded.

"I'm Flea—"

"I know."

He sounded brusque, but why wouldn't he? His son had just been cremated. The emotion of the moment, again. She knew this could take different forms.

On the other hand, he'd never responded to her phone call. She'd dug his number out from a form at work, Liam's next-of-kin contact. Couldn't recall exactly what she'd said. But he'd never called back.

What he said now, though, was, "You rang me. Thank you."

"You live abroad."

This sounded disjointed even to her own ears.

"Liam told me," she added.

How else would she have known? She was coming adrift from this exchange already.

"I'm so sorry, I hated to tell you like that, but I didn't know what else to do—"

"You did the right thing."

"I know you hadn't been getting on. I mean, Liam said you didn't—hadn't—"

"We hadn't been in touch," Bettany said.

His gaze left hers to focus on something behind her. Without meaning to, she turned. A small group, three men, one woman, still lingered by the chapel door, but even as she registered this they began to move off. Instead of heading for the gate they walked round to the front, as if heading back inside. One of the men was carrying something. It took Flea a moment to recognise it as a thermos flask.

Liam's father asked her, "Who was that you were talking to?"

"When?"

"He just left."

"Oh . . . That was Vincent. Vincent Driscoll?"

It was clear he didn't know who Vincent Driscoll was.

"We worked for him. Liam and I did. Well, I still do."

She bit her lip. Tenses were awkward, in the company of the bereaved. Apologies had to be implied, for the offence of still living.

"So you were colleagues," he said. "Doing what?"

"Vincent's a game designer. *Shades*?"

Bettany nodded, but she could tell the name meant nothing.

Distantly, music swelled. The next service was starting. Flea Pointer had the sudden understanding that life was a conveyor belt, a slow rolling progress to the dropping-off point, and that once you'd fallen you'd be followed by the next in line. An unhappy thought, which could be shrugged off anywhere but here.

If Tom Bettany was having similar thoughts you wouldn't know it from his expression. He seemed just barely involved in what had happened here this morning.

"Thank you," he said again, and left. Flea watched as he headed down the path.

He didn't look back.

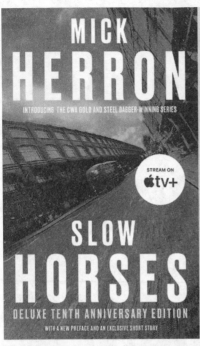
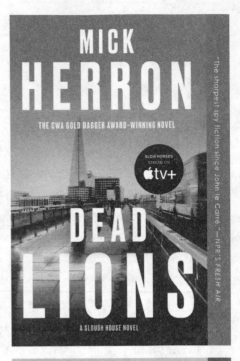

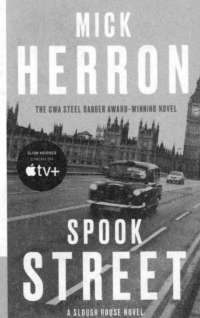

MICK HERRON

CWA GOLD AND STEEL DAGGER–WINNING AUTHOR OF *SLOW HORSES*

SLOW HORSES
STREAM ON
tv+

LONDON RULES

A SLOUGH HOUSE NOVEL

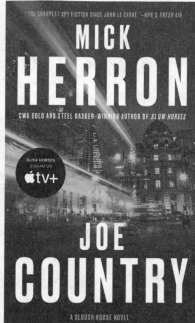

"THE SHARPEST SPY FICTION SINCE JOHN LE CARRÉ." —NPR'S *FRESH AIR*

MICK HERRON

CWA GOLD AND STEEL DAGGER–WINNING AUTHOR OF *SLOW HORSES*

SLOW HORSES
STREAM ON
tv+

JOE COUNTRY

A SLOUGH HOUSE NOVEL

MICK HERRON

THE CWA GOLD DAGGER AWARD–WINNING AUTHOR OF *SLOW HORSES*

SLOW HORSES
STREAM ON
tv+

SLOUGH HOUSE

A SLOUGH HOUSE NOVEL

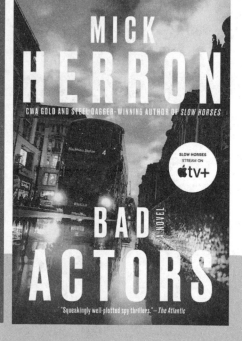

MICK HERRON

CWA GOLD AND STEEL DAGGER–WINNING AUTHOR OF *SLOW HORSES*

SLOW HORSES
STREAM ON
tv+

BAD ACTORS

A NOVEL

"Squeakingly well-plotted spy thrillers." —*The Atlantic*

"Confirms Mick Herron as the greatest comic writer of spy fiction." —*THE TIMES*

"John le Carré with an extra dose of dry humor." —*THE SEATTLE TIMES*

"Confirms Mick Herron as the best spy novelist now working." —NPR'S *FRESH AIR*